To Kath, with thanks
Meg

The Causton Series

The Army's Daughter

At seventeen, Louisa is married off to brutal R[illegible]t. A determined survivor she lives her new life with an i[illegible]ted chin. When the chance of a respite app[illegible]m tastes sweet, and never lacking co[illegible]en that too is ripped away, now [illegible] protect, her determination to surv[illegible] Hawksworth offers a chance of a lat[illegible]in and grasp it?

The Army's Son

Eleven-year-old James has always known that the Army is his destiny. Big boned and well nourished, the Army takes his shilling. Years later Hal finds him left to die on a quayside and nurses him back to health, and a return to service. After the battle of Waterloo James is seriously injured again. When he meets Mary, he believes that his only possible future is to die in uniform, still serving his country. As china ornaments whizz past his ears, might he take a chance on a very different life? One of love and children?

Chantel

A mathematics prodigy, Chantel solves her first coded message at eight-years-old. Ten years later she enters society and the marriage mart. After four years she is bored until Joshua, Duke of Daughton, offers her marriage and a challenge to last her a lifetime. Marriage is literally, 'Until death do us part'. When Joshua tires of her and her childhood friend, Daniel reappears, how far can social rules be pushed aside to allow her and Daniel to be together?

Elena

Louisa's daughter, Elena, is born while her mother is still legally married to the brutal Rupert, making her the legitimate heir to his title and fortune. Unprepared, she is thrown into society, which does not go well. Wounded, she wraps her independence around herself and strikes out into the world by going into business with Harrison Weeks, an iron foundry owner. A female earl, and a working man, surely a romantic relationship is impossible? Except no one told their hearts.

Samantha

Samantha writes and solves codes like her Aunt Chantel for the spies in Whitehall. But she is too lively to want to help her country only by sitting at her desk. When life goes horribly wrong she offers herself in marriage to the one man she can think of. In his wildest dreams Toby never imagined he might ever be considered eligible to marry Samantha, but all he has ever wanted to do is protect and love her. Now he has his chance, except Samantha, knowing she forced his hand, wants to set him free.

The Army's Daughter

MEG BARBER

First published in paperback by
Michael Terence Publishing in 2023
www.mtp.agency

authormegbarber@yahoo.com

ISBN 9781800944367

Cover design by
GetCovers

Michael Terence
Publishing

Dear Reader

'Leave a review, feed an author', has more than a grain of truth in it. Writing for me is an unpaid labour of love, and the reward is other people enjoying the story. If you wish to be informed when the next Causton book is available, please send your email to authormegbarber@yahoo.com. You will not be bombarded with emails; I have neither the technical know-how to do that, nor the time. That is a promise. When people say that they like my stories, I light up like a neon sign, so if you praise The Army's Daughter, glance out of the window; there is a multi-coloured glow out there somewhere.

Happy reading.

PART ONE

Louisa: 1800 Portugal – A New Century and a New Life.

'What is the army, lad?
Why, tis nowt but drillin an killin.'

Chapter 1

The first time Louisa fell in love she was nine. She was playing catch and ran into a cannon because she was looking back to see how close Billy Tyler was. Her giggle of laughter was cut off and she was felled like an oak. Billy and Pump (his family name was Waters) shoved through the legs of the gunnery crew to reach her. Louisa was out cold. Despite the adults around him, fourteen-year-old Billy picked her up and carried her back to her mother; Pump running interference, in that, he wasn't going to let anyone of any age or rank pluck Louisa from Billy's arms. They had caused the accident. They would own up and take her home.

Louisa woke up with a lump the size of a pigeon's egg on her brow and a black eye that reached half-way down her cheek. In later years, when her father told the story, the bump grew to the size of a hen's egg and she was out for a week. No matter, from that moment on Billy, could do no wrong in her eyes. She helped him steal baccy for his pa and whisky for his ma and food for the gang of them. Life for an army child was good more than it was bad and with Billy to hero-worship Louisa was as happy as any.

It didn't last. Before she had time to fall out of love with Billy, she was packed off to school in England for four years and not allowed to return until she was sixteen. She hadn't minded school once she had got past the first months of home sickness. Until she experienced it, she had thought those words were only that, but she learnt otherwise. The agony of missing her previous life and most of all her parents had been grim. Like a soldier on a long, wet march with a loaded pack she had taken first of all each minute, and then each hour, and then each day, with a set jaw and dogged determination. And in time, she had settled in, learned to enjoy learning, and made a few friends. But Billy had haunted her dreams for a long, long time.

And today was her wedding day, and she was remembering Billy Tyler. He had been forgotten when she had tumbled into love with Lieutenant Charles Cowper. Charles was not above average height, but was solid, with a chest as deep as his shoulders were broad. He had thick crinkly dull blonde hair that shone with gold lights in the sun, a snub nose and a solid round face smothered in freckles set off with laughing clear blue eyes that never seemed to be serious. He had joined the regiment a year after her return from school, a mature twenty to her seventeen. But then, he had already experienced the bowel-loosening fear of battle and the battle lust of kill or be killed. Such things tended to mature one, she had noticed. Her own maturity had come from searching the battlefield for the injured rather than the dead alongside her mother. And before long, there was just one freckled face in a scarlet jacket she feared most of all to find.

Her mother had noticed her blushes when Charles hove near and smiled indulgently. Louisa now wondered how transparent her feelings had been. Had the see-saw in her guts when he was near, or the lightning bolt of sensation that shot through her hand when he touched her even negligibly, been obvious to all? She gasped down air and hoped beyond hope it had been so. Perhaps then there was a chance, that the Colonel's choice might align with hers. It was he who had, with clear distaste, taken on the task of finding her a husband.

Louisa's father, knowing that neither he nor her mother had any living relatives, had willed her to the regiment, the regimental Colonel to find her a husband in the unlikely event of both of her parents dying. And now the time had come, both she and the Colonel were honouring her father's wishes. Not that she had much choice or any for that matter. As far as she could see, seamstress, washer woman or whore were her only other options.

The French, as throughout history, were annoying the English, and so she, along with her part of the army, remained here, caught between Portugal and Spain, in an effort to keep them within their own borders. As she stood waiting to know her fate the wind rushed down the peaks and through the wool stuff of her outfit right to her skin. It was a soft light green that her mother had always said set off her rather dull dark-blonde hair. English hair. Neither fair nor dark, just sort of middling. It was her very best outfit, the pelisse being edged with fur that was supposed to be squirrel but she feared was cat, and it was already nearly three years old. It did suit her, she supposed, but it was a long way from new, or stylish.

And so she stood in the wind and embraced the chill. This wind could not be colder than her frozen emotions. Below her tumbled the stream that had taken her father. Icy with snow melt and a dozen times its summer size it rushed and roared through a miniature canyon not ten feet below her. A small part of her mind wondered about stepping forward and joining her father. But she was days from being eighteen and he had been fifty-four. That, she found, made a difference. At least at the moment. But dear God how she missed him, and her mother. For a brief moment, she let the pain roar through her before forcing it back into the hidden place in her core. Now was not the time. Perhaps never would be the time. The Army didn't do grief. There was never time and it was unbecoming. Stoicism had been invented by armies and hers was no different.

She was so deep in thought his voice startled her.

'Miss Jenner, how are you?'

Louisa turned her head and found that Charles Cowper's laughing eyes could indeed be serious. For a moment she simply drowned in their blue.

'Well, I believe,' she said softly. What else could she say?

'There are three applicants for your hand, I believe.'

Louisa came back to the present. 'Three? Do you know who they are?' Please let one be you, she pleaded internally, please be one of them, oh, please.

'No, the Colonel is keeping it a private matter.' His voice was sombre.

'You really don't know even one of the names?' It was the closest she could get to asking him outright.

'No. I wanted to wish you well. We all held your father in high regard. He was a good man. And your mother was a wonderful lady. We all admired her and her loss to us is as great as your father's.' He paused as if about to say more, then bade her farewell and walked away.

Louisa watched his back and screamed inside, come back! Hold me! Don't leave me! But his scarlet back kept retreating, and she knew, she just knew, that he wasn't one of the names. So exactly who was she to end up in bed with tonight? Would she even be fortunate enough to have a ring put on her finger to show her altered status? At least the Colonel would not let her be completely dishonoured; his own reputation might be besmirched otherwise, she thought bitterly.

Louisa tipped her head back and swallowed down her pain. Life had turned on her with a vengeance. Her father had joined the army as a boy but had never had the money to buy a rank above Major. Her mother had been a milliner in Bath and they had met by accident when he had been on furlough. Her mother had tripped over a paving stone and fallen hard to her knees. Her father had helped her to her feet and then escorted her home. She had been told the story many, many times. How they fell in love and, when they married, she had sworn to follow the drum beside him. How he had given her three months before she would return to her mother and that they had lasted tight together for nigh on thirty years. She had been a late and much longed-for, surprise.

And now she was alone. Her mother had died suddenly and without warning only three weeks ago. One minute she was hale, and the next she was gone. No one knew why. She had just taken to her bed and then stopped breathing. At first, her father had been too shocked to react, then he had hit the bottle. Night after night, as she stripped off his outer clothes and lay him in his bed Louisa had bitten down on her own grief in fear of what his might bring about. She had seen her father slightly worse for drink, laughing and teasing her mother as she scolded him, but he had always had most of his wits about him, but not now. Now he drank to unconsciousness. And before he passed out, he had been angry and foul-tempered, even to the point of throwing things at her. Terrified, she had waited for the storm to pass.

Instead, he had drunk himself into a semi-stupor and engaged in a card game, where he had rapidly lost his best uniform, all of his blunt, both his swords and his pistols along with her mother's jewellery. Then he had fallen into the very creek she stood over and been found dead and cold as dawn had broken and the sentries had made their rounds. So, she was not only orphaned but totally impoverished. She was hardly a gift for any man.

Her mother had insisted her height had not mattered, but she felt it keenly. She was five foot eight, and many of the troops were shorter than her. She had been called every name under the sun at one time or another, lanky, long Meg, legs, the list went on and on. And now she wondered with dull misery if she was to be taller than her husband. It shouldn't matter, but she was seventeen, and it did. Charles Cowper was only slightly taller than her, but she had known his shoulder would have been perfectly placed for her to rest her weary head upon. But he wasn't one of the three names who had volunteered to take her, she was now certain of that. That he wasn't, was one more heartache to add to the list.

Eventually, when the cold had shafted into her very bones, a valet came to fetch her. Louisa simply gave him a nod and turned and followed him. When all of this was long over, the mountains she had been gazing at would remain, still covered in snow each winter. The thought should have been comforting, but wasn't.

The Colonel was waiting in the tent that acted as his office and command centre. To Louisa's relief, he despatched the valet so that they were alone. Like a bee in her hive, he was normally hidden under a flurry of officers; the young hurrying out to carry orders while the older ones leaned in and offered counsel. Louisa had seen him rarely, and only in heavy company. It was her first opportunity to properly examine him, and he, her. They stood gazing at each other until Louisa remembered her manners and dropped a small curtsey.

He didn't bother with a preamble. That he was somewhat disgusted by this whole business of marrying off one of his officer's daughters was clear.

'Three men offered for your hand. One I dismissed out of hand as unworthy in the light of the other two you had received.'

'Corporal Daly?' she suggested.

'Indeed.'

He gave her a sharp look but didn't enquire as to how she might have guessed one of the names. Daly was a small rat-like man with lank greasy hair who had made suggestive comments in her direction for a long, long time. Sometimes when she was alone, he would mysteriously appear and although he had never reached out to touch her, he had filled her with fear and revulsion, and if by some chance he could force her to push past him, he would. Her father had been keeping an eye on the problem but she swallowed in relief that she was not to be handed to the man on a plate.

'As the daughter of a respected officer, I am pleased that the other two offers are both respectable and from gentlemen. I have selected one.'

Louisa couldn't stop her small gasp of surprise. 'Do I not get to choose?'

The Colonel sniffed in disgust. 'Certainly not girl.'

'May I know who the other gentleman is?'

'I think not,' was the curt reply.

Louisa bit the inside of her mouth hard. They stood holding eye contact for a while before Louisa's dulled mind came up with a suitable question.

'May I ask if the second gentleman's name begins with the letter C?'

'Why girl? Has someone been making you promises?'

'Absolutely not sir,' was Louisa's crisp response.

The Colonel remained frowning at her, and then he sighed. 'You are very young, I suppose, and girls have silly dreams.'

Louisa lifted her chin and said softly, 'Indeed.'

He seemed to like her reply and said suddenly, 'No, I give you my word. It did not.'

'In that case, I shall be grateful to accept the offer of the gentleman you have chosen for me. I have only one question, is he able to financially support a wife? I have no wish to be a burden and I have no dowry.'

'Yes. I have acted indeed in *loco parentis*. This is a man I would have accepted for any daughter of mine.'

Louisa managed a weak smile of thanks. 'I am truly grateful Colonel. I realise this is a distasteful business that has been forced upon you. But I am grateful.'

'Come along then. Let's get this business over with. I will, of course, give you away in lieu of your father.'

The small chapel in the village smelt of animal ordure, which Louisa had not expected, and incense, which she had. Clearly, the space had been recently used to house animals. Which raised interesting questions. All armies simply took what they needed. Only an idiot, or a crook, liked an army near to their fields and families. But tomorrow the army was moving out as they had 'purchased' every edible item for miles around. Clearly, 'every', was not totally accurate. Louisa didn't mind. Even buying foodstuffs wasn't much help to the locals. No one could eat money, but anyone could eat grain, hens or cows. It was a brutal reality. And having a regiment camped nearby was definitely brutal.

The officiating priest was Catholic. It was his chapel and he insisted on being in charge, she presumed.

'Will the marriage be legal?' she whispered to the colonel.

'Your husband is Catholic, so definitely yes. This is best, believe me.'

Louisa shot him a sharp glance. The man seemed to be doing his best by her, and she was grateful. Perhaps she had become slightly less of a nuisance once he had actually looked her in the eye and seen a real person, not simply an irritant mentioned in a will. Also, she was a daughter of his army. She hadn't been wailing in hysterics. Perhaps she had confounded his expectations.

They were standing at the entrance to the chapel. Louisa looked at him as she took in a breath to calm her nerves. To have him beside her in his full uniform was comforting. To her surprise, the colonel shot her a tight smile back and patted the back of her hand.

They had walked from the camp to the chapel, escorted by their troop, polished up as much as was possible while on the march in a foreign mountain range between two suspicious countries, both of which were armed to the teeth with weapons not seen on battlefields in England since the War of the Roses, but still as deadly. A hay fork could eviscerate a man as effectively as a sabre.

First, they had stopped at the graveside to inter her father. He had been sewn into canvas and lowered gently by six infantrymen into the hole, alongside the grave of her mother that was still raw with turned stony soil. A bugler had played and a drummer boy with tears sliding silently down his round cheeks had beat a soft, low, tattoo. Louisa had stood, frozen-faced, and wondered what the men around her thought about her. Her father had been well-liked; more likely to knock back ale or a whiskey with his men than linger with the other officers late into the night. It hadn't made him popular in the Officer's Tent, but he hadn't cared. He didn't have the money for any more promotions and unless a purse from a battle came his way, wasn't likely to ever gain any. Rank was by preferment or hard cash. Skill was not a consideration. Being a good soldier didn't raise you up the ladder, it was who knew you, and how much gold you could hand over.

The chapel was filled to the left with officers' wives, to the right with the officers of her father's regiment in full honour dress. The 44th Regiment of Foot prided itself on being the oldest regiment in the army, and they were burying and marrying one of their own. Outside stood her father's men, drilled into strict rows by their sergeants, all of whom looked ahead, grim-faced. The sergeants had wanted to take her into their care, subsume her into their families with their own wives and daughters, but the Will had been clear and the Colonel determined to respect it. And it wouldn't have worked. Before long one of the wives, perhaps one of the younger ones, would have become convinced Louisa was after her man, and a row would have brewed. Louisa's own actions would have been immaterial. No, marriage was her only saviour.

And, by any measure, the Colonel had done brilliantly by her. Her husband-to-be was Lieutenant Colonel Lord Rupert Douglas McCloud, head of the battalion. She was to be elevated to be Lady Douglas McCloud. She wondered if her father was revolving in heaven. He had had scant respect for the aristocracy. She didn't know the man; had never seen him. Now, in the gloom of the tiny chapel, he stood not twenty feet away at the small altar waiting for her. As the bugler now played a more lively tune, nicely judged she thought, not too slow, not too fast, she tried to make him out. He seemed, to her relief, to be well over average height with thick black hair and matching heavy dark eyebrows that slashed across his face. He was in his scarlet regimentals like the other men, but with a length of green and black tartan swagged around his waist and over one shoulder. It was held in place with a huge diamond-encrusted star brooch that was the only glitter in the place. Certainly, she had nothing to match it.

She just had time for the thought, 'Why on earth is he marrying me?' before the Colonel stepped forward and she began to be moved firmly down the aisle.

All through the service, Louisa was trying to remember the name of the village. How would she ever find her parents' graves again here in the Sierras? She had been trying to imprint the pattern of the mountain tops in her mind; perhaps one day she might be able to return. When this war was over, or the next one. Being given as the legally owned chattel to a man she had never met seemed unimportant by comparison. Her thoughts were far from her present and her responses to the priest were automatic. She had attended enough weddings; she knew what to say.

The dinner in their honour dragged as Louisa sat numbly in amongst her father's brother officers and the wives who had followed them. Few did. Louisa's mother had been in a minority. Louisa knew who all of them were but the wives of the more senior officers had always ignored her. Their sudden keen attention now bewildered her and she was far from any kind of emotional state to find suitable responses. So she nodded when it seemed appropriate and picked at her food. She could never remember when she had before felt so exhausted.

Lord Rupert's accommodation was far superior to the one her parents had enjoyed. She hadn't thought that the village was large enough to have a mayor, but when she heard one of the servants mention the *Alcalde*, she assumed that this had been his house. She doubted that he had handed it over willingly. The bedroom was large, which surprised her, and dominated by a massive, heavily carved, four-poster bed in a wood so dark that was almost black in the candlelight. There was a padded screen, so she went behind it and stripped naked. Slowly she washed every inch of her skin until it glowed. She would not go to her marriage bed begrimed with road dust. If her husband took a distaste for her, it would not be because she was dirty. The story of how Henry VIII had complained that Anne of Cleves stank on his wedding night had dug deep into her mind.

She sat on the bed in her neck-to-toe white calico nightdress and waited. She never touched wine but had sometimes sipped her father's ale. It was not a lady's drink, but she had rather liked it, compared to the wine, watered or not, that she was supposed to get used to as an adult. To her, the ale had tasted thirst-quenching and refreshing and decidedly not sweet, like some of the horrendous drinks 'ladies' were often expected to consume. But right now, she thought she could have downed a pint of decent ale as fast as her father had. She wasn't particularly nervous. She knew roughly what to expect. No one could have experienced the childhood she had in following the drum and not worked out what was what between men and women. So, she waited in the soft light of a single candle, before suddenly losing her nerve and lighting two more. She needed light to retain her nerve, she thought; deep shadows suggested too much that might be unknown.

Downstairs a door slammed and loud boot steps could be heard clattering up the stairs. Louisa stood and waited by the bed. Lord Rupert came in with a clash of the door against the wall, and she wondered how drunk he was. It was his wedding night too, she supposed. And if he was seriously drunk, all he would be capable of would be sleep. He stood in the doorway and gazed around the room and finally at her. She was standing tall now at the side of the bed, with her chin up, her fists clenched by her side.

'Huh,' he said. And strode to sit on the other side of the bed to her. 'Geordie!' he yelled.

Louisa didn't move but waited as the valet came in and divested his master of his boots and the tartan sash and brooch.

'Lock that away,' he gestured at the brooch, 'and bugger off,' was the noble lord's instruction.

He then began to undress with efficiency and speed. He had his back to her and was throwing his uniform and under-clothes into a corner with gusto. Poor valet, thought Louisa. All the clothes would look like rags in the morning. The coat would need brushing and pressing, the shirt probably a wash and iron. As his shirt came off over his head, she regarded his back. It was broad and fleshy with a couple of healed sabre slashes on one side. His buttocks were square and solid-looking as were his thighs. He had no hair on his back, she was relieved to see. Hairy backs revolted her, though she didn't know why. She didn't mind the thick pelt on his thighs or chest, they by contrast seemed manly and acceptable. Naked, he turned to face her and then strode off to the screen. She heard him piss, and then tip some water into a bowl and then came the sounds of washing. Louisa did not move. She was no longer sure she could.

He emerged eventually and strode towards the bed. It took all her self-control not to wince, but she managed it. Swinging his head sideways to look at her he hauled the covers back to reveal good white linen sheets and said,

'You can take that bloody thing off,' nodding towards her nightgown.

Now Louisa wished she had found the guts to blow out all of the candles. Silently, she pulled the nightgown over her head and folded it neatly and lay it on a chair. Her mother had made it for her, placing every stitch with care. Rupert had walked to the other side of the bed again. He stood there, hands on hips, and regarded her.

'Good body,' he said, non-committedly. 'Colonel tells me you are a virgin. Are you?'

Louisa swallowed and lifted her chin a little higher. 'Yes.'

'Any proof?' he asked.

Louisa stood frowning at him; her fists clenched so tightly by her sides that the knuckles must have been bone. After a long while, she said,

'I am not sure it is possible to prove a negative.'

'No, suppose not,' he said, 'get in.'

As naked as the day she was born, Louisa slipped between the sheets.

Chapter 2

She woke to the sounds of Rupert moving around the room. When she looked up, he was pulling a clean and pressed shirt from the dresser and tugging it over his head. When he saw she was awake he instructed, 'Get up.'

Louisa did so. She had slipped back into her nightdress when she had been sure the man beside her was asleep, so now she rose and stood again beside the bed.

'Throw back the covers,' was his second instruction.

A man used to giving orders she thought. No surprise there, she supposed. When she had done so he came towards her and pulled them even further back. He looked the sheets over thoroughly. Then he turned and looked her in the eye.

'Thought you said you were a virgin.'

'I was.'

'Then where's the blood?'

'What blood?'

'There should be at least spotting.'

'Spotting?'

'Blood. Blood spotting.' His voice was harsh.

Louisa was still utterly lost. Her mother had warned her the first time would hurt, and it had, but she hadn't mentioned anything else.

'Should you have wounded me? Is that what should happen?'

He leaned into her and stared at her intently. It was clear he was beginning to lose his temper. She could feel the colour rise in her cheeks but was at a total loss for what to say.

'Virgins bleed. I have a notion I have been short-changed. If I have, the wedding will be annulled.'

Louisa stood for a long while utterly numb. Had he pulled some kind of trick on her? Had she been a fool to trust the Colonel? Meanwhile, Rupert continued to dress as the door opened and the valet brought in coffee, rolls and butter. Louisa fled behind the screen. She hauled off her nightdress and began to wash the stickiness from her thighs. The white cloth was slightly smeared with something brown. In the dim light behind the screen, Louisa peered more closely. Then she realised what it was. She made sure the cloth was well soaked, then pulled on her chemise and a skirt and strode, bare footed back into the room. Walking over to Rupert, who was slouching over his breakfast and reading some kind of report, she dropped the sopping cloth onto his groin. Onto his uniform trouser-clad groin.

'You should have checked my thighs. I am an army daughter. I have not been out of someone's sight since I was in leading strings. If I had so much as touched a man's hand it would have been all round the regiment, let alone had I allowed any man close enough to poke me. In any case, one whisper about my reputation not being absolutely without stain and my father would have whipped me to within an inch of my life.'

The latter was a lie. Her father had adored her and would have forgiven her anything, but this lout wasn't to know that.

'Do that again,' he said, tossing the cloth onto the floor, 'and I will be the one whipping you.'

'So, is there to be an annulment, or do you accept me, as I have had to accept you?'

He stared at her for a long while, then said, 'No annulment,' before standing and striding out of the room, wet trousered and half breakfasted.

Louisa sat down and polished off the rolls and milk. She was hungry. And shaking.

The days had always flown by. She and her mother had 'kept house' with as little help as possible. They had used a washerwoman, when necessary, but their lodgings were usually basic and plain and took little cleaning. It was never as if it was ever their own house, so they did not feel inclined to polish and primp to any great degree. It had been different in India of course. There they had been swamped with servants, but here in the Peninsula, it was different. Staff were both hard to come by and expensive. It hadn't mattered. They had all been content and the present had slid into the past easily. Both she and her mother had loved sewing, and in the afternoons, would often sit for an age silently together, simply content to be in each other's company, her mother often making clothes, such as her nightgown, while she had enjoyed experimenting with decorative embroidery.

But now, as the valet, Geordie, was it? bustled in Louisa was at a loss for what to do with herself. From the furtive glances the valet was directing, it was clear that she was decidedly in the way so Louisa left the room and made her way out into the village. As she stepped outside the crisp, clean, mountain air hit her. She took a deep breath. The sun was high. Both she and Lord Rupert has slept late. Now, despite the cold, the light was brilliantly clear and was casting deep and vivid shadows in amongst the huddle of whitewashed homes that made up the village. Most were thatched, but a few were roofed with flat red clay tiles. High-walled sties were scattered in no apparent pattern, and as she passed more than one curious snout poked above the structures to see who she was, and no doubt whether she had food with her or not. She quite liked pigs. Louisa had often thought that they had brighter minds than people generally gave them credit for. She could not see another human anywhere and the silent emptiness of the village with its brilliant light and impenetrable shadows was oddly unnerving.

At a loss, she headed down the narrow lanes towards the army camp across the river. The village sat on higher ground and some of the pathways were so steep she felt she might lose her footing, but eventually, she found the bridge. It was guarded by two sentries she didn't know; they were not men of the 44th, not that she knew every one of them. To her surprise, they both snapped to attention and saluted as she reached them. Louisa stumbled to a halt feeling bewildered. Normally she would nod and exchange a general greeting before going on her way. It was a rare occasion that she would be asked who she was.

'Lady McCloud,' snapped one.

Neither sentry looked at her, but both fixed their gaze past her and into the middle distance. Louisa felt herself go bright red. Feeling horribly exposed and uncomfortable she nodded and carried on walking onto the bridge. Should she have given the order to 'stand down' or 'stand easy'? Was she authorised to do that? She had absolutely no idea and supposed she should ask Lord Rupert tonight.

Army gossip had it that the bridge had been a flat wooden construction, wide enough to take a man and a donkey, and with wooden walls on each side to waist height. Considering her father had died further up the river in one of its streams, and he had been a large, grown, man, no doubt the walls had helped to let the women and children cross safely in winter when there was ice and in spring with the snow melt roaring below. Apparently, the army engineers had taken one look, and then with their second felled it into pieces within minutes. The new bridge they had constructed would easily take a carriage or an army waggon full of supplies. It was wide and sturdy but lacked the wooden sides. She supposed if the locals wanted, they could add those once the army moved on.

Down on her left in a sandy curve, the army washer-women were smashing clothes against the rocks with gusto. With skirts hauled up to mid-thigh and arms that could take on a male wrestler, they were gossiping and laughing as they worked. Louisa paused and watched them a moment. Should she have joined them? Was Lord Rupert really a better option? But she knew the answer. The water they were standing in was freezing, and their strength was formidable. She would probably have died of cold and exhaustion the first winter! And he had taken her on. She owed him her loyalty and gratitude.

The instant she stepped off the bridge the world changed. Gone was the eerie shadowed silence of the village up on the hill, here was activity incarnate. Everywhere men hurried to perform one task or another, in odd spots army comrades smoked a pipe companionably together around a small fire, and children darted hither and yon, just as she had with Billy and Pump all those years ago. Here and there, women stood talking as ranked soldiers marched pass on their way to sentry or other duties. And tents as far as the eye could see.

Louisa moved forward instinctively heading for the encampment of the 44th. She saw Genine scolding her two eldest daughters. On spotting her, Genny dropped to a curtsey. Louisa swallowed and gave a brief nod.

'Lady Louisa', Genny greeted her.

'Mrs Hawthorne,' Louisa murmured. Yesterday they had been Genny and Lou!

Genny was gazing hard at her. She dropped another curtsey as if to take her leave but used the movement to step closer to Louisa. As her head went down, she hissed, 'Chapel. Ten minutes.'

Louisa gave another nod and moved on as if no communication had been undertaken. As she moved away, she could hear Genny instructing, 'Alice, Maria, take the little ones for half an hour.'

She could then hear Alice protesting. Alice was lovely, with pale blonde hair that waved naturally around her face; and she knew it. Maria was as plain as Alice was pretty, but her smile was the sweetest ever seen giving her face the otherworldly loveliness of an angel. Genny always moaned that Alice would break a dozen hearts as she had not one herself, but Maria was likely to love once and have her heart smashed to pieces. Proud as she was of all her children, Genny reckoned to be a mother was to enter a world of worry. That was something Lord Rupert could give her that washing clothes couldn't Louisa thought; a child and a home for that child. There was now that hope.

Louisa made her way out of the encampment to the small knoll where the chapel stood. She slipped into the interior gloom and found her way to the back left-hand corner where she sat on a rough, hard, pew and waited. She remembered how her nose had itched during the service. Skirmishers had taught her as a child that if an itch was ignored, it would eventually stop. She had learned well. Even if a scorpion or snake moved over them when they were behind enemy lines, they would lay absolutely still, until eventually, the irritation would cease. After all, any movement might bring the enemy down on their heads. So she and Billy and Pump had practised and practised. It was a small skill, yet one she was proud of. So she hadn't scratched at her nose as she had repeated the vows that placed her in the charge of a stranger.

As she sat in the quiet gloom, she looked around the rough, whitewashed, walls with its small altar and one glazed window high on the altar wall. She was without thought. Without movement. It might have been forty minutes or an hour before Genny joined her, but Louisa did not fidget, did not move at all. Eventually, the door opened letting in more light, and Genny bustled over to sit beside her.

'Sorry love. Kids!' Genny peered around Louisa who still didn't move to frown up into her face. 'How are you love?' Louisa licked her lips, but only gave a small nod. 'I didn't know what your ma had told you, like what to expect last night.'

'I'm alright,' she said softly. 'I wasn't too naive. When I was quite small mama and I walked past the end of an alley. Infantryman Drummond had a girl pinned up against a wall in the shadows. She had her legs round his waist and her arms round his neck and he was pumping away at her. His bare arse was on view.'

Genny gave a snort, 'Drummond hey. Nothing that big brute did would surprise me. Well, at least it wasn't too much of a surprise.'

Louisa didn't say anything for a moment. What she most vividly remembered was the girl's face screwed up in pain as her back thumped against the ale house wall and how she had looked out for a brief moment straight into Louisa's eyes. Then she had fixed a smile on her face and turned towards Drummond. It had been a sharp lesson in the duties of a whore. Slowly, Louisa bent forward at the waist, her mouth open in a silent howl, and burying her face in her hands, began to sob. Genny pulled her over gently so her face was in her own skirts and stroked her back as the tears shuddered from her.

It took a long while for the storm to pass. When Louisa eventually heaved herself upright the lap of Genny's brown skirt was dark from the tears. Louisa looked at the large damp patch and muttered, 'Sorry.'

'I'll say I pissed myself,' Genny murmured, trying to lighten the moment. It worked in that Louisa gave a small gasp of a laugh. 'Did he treat you alright?' Genny asked.

'He came in and he stripped and he ordered me to strip and then he rolled on top and poked me. Then in the morning, he got in a paddy because there was no blood on the sheets. Do women bleed every time a man does that?'

'Ah,' said Genny and went quiet for a while.

Louisa interrupted her thoughts, 'But there was some blood. It had dried down my thigh, so he said he would not annul the marriage. Could he have done that?'

Again, Genny went very quiet, obviously thinking. 'Well,' she said, 'it is said that a virgin bleeds her first time, but I never did and I have never been with anyone other than my Frank. Mind you, we had done a lot of fiddling around before we managed to get to the aisle. Frank knew he would get a thick ear if he doubted me; I had been all his since

I was fourteen. Never looked at another boy or man.'

'Do you, I mean,' Louisa was clearly flustered, 'do you do it much?'

Genny patted her hand, 'Quite a lot,' she said calmly.

'But how can you bear it! It hurt so much!' The whore's grimace of pain was in her mind's eye again echoing with her own pain of the night before.

'Ah,' said Genny. 'See, I loves my Frank. I like to cuddle him, be close to him and, well, I like to touch him and be touched. When there ain't no love, well, it is up to the skill of the man to make it, I don't know, comfortable.'

Even in the dark chapel, Louisa could see that Genny's cheeks were quite red now. Louisa sat and absorbed this. 'I see,' she said, but she didn't really.

She had been quite besotted with Charles Cowper, but her mind had not gone past the hope of touching his hand one day! She had loved to catch sight of him, a glimpse had made her day wonderful, and to stand nearby while her father spoke to him with her eyes downcast but her ears catching every cadence of his voice had thrilled her to blushing confusion. How green she had been! And she had thought she knew it all!

Genny's voice interrupted her thoughts. 'It shouldn't ever hurt that much again,' she said softly.

'Well,' said Louisa briskly, 'I certainly hope not.' And then she came out with one of her mother's favourite phrases, 'And this will not get the baby a new bonnet!'

This bizarre phrase meant that the day was idling away when there was work to be done. Genny took the hint, rather too rapidly for Louisa's liking.

'Yes, well, I need to get on.' She began to fuss with her skirts. 'You do know that this may be the last time we ever get to speak to each other, don't you?'

Louisa nodded. She was now Lady Louisa, and her conversations must now be with ladies that were appropriate to her husband's rank. Her contented past life was now gone. Time to move into the new.

'I'll go first,' Genny offered.

As Genny stood Louisa asked softly, 'Why do you think he married me?'

Genny gave her a sad look. 'No idea, love. Odd though, ain't it? Grand man the likes of 'im.'

And then she was gone, and a long and loving friendship was probably over.

It was early afternoon and Louisa had no idea what to do with her day, so she made her way back slowly to Lord Rupert's dwelling. The path from the bridge seemed impossibly steep, but perhaps that was because her heart weighed so much! To her surprise, Rupert was in the house. He was slouched in a chair in the large downstairs room to the right of the front entrance. He greeted her by tipping his whisky glass in her direction. Louisa swallowed her nervousness and went to sit in the room with him. If they were to be together for the rest of their lives they needed to at least rub along together.

'I have had Geordie lay out your clothing on the bed. It is disreputable, to say the least,' was his opening remark.

Louisa was so taken aback all she found to say was, 'On the bed?'

'Not much, is there?' His voice was deep and amused, as was the twinkle in his eye.

Louisa didn't trust that twinkle one bit. She had no reply to that. So she changed tack. 'I thought we were moving out today and heading north.'

His face lost its good-humoured look. 'What do you know about that?'

'Just that there was a rumour that today was the day we would move on, but clearly, nothing is happening. No tents have been struck.' She looked at him curiously.

'Army events are none of your business,' he snapped.

Louisa wasn't sure what to say. Moving out was a massive undertaking and everyone, men, women and children would be involved and affected. Such a huge event was hardly likely to be a secret.

'My father always discussed army matters with me and my mother. We needed to pack up as much as the troops did.'

'Ah, of course. Your mother marched with your father, did she not.' It was a sneer.

'We both did,' Louisa said flatly, 'and he kept us as informed as he considered suitable.'

Rupert's reply was a drawn-out, 'Hmm.'

Louisa was annoyed. 'I suppose,' she said, 'the skirmishers or the scouts came back with information.'

'What do you know about that?' Rupert's heavy brows were drawn down now.

Louisa sighed. 'I was born into the army, apart from four years away at school I have witnessed just about most of what the army is about. I am not blind.' Or stupid, she wanted to add but didn't feel she could. He might disagree!

Rupert gave another, 'Hmm.' After a while, he said, 'Not like other officers' wives, are you.'

Louisa felt herself go red. 'On the contrary,' she offered softly, 'it has always seemed to me there are two types of wives of every rank. Those who stay at home and those who march. My mother and I were not unique in following an officer.'

'Suppose not,' grunted Rupert.

'Why did you marry me?'

Rupert stayed silent a long while. 'Dj'know Carstairs? Simon Carstairs?' From his slurred voice it was clear the afternoon had included more than the whisky he was currently drinking.

'No.'

'Got the pox. French disease. Got it bad.' Rupert had closed his eyes.

'I believe the French call it the English disease,' Louisa offered softly.

His response was a snort of laughter. Somehow that cheered Louisa immensely. After another long pause where Louisa sat frozen wondering if he had dozed off, he seemed to recollect that they were in the middle of a conversation.

'Well, I don't want the pox. Bad business that. Thought a virgin was the answer. Was drunk and upset about Carstairs when I offered for you. Colonel wouldn't let me back out after. Clever bastard on the quiet. Probably thought marriage might settle me down.' He closed his eyes again.

Louisa's blood ran cold. She wasn't at all sure how to follow that. 'What about children?'

'Oh, shouldn't think we shall have any.'

Louisa raised her eyebrows. How he was going to manage that if he intended to continue bedding her. she wasn't sure. But he hadn't finished.

'Women tend to die in childbirth. Known fact.'

Well, that was true, but the comment didn't warm Louisa's blood any. A loud snore came from the opposite chair, so Louisa slipped from the room while he slept. She climbed the stairs quietly. As Rupert said, all of her dresses and outerwear were spread out on the bed. Slowly she began to refold everything and put it all back into her clothing trunk. She had only just begun when Geordie came in.

'Now then,' he said with a tut, 'that is my job. His Lordship has sent for a sewing woman. Says you are to have new duds. Asleep, is he? Can't keep off the stuff, silly bugger.'

Louisa blinked. This was not the sort of valet she had expected the domineering Lord Rupert to have. But he hadn't finished,

'Got this for you, I have.'

To Louisa's surprise, he handed over her sewing basket. Her heart leapt. Her father had staked 'all his worldly goods' on his last card game and when the men had come in to claim their winnings, they had left her almost nothing. She had been lucky to be allowed her clothing trunk. The sewing basket had gone out the door along with all their bedding, spare food, her father's weapons, everything.

'Young officer handed it in. Fair chap. Lieutenant.'

Charles! thought Louisa as she rummaged in the basket to see if anything was missing. Thankfully enough it all seemed to be as it should. Some of her sewing silks had come from their time in India, along with gold thread and tiny mirrors that the local woman had so skilfully sewn into their saris. Louisa would have hated to lose it all. In some odd way, it was a kind of contact with her parents.

'You are eating in the mess. His Lordship says you are to behave better this time.' Geordie's voice was disparaging.

'Better?'

'Never said boo to a goose, he says.'

Quite, thought Louisa, but then I had just buried my father, who only survived my mother by three weeks, and been married off to a stranger, who it seems is a drunken sot!

'What you need to remember is that his title is the most senior in the mess.' Geordie's tone was lecturing. Louisa was beginning to dislike him. 'Came over with the Conqueror his lot did. Got sent north again and again until they ended up in Scotland. Weren't always called Douglas McCloud. That was for politics, see? All them other lords and ladies, they have to give way to him, see, as he is the most regal, like.'

A less regal man Louisa had never seen, when she thought of the drunk downstairs catching flies with his mouth open and snoring fit to burst. She sighed, picked up her sewing basket, and made her way out onto the narrow balcony at the back of the room. There was a good light there and she could amuse herself by creating pictures with her stitches and coloured threads.

Dinner that night was utterly boring. Her mother had occasionally attended mess meals, but her father had always refused Louisa's invitation on her behalf, and now she understood why. Nights with her father would mean him sitting smiling and sucking on an old clay pipe, a fiddler making a tune, a couple (often two troopers playing the idiot) dancing, a few dealing cards, and most of the women talking non-stop about their children and what they were up to. There had been laughter, good humour, and comradeship. Now she sat while both men and women fawned over her and slid sly comments to her disfavour that they seemed to believe she could not hear behind her back, while all the time she was expected to smile and give every appearance that she was both impressed and happy to be there. Rupert was opposite her and sat for the whole time downing whisky and watching her with half-closed eyes. Louisa sat as upright as she could, lifted her chin, and answered each and every question politely while giving away as little information as possible. How she stopped herself yawning she didn't know.

Gradually, the bottles emptied, wine-soaked the damask cloth, cutlery scattered and porcelain clashed as the tenor of the evening altered. Jokes became bawdier, comments cruder. When some of the more senior ladies made to leave, Louisa joined them with alacrity. If this was to be her future, heaven help her.

She was in her bed asleep when Rupert came in. He whipped back the covers and stood looking down at her. Louisa came to blinking, for the moment unsure of where she was. Her father had been a large man, equally as large as Lord Rupert, yet she had never been afraid of him. Suddenly she felt as if there was not enough air in the room for her to breathe, the man in front of her seemed to fill the space entirely.

'Get that bloody thing off,' he instructed gesturing to her nightgown.

Louisa slipped from the bed and did as instructed. Her heart was pounding, and she felt real fear of her husband for the first time. Animosity seemed to come off him in waves. Nervously she slipped out of the garment and moved to fold it onto the chair. Rupert grasped her wrist harshly and tugged her back toward the bed, so she sat down sharply. Her shoulder ached from his yanking. The nightgown fell to the floor in a heap as he pulled his shirt over his head and shoved her so she fell onto her back. With harsh fingers, he ensured her thighs were open and rolled on top of her. Louisa was sure she was not going to be able to breathe. He stank of old sweat and stale whisky and she, used to most scents of bodies and animals, almost heaved. He shoved inside her and she couldn't stop the high-pitched noise she made against the pain. His chest was hard against her, his shoulder jammed in her face so she could hardly breathe. In panic, she clenched her fists and bit down on her lower lip until she tasted blood. Her world was his weight, his heat, and the pain deep inside. Teeth tightly clenched she grunted in agony every time he thrust forward.

When he had finished, he rolled to one side. Lying with one arm over his eyes he muttered, 'Whores are more interesting.'

'Whores are whores by profession. I am a whore by necessity,' she snapped.

She had sat up to reach for her nightgown intending to pull it back on. His slap took her breath away. Her jaw shot backwards and the pain exploded behind her closed eyes.

'I'll have no backchat from the likes of you!' was his comment, before turning and casually blowing out the candle.

Louisa's tears shamed her and she bit them back as hard as she could. When he began to snore, she reached to the floor for her nightgown and tugged it over her head.

He was gone in the morning when she awoke. Which, considering she had not fallen asleep until near dawn, was no surprise. Geordie was clattering about removing Lord Rupert's breakfast items.

'Milk and rolls do for you, miss?' he asked cheerily.

Louisa nodded and padded behind the screen to hide and wash. She was shocked at how much the slap had affected her. She had never been hit in her life before. The knowledge that her husband not only could strike her but would, left her feeling shaky and lost in a world she now knew she did not understand. Clearly, her parent's marriage was no use as a guiding template for her own. Worse, she had no idea what she had done to bring about his censure!

The army was not going to move onward for another two weeks. Louisa felt offended that it was her husband's valet who gave her the information and not him himself. To her absolute surprise, a seamstress arrived when she had only just finished her breakfast. How Lord Rupert had rustled her up she did not know, but clearly, he intended to use the delay to dress his new acquisition in a way he considered more fitting. The woman was clearly French, with a heavy accent to her spoken English.

'Why are you working for us? Doesn't your revolution make us the enemy?' Louisa asked her.

'Huh. I work for who pays,' was the brisk reply.

When the woman then called her 'Miss' Louisa stared her hard in the eye. 'I am Lady Louisa, and you will refer to me as My Lady if you need to refer to me at all.'

One thing the slap had achieved was that Louisa was now going to stand on her status whenever possible. She could not afford to make friends with people Lord Rupert might consider of too lowly a station; that could definitely lead to another chastisement. The woman dropped her eyes but not before she had glimpsed the look of resentment there.

On instinct, Louisa strode to the door and swung it open. Geordie stood there eavesdropping, completely unabashed.

'If I catch you again, I will tell Lord Rupert you were trying to see me undressed,' she hissed at him. The only way to describe Geordie's departure was as a flounce. Louisa wasn't sure, but she thought she heard him say,

'Don't know why he needs you when he had me!'

As Louisa stood to be measured and pinned, she gazed into the middle distance and thought. Two phrases came to mind. The first was Genny's; It is up to the man to make it comfortable for the woman, or something like that. It sounded as if the pain Rupert was causing her was either deliberate or through lack of skill. Neither made much sense. If he had contracted her in order to have the comfort of a marriage bed with a known woman, why not make that bed comfortable for her, so that she might be more willing? The second phrase was Geordie's, and that helped her to make sense of her new life even less. That men sometimes preferred other men to women was of no surprise to her. For one, she had read more about the ancient Greeks than her parents or her school suspected, but her understanding had been driven by the whispers she had overheard and the observation of her own eyes. That there were on rare occasions men who cared for each other rather beyond the limits of military comradeship had been clear to her since childhood, especially when they had been in India. As a child, she had accepted such couples as natural. It was only as she began to grow that she realised that such relationships were forbidden and never acknowledged. That didn't mean people didn't suspect, it was just that it was crucial never to refer to such affections. But when one of the couple had been transferred, killed in battle, or died of illness, the grief of the remaining partner had been awful both in its extent and in the way it had to be hidden from view.

But again, that made no sense. If Geordie and Lord Rupert were such a couple, why did he worry about the pox, and why marry her? But then his words came back to her. Something he had said about the Colonel being a wily fox. Also, about the Colonel wanting to settle him down. She wished she could remember the exact words, but they had slipped away in amongst the waves of pain and fear.

Once her size had been taken, the French woman began to lay out fabrics and suggested styles. Louisa had always chosen green as her favourite colour as she considered it showed off her rather boring hair, and brown when practicality had been foremost. But the seamstress went straight to a rich royal blue.

'For you, the colours of sapphires, rubies and emeralds,' she declared.

Louisa blinked in surprise. The modest moss and sage greens of her wardrobe were nothing like the colours this woman was suggesting. Louisa began to change her mind as a swathe of rich, deep, blue was draped across her shoulders. In the rather spotted long mirror in the room, she was amazed at how it lit up her hair and even made her hazel eyes look more interesting. It seemed she was to have two evening gowns, two day gowns and a riding habit. The styles were simple and to Louisa's taste and she absolutely fell in love with the heavy wool in a deep, rich, red that was to be her riding habit. The fact that she didn't have a horse seemed irrelevant at the moment! Although she still viewed the French seamstress with suspicion, it seemed she really did know her trade. However, she found it impossible to warm to a woman whose countrymen would willingly kill her own and whose presence behind enemy lines she viewed with mistrust.

Her second surprise of the day was the arrival of a small Portuguese girl who, it seemed, was to be her maid. Louisa breathed a sigh of relief as none of the new gowns fastened at the front as all of her old ones had, and she was thoroughly tired of trying to make her hair look smart for the endless and tedious mess dinners.

The days slipped by and Louisa made cautious friends with some of the other officer's wives, not now as her mother's daughter but as Lady McCloud, a person in her own right. Unbeknown to her she was developing a reputation as an elegant and impressive woman. The luxurious gowns in simple styles and deep rich colours were being sketched and copied and now her hair was heaped up into formal styles her appearance was, in the eyes of those interested, considered entirely to be admired. Many a man gazed at her over the candlelight and came to the sudden and surprising revelation that the insignificant Major's daughter had a delectable profile, a long elegant neck, and calm exquisite manners they would enjoy ruffling.

The main reason for her rise to fame, a rise she was wholly unaware of, was her complete composure. Louisa felt as though she was swimming in a sea of sharks. One wrong move on her part and the company around her might tear her limb from limb. So she kept her own counsel and made no especial friends. She was unfailingly polite, but always somewhat distant. When she completely failed to respond to the rather ribald comments always made to new brides, her stock rose even further. What they were all looking for, and prodding for, were the blushes of a young woman who was discovering the pleasures and sensations of the flesh for the first time. What they received was the iron self-discipline of a woman suffering brutality each night. On his part, Lord Rupert always insisted on sitting immediately opposite her, a sign to onlookers that he was besotted and a sign to Louisa that he didn't trust her an inch. As he watched her each evening from hooded eyes and the inevitable glass of whisky, Louisa felt as though she was an insect pinned to an inspection board.

Life slipped into a routine and the army packed up and moved with all the upheaval, efficiencies and inefficiencies that involved. Louisa planned to walk in the train as she and her mother always had and was again surprised by her husband when a glossy chestnut-coloured cob was brought over to her. Louisa fell in love at once. Her horse was sturdy, with feathers around her hooves, and a gentle and solid manner. In her rich, red, riding habit, settled on the chestnut cob that was a size appropriate for her height, she was entirely unaware that she looked like a queen. Louisa felt her first glimmer of happiness in a long while. Riding freed her and gave her someone to love who could show affection back. Rupert hadn't hit her again and life was settling on an even keel that was beginning to feel like an acceptable existence.

Then, on the second morning of the march, Rupert had stood eyeing her for a while as she ate her breakfast. His inspection had caused a faint blush of discomposure to rise up her neck but she had continued chewing slowly and hoped he would go away. To her utter surprise, he had muttered, 'You are a good lass,' before striding out. That comment had transformed her. It suggested that there was a glimmer of hope that this marriage might, eventually, turn into something they could both be comfortable with. The whole of that day, with a lovely horse below her responsive to her voice and movements, the sunshine, the crisp mountain air, and Rupert's apparent approval to buoy her, Louisa found herself happier than she had felt in a long time. The dust, the noise, the confusion, the hold-ups, and the indifferent food were all normal to her, and nothing could lower her. She was determined to make the best of things.

At one of the stops on the third day, Charles Cowper came to find her. She was standing by the neck of her horse, patting and whispering loving words to her as the army trailed by. His voice took her by surprise. She turned to meet his gaze.

'Lady Louisa,' he greeted her, 'how do you do?'

'Very well, Lieutenant Cowper, thank you. I hope I find you well.'

Louisa regarded him with sadness. Not so long ago she had craned her neck all day in the hope of a glimpse of him. A simple acknowledgement would send her to sleep with a smile on her face for days. He hadn't changed, she supposed, she had. Then she remembered.

'I believe you returned my sewing basket? Thank you, I missed it dreadfully and was glad to have it returned to me.'

'Charles now, please, and it was my pleasure.'

Charles, she thought. Yes, I suppose so. I am so fearfully elevated.

For his part, Cowper was amazed. The sweet, shy and, he had thought, gauche girl who had amused by blushing at the sight of him was gone. As were her threadbare skirts and the plaits she had always worn wrapped around her head. Now he was faced with a pale, composed woman whose reserve was plainly evident. Louisa watched him with increasing cynicism. His admiration was obvious. But then, she supposed, everything had changed. Now she was dressed in costly fabrics, cut with skill to show off her figure. Her Portuguese maid, unbelievably called Millie, had styled her thick and heavy hair into a complex pile of interlocking coils that while not English in style, was undoubtedly stylish and suited her admirably; she had never been, nor ever would be, a candidate for the fussy curls so many women forced upon their hair. What no one could see, of course, was that Lord Rupert, her literal lord and master, had sprung for what was externally essential for his status, but nothing that he considered non-essential. Such as her worn and darned undergarments. After all, only he and Millie saw those.

'Louisa, I am so sorry,' Cowper blurted out.

Louisa played dumb. 'Sorry?' she enquired coolly.

He reached out and grasped her hand. Louisa tried to pull away but he held her fast.

'I believe I have made the biggest mistake of my life!' he declared.

'Indeed,' she said calmly, surreptitiously tugging her wrist to try to make him release his grasp.

'I should have bid for you!' he declared with passion. 'But I have two brothers! All we would have had to live on would have been my army pay. I have no expectation of any other funds!'

Louisa thought of her parents, who also had managed on only army pay. And of the stretching of every penny to make it do the work of two, and of the patching and mending and of the deep contentment they had found together and in her. Disgust roiled her stomach. She was not as naïve as she had been. She was now a target for Cowper and others like him, married and unmarried. Any child she conceived with an illicit relationship would have to be claimed by her husband. She was now far riper game than when she had been the regiment's darling child and an innocent. Cowper's oh-so-blue eyes were now very close to hers, and they moved her not at all. Leaning forward she hissed in his face,

'Let me go, now, or I will scream blue murder.'

'But Louisa!' he protested.

So, she stamped on his foot. His boot protected him, but the shock of her attack caused him to reconsider and he released her wrist.

'Don't you ever call me Louisa again. I am Lady Louisa. I have never been nor will I ever be just Louisa to you.'

Cowper's face sneered. 'Got too high for the likes of me, have you?'

And Louisa thought, Rupert might be a pig, but he is at least an honest pig. He put a ring on my finger, admitted why he did so, and has clad me and fed me and housed me.

When he walked away, clearly angry at how the exchange had gone, she watched his back for a long time. It now seemed clear that, because of her earlier infatuation, he had expected her to fall into his arms. Marrying him would have been a huge mistake. It was now clear that he was not a man inclined to respect marriage vows, certainly not those of others and, she suspected, not his own when he made them either. Turning, amidst the clamour and noise and confusion of an army actively on the move, she found Geordie staring at her. Sighing, she used a nearby log to help her remount and re-joined the muddy trail. Early spring was never an easy time to travel.

Louisa didn't see Rupert for the rest of the march. She was billeted with other officers' wives in various farmhouses, all poor, all basic, all smelling of various beasts, along the way. This part of the continent, caught between Spain and Portugal, seemed an unlikely trophy for any country to go to war over, despite its mountains, but everyone seemed convinced that the French bandits, most of whom had walked away from their army, were the forerunners of a future French invasion. Rupert seemed certain that at some point, the French bandits would be called to order and would then march along these mountains not as a rag-tag of looters, but as drilled troops. The Portuguese rulers were afraid, too, that revolution might infect their population. How the British army could help, she wasn't sure, but that was their alleged role.

She pitied the locals, and at times, when tired, pitied herself. Most of the wives had said farewell to their husbands and sailed from the Portuguese city of Oporto as the army vacated their winter quarters. The ones who remained were the older ones, often with grown children who, like Louisa, were experienced and hardened to army life. As the youngest by far, but also the one, courtesy of Rupert, with the highest status, she was in an ambivalent position. The other women were kind but in a somewhat disinterested way. Louisa suspected they didn't like Rupert much; he was a heavy drinker and louche, not that that was unusual, but he had a streak of cruelty that made them wary of him. Every so often she caught a look of pity in a woman's eyes and lifted her chin and hardened her gaze. She wanted no one's pity. Her marriage was her own affair. Certainly, there was no one in the mess so far that she wanted to befriend in the way she and Genny had been friends.

When they arrived at their new encampment Louisa was amazed, as she always was, at how the long trail of marching soldiers, dragged cannons, supply waggons and the ragged tail of wives and children, settled so rapidly into an organized camp of tents, stores and the inevitable officer's mess. Her nemesis. She and Millie, who had found a baggage cart to travel on, were shown to a large, square building, not unlike the one Rupert had been allocated for his winter quarters. The bed was not unlike the previous one. Huge, and in a heavily carved dark wood. She and Millie proceeded to wash themselves thoroughly, road mud crept everywhere, and settle in by unpacking clothes and moving some of the furniture around. When Geordie showed his face, Louisa had him shoving some of the larger clothes trunks and tables around. Perhaps that was what caused what happened next.

Rupert appeared to inspect his new quarters. He strode in and immediately faced up to Louisa. Her father had been a big man, not unlike Rupert, and she had become accustomed to his size. He had slapped her once in their early days, but that wasn't out of the ordinary within marriages, she knew. Her father had been unusual in never lifting a finger to her or her mother, but looking up at Rupert now she felt real fear. He stank of stale sweat and whisky and horse, and it was so strong she had to force herself not to flinch, and he was only inches from her. She tipped her face to look up at him, bewildered by his belligerence, uncertain as to what she had done wrong.

'Holding hands with that worm Cowper!' he bellowed.

Louisa's mind went blank. She had no idea what he was talking about. Then the punch came. Low and hard and straight to her gut. She folded forward as black and white explosions of pain filled her head and body. She fell to the floor, vomiting when his boot followed up and hit her in the same place. She came to lying on the floor, her face in a semi-dry pool of her own stomach contents. It smelt foul and her head span as she tried to sit upright. Millie was hunched in a chair and had clearly been crying.

'I not allowed to help!' she wailed.

Louisa waved a hand weakly in understanding. Millie now rushed forward and supported her as they made for the washbasin. Once clean again, Louisa fell onto the bed and slept. Her body hurt all over, in far more places than simply her stomach. She felt Rupert fall onto the bed beside her sometime during the night but felt too awful to care. Vaguely, she heard the murmurings of Geordie and her husband as his boots were removed and he was stripped ready for his sleep. For two days and nights she kept to her bed or their room while Rupert ignored her.

On the third morning she awoke before Rupert and headed for the wash basin and chamber pot. Walking was remained painful, as was standing, as was sitting still. When Rupert woke, she was sitting beside him on the chair he used for his uniform, that stood by his side of the bed. As he blinked into consciousness, she asked calmly,

'Why did you hit me?'

'Flirting with Cowper. Geordie saw you.' His voice was rough with sleep and his breath stank of stale whisky.

'And I saw Geordie,' she said quietly.

Rupert frowned at her.

'I always see Geordie,' she added, 'he watches me constantly, and he was watching me that morning. I thanked Lieutenant Cowper for returning my sewing box, that was all. I most definitely was not flirting with him.'

'Holding hands,' Rupert muttered, as he scrubbed through his hair with his fingers in an attempt, probably, to rub away his hangover.

Louisa sat quietly for a while. If she told Rupert Cowper had grabbed her wrist, he might go to fight Cowper. Or shoot him in the back in the middle of a battle, who knew what Rupert might be capable of? If she didn't, then she stood falsely accused of flirting with the man. At that moment, Louisa changed. As she sat there even swallowing was painful. Her body hurt all over and her head was pounding like a kettle drum. She knew that it would be two or three days before she was even partially recovered from Rupert's beating. Until now she would have instinctively covered for Charles Cowper, but as a coin spins before landing, her mental coin turned. Cowper would have to look after himself. She owed him nothing and he had brought it on himself. Bed with Rupert was now bearable and she just wanted to survive.

'He grabbed my wrist,' she said eventually, 'so I stamped on his foot to make him release me. If you had asked at the time, I could have shown you the bruise where he grabbed me. If Geordie is to spy on me, at least ask him to tell the truth.'

Louisa left Rupert to mull matters over. She had already worked out he wasn't the quickest of thinkers. There had been no bruise, Cowper hadn't gripped her that hard and she was tougher than that, but as the event had been days ago, she was confident her exaggeration would never be found out. She limped her way downstairs. She was hungry, and Geordie had better have some decent food waiting for her after his lying betrayal.

Louisa spent the rest of the day sleeping and walking gently around the house as the pain gradually eased its grip. As darkness fell, she retreated to the bedroom and lifted out all of her clothing and released the catch at the bottom. Inside was the knife her father had given her when they had left India. He had told her that it was sharp enough that he could shave with it, and to keep it safe. She vividly remembered how he would smear the local red mud on points of his body. She would laugh at the dot on the end of his nose, but with that remembrance came the memory of where else he had placed smears, one on the side of his neck, one on his shirt over his guts, the one in his groin.

'Put your knife where it matters, and if your knife is gone, shove out an eye with your fingers or up a nostril. Anywhere sensitive.' He had especially liked the gut. 'Shove in deep and twist. Force the blade up if you can. A man with his guts hanging out won't last long.'

She wasn't a daughter of the army for nothing. Resolute, she shoved the knife under her pillow. She had made Geordie find her a bottle of brandy for the pain, so she drank a draught and went to bed feeling a little safer.

Rupert woke her with a slap on her still painfully bruised face. She came to in candlelight to find him leaning over her still wearing his shirt. Her knife was in his hand. Idly he worked it through his fingers, faster and faster until the silver metal flashed and sparked like insane lightning. Louisa licked her lips.

'How did you know?' she whispered.

'Been waiting for you to dig it out of your chest. I have been in the army even longer than you, my little bird, and I gutted my first man when I was fourteen. And what do you think would happen to you if you did cut my throat?'

'I'd hang,' Louisa said bleakly.

'Oh, I have made sure worse than that would happen my little pet.'

With a smug smile, he threw the knife so it dug into the wood panelling across the room. Louisa spent the rest of the night staring into the itchy darkness as Rupert snored beside her.

The following morning it was clear that Millie hadn't just stayed away for a while but had vanished. There was no trace of the little maid anywhere around and, when questioned, Geordie swore he knew nothing; Rupert's response was to send him off to find a replacement. The replacement was a gangly, freckled girl with coarse reddish hair, called Gladys. Louisa hated her on sight. Perhaps because she was dirty, probably untrustworthy and definitely lazy, and perhaps because Geordie chose her. Louisa hadn't realised how much the little Portuguese maid had cheered her days until she was forced to have Gladys around her.

When, eventually, she was sufficiently well to once more accompany Rupert to the mess dinners, she brushed off enquires about her absence as a touch of the grippe caused by the travelling. Rupert watched her from across the table as ever with half-closed eyes and a half-smile when his gaze caught hers. For the first time, Louisa began to feel real fear of him. She considered whether he was getting bored with her and wondered if an 'accident' was somewhere in her future. Her earlier hope about their marriage felt like a wisp of a dream.

As if to confound her, when they retired to bed, as he came on top of her, he murmured, 'I have missed this. Missed you too.'

When he settled to sleep, he pulled her against him and nestled her into his body, one extremely heavy arm lay across her mid-section. It was only when confident he was asleep that she had the nerve to wriggle out from under the weight and allow herself to slide into her own rest. Over breakfast he was cheery and seemed content to be in her company, mentioning one or two matters he would need to deal with that day. Louisa breathed in deeply and felt immensely lighter.

Two nights later Rupert was in a bad mood. 'Your hair,' he complained. 'Looks an utter mess.'

'Millie, the maid you found me, was wonderful with hair. Gladys, the one Georgie found, has absolutely no idea. No woman can do her own hair and have it look reasonable, it simply isn't possible.'

Louisa had, in fact, learned a great deal from Millie and could probably now manage her own hair, not to Millie's standard, but to a respectable one that would pass muster, but she held her breath as she placed the blame firmly with Geordie and by inference, praised Rupert. When she wondered, had she become sly? What was clear was that Rupert might treat her as he would, but he set store by the woman who was his wife setting the right tone to accompany his own sense of status.

The result was an older 'maid', a widow called Mary, who had once been a dresser for a Lady Honour. She was quiet and reserved and Louisa far preferred her to the obnoxious Gladys.

At the winter quarters, Louisa had felt circled by sharks because of the way the other officers' wives had watched and fileted her behind her back. Most of those women were now safely either back on their husband's estates or enjoying the delights of the London season. The few who remained were hardened campaigners, like their husbands. Now the sharks circling Louisa were all male. Even the Colonel put his arm around her back for a moment and had a glint in his eye. Louisa sent a panicked glance to Rupert, but it didn't help. That night he showed his displeasure with his fists once again, and Louisa wondered how long she might survive as his wife. At least this time he had pulled his punches and she did not miss any mess dinners. She wasn't sure she could lie so smoothly again. Perhaps Rupert thought the same thing.

Spring arrived suddenly. One minute, it seemed, the meadows around them were stones and hard brown soil, the next they were hazed with green. Even the snow on the peaks had retreated a little. What had once been a white coverlet in the lower slopes was now black stones and filigree of glinting light. Louisa breathed in the air deeply, and it occurred to her, that she had survived four months of marriage to Rupert. He beat her less and she had come to understand when it might happen. He was not a man who could suffer frustration, and his first instinct when thwarted was to take his fists to anyone he considered his. She certainly did not love him, but she had come to respect him. He dressed, fed and housed her. At mess dinners, he appeared to be more relaxed, now confident that she would not play him false. It was not surprising he had wondered if she might; there were far more men than women with the army but she had become skilled at lifting her chin and giving an icy stare to any man who seemed to be considering taking liberties.

Rupert always watched her and had once given her a nod of approval. She was aware of his possessiveness, and it gave her some confidence that he would keep her safe, if not from himself. Within a week or two, these meadows would be wild with flowers of every hue. She felt rather like the meadow. She had been ground down first with grief, and then with the horror of the reality of marriage, hard and brown. But her marriage was the reality of her life now. She needed to alter it to suit her rather more than it did. Rupert didn't hate her, but he did mistrust her and view her with suspicion still. Well, she had had enough. She had grown up hard, but Rupert's treatment of her was becoming dangerous.

Like the best of generals, she began to plan. First, she filched coins from Rupert's pocket, having little coin of her own. Then she began to hunt for some sheer fabric, something cheap in case he simply ripped it to pieces, and soft enough to lay against the skin in case he didn't. She needed bed wear that wouldn't set his anger tripping immediately. Then she picked her evening; Rupert needed to be quite drunk, but not too drunk. Then she set her scene and waited.

He came in just as she had hoped, walking steadily, but clearly a bottle of whisky down. She sat in the bed in her new nightdress. The truth was, she had known that she couldn't confront him naked; she didn't have the courage. Although it covered her, it was transparent so he might not be too annoyed, at least, that was the plan. He did as always, going behind the screen to piss and splash some water about, then he emerged and hauled off his clothes, throwing everything onto the floor. The room was a mass of shadows, blacks in the corners, lighter in some areas and golden around his side of the bed where the single candle burned. Outside a bird sang. Rupert strode towards the bed and pulled back the covers and then blinked. There, nestled on the white sheets were three huge toads.

'What the…?' The word he used Louisa knew, but it had never been directed at her. She knelt up on the mattress. A toad croaked, startled by the light.

'I am your wife,' she stated, 'wife, not whore. They both start with the letter W but are quite different. I don't mind lying with you. You are my husband. I do not do it for a coin and then forget you, I am here for good. It's about time you stopped rolling on top of me and simply poking me. It hurts. As a man, it is up to you to ensure it doesn't hurt. So be a man and be my husband.'

A toad croaked again; it sounded cross. Rupert tipped back his head and roared with laughter. Picking one up he strode to the window. Louisa had tried to open it beyond a crack earlier in the day but found it firmly stuck. Rupert simply pushed it open with one hand. The toad went flying out into the night. Walking back, he picked up the other two and they rapidly followed the first.

'Geordie!' Rupert bellowed. Geordie opened the door, rubbing his eyes. 'Change the sheets.'

'Now?'

Rupert's answer was a quick stride and a sharp backhand. Geordie vanished, presumably to find the linens. Rupert vanished behind the screen and reappeared wearing his robe. Tossing hers to her he went to sit at the table. 'And bring whisky!' he bellowed.

Louisa shrugged into her robe and crossed to him. She lit a candle on the table and then sat quite deliberately on Rupert's lap. He showed her his teeth in what she hoped was a smile.

'You have nice teeth,' she told him, 'very white and even.'

His chuckle almost unseated her, so he brought one meaty arm around her waist. 'Wife,' he murmured in her ear, 'not whore. I'll remember.'

Inside Louisa was quaking. She had told herself if whores could please dozens of men, she could please one. And hopefully, persuade him to at least stop treating her like a piece of oak he had to bore holes into. Behind them, Geordie bustled about, silent about his work for once. Rupert offered the whisky glass to her, and Louisa sipped, passing it back to him. Rupert buried his nose into the hair beside her ear, 'Witch also begins with a W,' he whispered. Louisa snuggled into his embrace and he let her. For the first time since her parents had died, she felt secure.

That night Louisa experienced her first kiss. It was not unpleasant. There was a great deal to admire in Rupert if he could only be persuaded to keep his fists to himself. Life could be a great deal worse.

The following day she tackled Geordie. When he flounced around, smacking her breakfast down as if it was below him to serve her, she stood and faced him. Stepping forward with her left foot, she swung her right hand flat against his face, powering up from the sole of her right foot with all the strength she had. He yowled and gazed at her with wide disbelieving eyes.

'I am Lady Douglas McCloud, wife of Lieutenant Colonel Rupert Douglas McCloud the second most senior man in the regiment, the most senior woman in the mess and the daughter of a senior officer. From now on you will treat me with respect or I shall have you whipped. In fact, I may do the whipping myself. Believe me, I know how.'

Her little finger had caught the corner of Geordie's eye and it watered, making him appear to be crying. Geordie had fled the room, but from then on, he called her my lady or ma'am. She had never thought she would be a 'ma'am' and certainly not at eighteen, or that it would be something that she would wish to insist on, but right at that moment, she felt hot and fierce about her rank and the respect it deserved. It was something Rupert had given her, something he was proud of, and she would not allow anyone to insult it.

The regiment, and Louisa, were to remain in their present quarters for the foreseeable future. Their job still was to support the Portuguese from dispossessed French who were roaming everywhere, with the constant fear that they might promote revolution. Life settled into some kind of routine and Louisa found religion, praying each day for her husband to be sent on manoeuvres. His moods remained mercurial, one minute he seemed quite content with her and they shared laughter, the next something would set him off and, if she was lucky, she might escape with a slap. If unlucky, walking was sometimes difficult.

It took Louisa some time to recognise the symptoms. Since her marriage, food hadn't really interested her. She was too tight with watching her dearly beloved husband to swallow comfortably. Nausea in the mornings she put down to the punches and slaps that came irregularly but like the dawn, always came. The fact that the smell of whisky revolted her she explained to herself as the result of breathing in stale fumes all night as her lump of a husband snorted and snuffled all over her, so her middle had begun to thicken noticeably before the fact that she was growing a baby occurred to her. The fear hit her like a thunderstorm, rolling around and sending out flashes of terrifying mental sparks as vinaigrettes of the past months came back to her in vivid detail. That Rupert enjoyed exercising his fists and boots on her didn't matter; she was inured to it. But her baby? That was something quite different.

Doors became objects to be feared. They might snap back and hit her gut. Weapons were to be watched with caution, even though she swam in a sea of them. Elbows were to be avoided. Louisa moved with frantic care, constantly protecting her middle. By the time Rupert noticed she was 'in an interesting condition' the baby was moving and tiny feet and fists were making their presence felt. He simply hadn't noticed her change in shape. Louisa's bump was small and high, and she had altered or renewed her clothes herself. He stood, head lowered and swinging from side to side as he took in what to him was news. That night she heard Geordie's screams as Rupert laid into him. It seemed he felt Geordie should have informed him.

The subject was not mentioned again. Rupert simply ignored the situation. As did the officers and their wives. Such situations were in polite society politely ignored. Perhaps if Rupert had proposed a toast, or made a joke about her shape, it may have changed matters, but he didn't. And no one teased Rupert.

As the days slipped by Louisa was in a haze of happiness. She sat stitching tiny baby clothes for hours, as did Mary her maid. Mary, of course, knew about the beatings but was wise enough never to mention them. There was nothing either woman could do so they had to be dealt with and brushed under the carpet. It was a conspiracy of silence. Theirs wasn't the only one. When there is no remedy there is no point in discussing one.

Louisa had genuinely begun to believe that Rupert would respect her condition. It could well be his heir she was carrying, after all. Fools, she thought later, often delude themselves. There had been a confrontation with leaderless French soldiers. Rag tag as they were, they had planned an ambush well and made off with valuable and difficult-to-replace rations. The butcher's bill was high and Rupert had lost a number of men and came back in a livid temper.

Louisa came to in the dark and on the floor. She had been knocked out cold. A rip of pain roared through her and then stopped. That was what had brought her around. The rip came again, causing her to try to bend in two, something that was now impossible. High in the rafters, an animal was screaming. Louisa listened to it and wondered what kind of beast it was. The scream came again and again. It was some time before she realised, she was listening to herself.

When the women came running, they decided to leave her on the stone flags but to lay mattresses and blankets under and around her. Her back was supported against an overturned chair and eighteen hours later she gave birth to a baby boy and passed out again.

She never saw him or held him. Born dead, he was wrapped and bundled away, she never knew where, no one said, and there was no one to ask. Mary, her third maid was tight-lipped, and Geordie was clearly wary of her.

Rupert came after a day or two. He stood in the room with his head lowered and swinging from side to side, for all the world like a bull in a field. Louisa didn't ask where he had been sleeping. She didn't care. When he didn't speak, she said, 'It was a boy.'

He didn't say anything for a while, just stood there swaying. Then he found his voice, 'Didn't think it would do any harm.' Then left.

Louisa stared at the closed door. Wouldn't do any harm? Kicking a heavily pregnant woman unconscious? And had he meant that as some kind of apology? It didn't matter what he meant. Nothing did.

For nearly a month Louisa lay in bed and slept and dozed and dreamed about her little boy. When she rose, she returned to her life, such as it was, on some kind of instinct that had little to do with thought.

Later, she would look back and the months between pregnancies would be simply a haze, a blank devoid of thought or action. She supposed she must have washed, dressed, eaten, and responded when people spoke to her, but she remembered nothing but a blur. It was the morning nausea that woke her up. With the cunning of a trapped animal, she began to plan her way out. She was acting less on thought than on blind instinct. She hunted Rupert's pockets for coins and squirrelled away some of any she found. She wasn't fool enough to take them all and Rupert was too drunk much of the time to know exactly what he did and didn't have. She thought about the diamond star he loved to parade on his plaid but knew she couldn't spend it, and besides, it was too well guarded. Before she had accepted that she could not change her fate, now she was desperate enough to go out into the world and starve if she had to. She had no friends or relatives and she was in the Peninsula in the midst of warfare. And then Rupert told her to pack up as they were going back to Scotland for a while.

The shock stunned her. Fate, for once, seemed to be on her side. Here, in the mountains, valleys and hills, far from the coast, she had nowhere to go. But back at home, she could run, hide, and even find help. She sought out Genny. Their conversation began with no preamble. Louisa found her behind the lines of the 44th.

'I need money,' she said.

Genny nodded and turned away. Louisa left her without another word and returned to her place, back where Rupert expected her to be.

Genny and the 44th had raised a small bag of coins. It wasn't much to support a pregnant woman illegally running from her husband, but Louisa wept with gratitude, biting down on her hand so no one would hear. It seemed they knew enough about her situation to help her. What gossip was running around she had no idea, but clearly, there was some, or the wife of the wealthy Lord Douglas McCloud would not be asking for coins from the lines of the men and families who lived hand to mouth and they would not have been offering them if they weren't aware of something.

The trip to Oporto was to take two weeks. Rupert had not explained why he was leaving his duties and she hadn't asked. It was clear from what the Colonel said over the evening dinners that he was expected back in a few months so, clearly, this was not a permanent expulsion but more leave of absence. Their departure was delayed over and over again and, as weeks slipped by, Louisa began to panic. Her pregnancy was becoming more and more apparent and she was expected to ride her lovely chestnut to Oporto, and if she became too unwieldy, she might be left behind.

Eventually, however, they did leave, and Louisa found riding side saddle while pregnant surprisingly comfortable. The baby was moving and seemed to love the rocking of the horse only becoming agitated at night when they either lodged or camped along the way and he or she was still. Then Louisa would walk away into the night crooning soothing noises and smoothing her bump until the baby settled and they both could sleep.

Rupert had never alluded to her pregnancy and not for the first time she wondered what on Earth went on in his head. At times he would ride back to her side, saying little but keeping her company. At other times she heard his laughter, a deep ringing tone that she always knew was his; toads had definitely been mentioned at least once and she smiled to herself and rubbed her bump. If he was telling tales and laughing, the future looked hopeful.

Their way was slow, on what felt like random mountain tracks that led nowhere, but at all times they had to make sure they avoided French looters, who seemed to be roaming the mountains with impunity. Their succession of guides seemed to have a second sense for danger, and twice they were pulled aside only to watch French bandits ride past just yards away. But their slow and seemingly random route led eventually to rather better roads and the way into Oporto.

As they rode, finally, into the town Louisa felt her spirits lift even higher. Because of the danger, she had enjoyed the journey. The risk of running into roaming French parties had forced them to travel with extreme caution which, for Louisa, had meant a slow journey through terrain that had delighted her with its initial wildness and views of untouched country rolling away into the distance, before they dropped down towards neat fields. The freedom and danger had thrilled and excited her. Instead of feeling unwieldy, as she did when on the ground, she had felt like a child again, moving free and excited about life, safe on the warm, wide back of her chestnut. Being caught by the French didn't worry her. Most of the roaming bands were ex-soldiers, and as a pregnant officer's wife, she knew there was a very good chance she would be treated with dignity and respect. In other words, far better than Rupert sometimes treated her. Life had improved, and she revelled in it.

Oporto was a maze of narrow cobbled streets winding away from the port itself. After over a year of being confined to an army camp, the tiny shops and street traders thrilled her with their colourful goods and huge piles of vegetables in wicker baskets. Embroidered shawls, lace, and wonderfully carved wooden utensils were also hawked by women as they roamed the streets. It was all life. People, trade, activity. Everything she had been denied for so long. It was her early childhood in India all over again and she breathed it in and rejoiced. And children. Running free everywhere. Shrieking at each other. Getting under everyone's feet. Laughing with sparkling eyes. It was the sight of them that made the tears choke her throat.

Their billet was a small inn up one of the narrow streets. Louisa had a room to herself with a small truckle bed for Mary, who gazed at it with disfavour and sniffed. Mary had been almost invisible on the trip, riding for most of the time in the rear with two sergeants, only appearing when needed. Louisa viewed her with curiosity as she unpacked the valise and wondered what went on in the woman's mind. She fulfilled her duties with scrupulous professionalism with no attempt at friendship with her much younger mistress. Louisa didn't much mind that. She was content to be left with her own thoughts. Friendship or even cordiality with anyone, man or woman, might bring Rupert's ire down on her head. Perhaps Mary was already wise to that and Louisa could only admire her perspicacity.

To Rupert's disgust, the ship would not be ready for a day or two. Geordie was more than disgusted. He was incandescent. Rupert had ordered him to stay in Oporto with their guard. The sergeants and lieutenants who had guarded them on their journey were authorised to buy horses while they waited for Rupert's return. The army ate up horses and could never have enough. A corporal Louisa did not know was to travel with Rupert as his valet so only the four of them would actually be making the crossing to Portsmouth. Louisa kept rigidly neutral as the row between them became a shouting match until Rupert back-handed Geordie and he retreated with tears sliding down his cheeks.

Louisa wondered if Geordie was being left behind as he simply knew too much. After all, if they were to travel to Scotland and Rupert's family, it was possible he didn't want anyone around to inform any interested parties that he had kicked his heir out of his wife's womb. Also, Louisa was fairly sure of Geordie's feelings for Rupert and a valet with his inclinations might end up with his throat cut in a strange land with protective relatives around. Rupert was at no risk, but others might not realise that.

That thought made her regard her rigidly self-contained maid anew. It was on the tip of her tongue to ask Mary if she was being paid off once they reached Portsmouth, but Louisa kept her words behind her teeth. What would happen would happen. And she had no intention of making the gruelling trip all the way to Scotland. All she wanted was to make dry land in her own country and she would be off. She needed this baby to be born in safety. If the Fates were willing! She doubted Rupert would harm his child once it existed out in the world, but she did not intend to take any risks.

Buoyed with hope, Louisa took a slow walk around the narrow winding streets of Oporto. Every so often a woman sitting by her open front door would nod or smile back at her. Every one of them was busy with some kind of task, sewing, lace making or preparing fruit or vegetables. Louisa found herself relaxing into a waking doze of contentment. The late summer sun was warm and bright, the shadows cool and dark, the town itself a maze of alleyways and interest. The very walls of the buildings seemed to breathe out age and vibrant history. Her baby was quiet, lulled by her mood and the rocking of being walked. She settled her hands protectively on her bump and wandered on, not caring where she ended up. She couldn't get lost; the port could always be found.

Eventually, as she was tiring, she came across a small sun-splashed square where three women sat together. One had a lace pillow and was throwing the bobbins with practised ease and two were engaged in some kind of vividly coloured embroidery. Louisa paused to watch, fascinated. Not able to help herself she leant forward to test the cloth between her fingers. She was unsurprised to find it fine linen of excellent quality. These women knew their fabric.

The oldest one grinned up at her showing ragged teeth. She patted the bench beside her inviting Louisa to sit. As Louisa settled slowly down, the woman patted her stomach and rattled something off to the others. Louisa's smattering of Portuguese couldn't keep up with the individual words, but she caught the sense. In halting words, she tried to say how happy she was about the baby and how long she had to go to the birth. To her delight, the women seemed to understand. She shut her eyes and leaned back.

When she opened her eyes, it was to watch the youngest woman, a girl really, at her sewing. Louisa frowned. Then she gently reached across and took the embroidery from the girl's hands. Her belly was almost as swollen as her own. All three women were gazing at her, wondering what she was doing. With firm fingers, Louisa rapidly unpicked the most recent stitches. With a gasp, the girl tried to pull her work back into her own hands, but Louisa made a gentling motion with her hand and the old woman with the dreadful teeth said something so the girl sat back, frowning. Louisa threaded three needles with threads, and then began to repair the work. After a few stitches, all three women leaned forward. The old woman clucked her teeth and chuckled. The middle one continued throwing her lace bobbins with a smile on her face, and the young wife sighed, closed her eyes, and dozed off contentedly. Louisa's work was far superior to her own!

Louisa had been working for a while and the piece was almost finished. She had been concentrating so hard and been so content to be sitting outside on a lovely day doing work she enjoyed, she hadn't paid attention to the chatter of the women, but suddenly something made her look around. Rupert was sitting a few yards away in the shade of a tree, his arms crossed over his chest and his booted ankles crossed at the end of his outstretched legs. Louisa started with fear. To her surprise, Rupert smiled and closed his eyes and made out he was dozing in the cool air under the tree. Uncertain and uncomfortable, Louisa carried on to finish the piece. The older woman made what appeared to be a ribald comment and the other two laughed. Turning to look over at Rupert she had to agree. He was large and muscular and dark-haired and good-looking in a rough-hewn way. He was very male. From here he was indeed a man to be proud of. She swallowed her disquiet and continued to sew. Finally, she lay the finished work down and thanked the women for their company. They all smiled and made warm farewells, even though Louisa understood little of the actual words.

As she crossed to Rupert he rose and bowed to the women before laying Louisa's right hand along his left arm. She had never seen him so relaxed. His uniform coat with its gold buttons and braid was hanging open, something he might well have one of his men whipped for, his neck was bare, and his boots smothered in dust. And he smiled down at her.

'Fond of sewing, aren't you.'

Louisa stiffened her spine. 'Yes,' she replied, cautiously.

He patted the hand that lay on his arm. 'You are a good lass,' he commented.

Louisa shot a glance at him and allowed him, despite his undress, to escort her formally back to their lodgings.

That night he took her to his room and pressed his mouth on hers before entering her. Their coupling was slower and gentler than usual and felt a bit less like a chore he had to achieve before sleep. He held himself up on his arms so as not to lay heavily on her stomach and the growing child. Louisa lay afterwards feeling more than a little confused. She had worked out long ago that, 'You are a good lass,' was high praise from her uncommunicative husband. She would decide when she would run another time. Perhaps she wouldn't have to. Perhaps this baby could be born with his support. And as she lay next to him, she realised that he didn't reek of whisky! She slept deeply that night.

Chapter 3

The weather was cooler when they headed up the gangplank to the ship. There was the smell of salt and fish in the breeze, and the rigging smacked above their heads. The deck was crowded with barrels and crates and trunks and what felt like dozens of mostly bare-footed men shouting and hurrying. Looking back the town shone in the morning sunlight and Louisa bade it a silent farewell with affection. She had enjoyed her time in Oporto. And oddly enough, she had enjoyed Rupert. He had been quieter, drunk little, and had sought out her company a time or two. Once to walk her about the town, and once to assist her in buying some lengths of superior linen for her embroidery. They still had never had what might be termed a real conversation; Rupert tended to grunt if asked a question, but they had been amiable together, and any day that didn't include a slap or a punch was a bonus in Louisa's mind.

The situation lasted six hours. Casting off was delayed. Rupert drank whisky. She smiled at a sailor who had shouted a ribald but flattering comment, and her husband's palm found the side of her face. Louisa dropped her head and hurried below deck to her cabin overwhelmed with a scalding sense of shame. Rupert's blows were usually in private and at night, never before in public. She sat and gazed out of the porthole and remade her plans to escape for the birth of her baby.

They eventually set sail, late, with Rupert in a foul temper, but the fact that they had left their mooring filled her with relief. Half a day out and Rupert was crippled with seasickness, as was Mary. The corporal who was his valet was more than engaged with caring for the two of them and Louisa found she was free of them all. Since the slap, the crew, especially the officers, were meticulously polite around her. Her solitude amidst the hurley-burley of a bustling ship heading into increasingly inclement weather was a joy to her senses. With the building storm, most of the few other passengers stayed below, but she walked the decks every day, and when the crew became concerned, she had them lash her to the rail rather than be forced to stay in her cabin. She loved to let the wind take her hair and make a net of tangles of it and blow her eyes closed as she would try to gaze into the ever-increasing gale. The baby loved her to be on the move. Just as he or she had been calm when she had been sitting side-saddle on the horse, her right thigh cushioning her bump, now she sensed that the tipping and dropping of the deck were what settled this little mite down. When she was still, the baby made his or her protest felt, by kicking her to pieces. Despite the discomfort, Louisa laughed. She was sure the men all around her thought her quite mad as she stroked and murmured to her rounded abdomen, but she didn't care.

When they arrived in Portsmouth, Louisa packed her valise with care. Only essentials. One thin dress. A brush. A couple of washcloths. Some of the baby clothes she had sewn with so much care. The ones Mary had made she deliberately placed back in her trunk. She was wearing her thickest dress and her warmest cloak. In the bottom of the valise, sewn into the lining, was about ten guineas she had managed to filch from Rupert over the previous few months and the regimental money. The coins she had in her pocket could be excused as pennies for ribbons or pins she might see on the road. She was sick with fear; so sick anyone might be forgiven for believing she too had suffered from the *mal de mare* on the crossing. Rupert was still dead-fish grey from seasickness and she wasn't sure she wasn't the same colour from nerves.

'Wait in your cabin,' he instructed her.

'May I not take the air?' Louisa pressed.

He gave her a surly look. His 'No,' was uncompromising.

As Louisa turned to return to her cabin, she saw Mary leaving the ship. Her trunk was being shouldered behind her by one of the seamen. As Louisa watched, the woman entered one of the hired carriages that plied their trade on the waterfront. Well, she thought, clearly, we shan't see you again.

When Louisa cracked her door open the corporal who was valet to Rupert for the trip was always in the passageway. She sat on the bunk and fretted. Eventually, the man must have needed to remove himself for some reason and finally when she peeped out the coast was clear. Gingerly, she made her way up the open wooden steps towards the deck. It was dark below and her eyes struggled to focus as she climbed into daylight. She squinted and concentrated on not falling as she manoeuvred her bulk upwards. She had only four or six weeks to her time, and she was far larger with this baby than she had been with her first. Perhaps it would be another boy. She hoped so. She so longed for little chubby arms to wind around her neck.

To her horror, as she emerged on deck Rupert was only a few yards away. She decided to brazen it out. She could say again that she needed air, and it was stuffy below, which was true. Rupert turned and she gave him her warmest smile as if seeing him was the nicest part of her day. He took two strides toward her and she could smell the whisky from the moment he turned to her. A bottle was hanging from his left hand.

'I gave you an order!' he bellowed.

Louisa stepped back reflexively. Her foot caught in the hem of her cloak and she toppled, the cloak strings jarring into her neck. For a moment the mast and spars swung through her vision until the shock of pain as she hit the deck closed her eyes. She was still on the edge of the hatch opening and her left hand shot out to try to save herself. Her hand found the handrail at the top of the hatch. Then Rupert's boot caught her smack in her gut and with a scream she toppled down, bouncing like a doll onto many of the wooden steps. She landed almost unconscious at the bottom when her valise smacked her in the right leg. Pain shuddered through her and both of her hands found her belly and grasped it.

When she could breathe again, she opened her eyes. Something made her turn her head. In the dark of the lower passageway, was a pair of hardened, grubby feet below the ragged hems of canvas trousers. She closed her eyes again. Was there no end to her humiliation? Neither of them moved and then two hard, calloused hands hauled her upright and helped her back into her cabin. Louisa was too shocked to speak or cry. The sailor shut the door quietly, and Louisa shoved her weight until it was supported by the bunk and tried to breathe through the pain.

A few minutes later there was a slight knock at the door, and Louisa assumed it was the corporal coming to check she was behaving herself. She didn't move. She couldn't. The door opened quietly and the man was back bearing a wooden bowl and matching spoon. She just looked at him. Silently he pressed the bowl into her hands. It was warm milk, with good fresh bread broken into it. Night slops, it was sometimes called. Made for little children to fill their tummies before bedtime. Louisa simply watched as the man withdrew as silently as he had arrived.

Oddly enough, the warmth and gentleness of the food were soothing, and an echoing taste of early childhood. The bowl was beautifully carved, as was the spoon. She vaguely wondered if the man had made them himself. A quarter of an hour must have passed when the door opened again. Numb, Louisa simply watched. She was beyond speech or emotion at that moment. She hurt from her fall, but even as the initial shock wore off she began to believe no real harm had been done. People fell all the time. The sailor was back. He lifted her valise and held out his hand.

'You want to go, missus?' he asked quietly.

Louisa looked into a pair of pale eyes in a weathered face framed with greying hair and stubble. She nodded. He took her hand and helped her stand, then took her the opposite way along the shadowed passageway. At the end, a different pair of hands took her valise and with a man behind and her rescuer in front she was helped up a rope ladder towards a different hatch. With strong hands on her backside and thighs and arms, she was manoeuvred up into daylight. There was nothing disrespectful in the handling, just arms experienced in moving unwieldy freight from hold to deck.

She emerged into daylight and realised it must be afternoon. Firm hands assisted her to a different gang plank that led down to a passageway between heaped crates, at the other end of the ship to Rupert; one he could only view a part of. Heads swung furtively left and right, and she found herself supported down the gangway surrounded by men hauling sacks on their shoulders. Then she was safe in amongst the crates, and the men turned and vanished. She took a deep breath and followed their example.

PART TWO

Ten years earlier:
Plymouth 1790: Samuel finds himself a mother.

'A princess is just opinion and clothes.
A mermaid now, a mermaid is truly magical.'

Chapter 4

Sam's hand was warm in his. William glanced down at the boy's head. He wasn't sure a boy of eleven should be hanging onto his papa's hand in public, but on the other hand, his lad was a bit different, and he was his, and besides, the place was crowded and fast-moving and he couldn't bear to lose the lad let alone face the impact that might have on young Sam.

He was tall for his age, his Sam, long and thin like a yard of pump water. Pale-skinned and with keen blue eyes, his fine fair hair, almost bone white, he always put him in mind of the young herons that stood around the pond at home. He wasn't paying attention to where they were walking, leaving William to pick a route through the hubbub as he twisted and tried to take everything in at once. He turned suddenly to smile up at William, and love twisted William's guts.

It had seemed a good idea to walk down to the harbour at Plymouth as so many merchant ships had berthed in the night. There had been a huge storm along with a spring tide, and a number of vessels had been swept into Plymouth as the only safe place they could head for, despite their itineraries and home ports being elsewhere. The tavern keeper, alight with the excitement of gossip, had talked about fights over the hiring of carts to take some of the cargos to London. With all the trouble going on in France everyone was fearful about cargo routes at present.

The sky was a mass of huge masts and cross pieces, with sails sometimes still hanging down in rags as men swarmed above and tried to cut or untangle a myriad of ropes and torn canvas shreds. The harbour was dense with barrels and crates, along with the men who were calling for work and trying to shift the various loads along the quay and onto the carts they had been forced to navigate through even to get this far. A young stevedore, big-boned and broad-shouldered, flung a curse at an older man who was struggling to haul a barrel. William watched the younger one direct a sly kick at the man whom he considered in his way. It clearly didn't occur to him that one day, when his body was worn out from hauling the crates and barrels, he now found so easy to lift, he too would be hunched and struggling. And probably hungry from being able to earn so little. William gripped Sam's hand tighter. At least his lad had a certain future.

Sam twisted right round, yanking his father's hand painfully. William looked over to see what had caught his attention. It was a neat pile of glass cases, each containing something green. Sam glanced up at William and the two of them moved across to look closer. A sailor gave them a warning glance, but deciding they were curious onlookers and not opportunistic thieves, he paid them no mind.

'Papa, they are all new!'

William peered closer. It was true, he had never seen leaves like them, but on the other hand, a leaf to him was a leaf. Some of the greenery was like fingers, some a blue-grey William had never seen before, stiff and hard-looking, some were as huge as dinner plates. If his Sam said they were strange, they probably were.

William had sent Sam to Eton when he had turned nine. Seven had felt too young for the boy, and besides, he would have missed his quiet presence. A letter had arrived after six months. Six months in which William, heart sore at missing his lad, had been trying on a daily basis to convince himself Eton was the right place for the lad, to help him grow up, teach him what he needed to know, lay the foundations of manhood. The letter said little, only that the headmaster would be grateful if William could find time to visit him. William had taken the coach rather than ride, riding being far faster but the coach was his instinctive choice, and his instinct had proved right.

Always slender, Sam had been bone-thin, his ribs and collarbone protruding out of his always too-pale skin like knives. Later, he had found the weals of regular beatings across his fine-skinned back and non-existent buttocks. 'Can't take discipline,' the headmaster, arrogant and overbearing, had declaimed, 'can't have a chap here who can't take discipline!' William had been too shocked to say anything. 'Send him back in a couple of years and we will see what we can do with him.'

It was clear to William that they hadn't wanted a dead boy on their hands. They had travelled home gently, Sam lying on his front with his head on William's thigh; they stopped often to spoon soups and soft stews into his small, reluctant mouth. Gradually the boy had absorbed sufficient food to allow him some sleep, and William had sat in the coach watching the countryside move by at a slow pace and holding his anger deep.

Sam was now taught what the local vicar knew three mornings a week. God knows, the man had little else to do. His sermons were hardly inventive. Sadly, his intellect wasn't either. It was clear to all of them that Sam could out-think the vicar even at eleven. Never mind, the boy would know enough to run the estate alongside and then after him.

A gust of wind blew, nearly lifting his hat off his head. William regarded Sam and worried the cold might be too much for the boy. They had been out a long while, both of them fascinated by the scurrying of the harried port. He looked around to check *how far they had come, wondering anew at how the men labouring to unload and despatch so much merchandise could cope with their bare feet and thin trousers on cold stone and biting damp winds. He smoothed the whiskers on his face with his free hand and then tugged at Sam's hand gently, determined to get the lad back for their lunch and a warm by the tavern fire.

As they turned to head back the hustling men parted and in front of them was yet another of the mini-dramas that had entertained them all morning. A woman, her back to them, was standing at the end of a gangplank arguing with a man who seemed to be one of the more senior sailing men. The woman was notable for her neat figure and her pale green and very stylish outfit. It was like finding a snowdrop hidden amongst the grey slush of an early thaw; something exquisite hidden like a jewel in a murky and muddy world.

As they drew close Sam tugged at William's arm to eavesdrop on the pair. Annoyed at Sam's bad manners, William pulled away, but Sam slipped free and stepped over to the couple. His head moved from one to the other, now listening boldly to the argument. Cross now, and rather embarrassed, William moved to remonstrate with Sam, but then Sam addressed the woman in halting French. Both parties turned towards him, and William paused, surprised. Sam turned to face him, and quickly he explained that the lady had expected to land in Harwich, but the ship had been blown badly off course. She was due to be met by people in Harwich, and now she did not know what to do, but the man was saying that the boat was badly damaged and she could not stay aboard. Flummoxed, William stared at Sam, who clearly expected him to step in and take charge.

Clearing his throat, William did so, and it was as Sam had described. Eventually, with Sam as interpreter, it was agreed that the lady would allow herself to be escorted to the tavern where William and Sam were staying and take a room there. William knew there would be at least one room. He had taken two, but Sam simply crept into his bed every night, so one was definitely free.

And so the small party, including two sailors shouldering two large trunks, presumably belonging to the woman, headed back towards the town. William had been more than aware of the woman looking him over and then deciding he was a safe escort less because of the exhortations of the seaman and rather more because of the eager young boy who called him Papa. Feeling awkward, he offered her his arm and was more than a little relieved she didn't snub him but gently slid her arm through his. Her gloves, he noticed, matched her outfit being the same soft green shade. Money somewhere thought William.

There was indeed a newly vacated room available and William called for luncheon to be served in the small dining room. With three of them in there, it was unlikely anyone else would join them. The woman had a small, sweet face, with large soft brown eyes and dark thickly curling hair. William knew he was little used to female company, and he couldn't guess the woman's age. She could be twenty or thirty as far as he could make out. When she smiled at Sam, her eyes crinkled as if smiling came naturally to her, so perhaps heading to thirty, but the lively way she chatted to Sam, drawing out his modicum of the French language, she might still be in her teen years.

It was Sam who William watched. It was the most animated he had seen him since before Eton. William had loved Eton. There had been siblings, but they had all died in infancy long before William had any real sense of their presence. Left an only child, he had relished the bombardment of the other boys, the jokes, the games, the rough play, and the anti-intellectualism had suited him. To be obviously clever was to incite approbation, but William had privately loved Latin. He had loved the logic of it, the way it was an ordered puzzle that if he worked at it could jump into clarity as if an image had been obscured and was suddenly clear. And they were a clever lot, the men who wrote the witty lines and the insightful comments that he had secretly enjoyed in dusty classrooms. Listening to the woman and Sam he was surprised to find he could pick out the odd phrase. He hadn't liked French as much as Latin, but some of it was returning.

He had thought Sam would come out of his shell at Eton, instead, he had almost lost him. Yes, he was tall for his age, but he was fine-boned where William was built like a barn door and always had been. At five-ten William was one of the tallest men around, and his big bones and solidity had always made him confident of his place in the world. But Sam, Sam always looked as though a breeze wouldn't so much as knock him down as blow him right away. His constant concern for the lad was eased as he watched the French woman draw him out into a warm and smiling stuttered conversation that included many smiles and hand gestures. Sam's glowing face warmed his heart. More of this, and in a year or two he would be more than ready to return to school.

The woman remained, however, an enigma. Her clothes were costly, and her trunks had been well made, with brass fittings rather than cheap iron ones. That she was used to servants doing her bidding was equally clear. So, who was she? And what on earth was she doing standing alone, alone for goodness' sake, on the harbour at Plymouth? If he and Sam hadn't been there, he wasn't confident she would have made it to the tavern without being robbed even of the clothes she stood up in! He could tell she and Sam were talking about their respective homes, so, lunch being over and the board cleared, he shoved back his chair and resting a reassuring hand on Sam's shoulder, he went to demand a slate and chalk from the tavern keeper.

Returning to the curious gaze of both Sam and the woman he wrote down Sam's name and two numbers, a one and a one, then William with his own age, a four and a two. He couldn't stand not knowing any longer. He passed the slate to the woman. She took it, giving him a long neutral gaze as she did so. He watched as she wrote Marie-Claire and a two and a seven, before returning it to him, again with that impervious and impassive look that was totally unlike the warm smiles and open encouragement she had for Sam. William nodded and felt his cheekbones warm a little, but at least now he knew.

The girl came in to clear the board, and William asked if the room promised to the lady was available. The girl gave her assent and William turned back to Sam and Marie-Claire who were opposite him. Marie-Claire was gazing at him.

'You, I understand you,' she told him. 'er,' she indicated to the door, '*Non.*' She shot Sam a brilliant smile, 'And you, *mon petit.*'

William's head shot back on his neck in shock. 'You speak English?'

'Of course,' she seemed affronted, 'but not too well.'

Sam was smiling like the sun had come out and he was responsible. It seemed Marie-Claire knew quite a bit of English, but her accent was heavy and listening was an effort. William and Sam, it seemed, spoke clearly enough, and slow enough, that she could follow most of what was said. Us slow-witted folk from the west country, William thought wryly, saying nothing.

After lunch Marie-Claire retired to her room to rest. She hadn't slept the night before because of the storm, and the ship had berthed early. She had a good room as the quarrel of people that had flooded the town as a result of the storm had flown like swallows at the end of summer. William and Sam took a walk around the town and up into the countryside a little way.

'I didn't realise she spoke English,' William told Sam.

'At first it was only odd words, Papa, but with my French and her English, we got along! She is a lovely lady, Papa.'

William looked down at Sam fondly. His face was animated and flushed, and he looked better than he had in two years. Silently William blessed the woman for the kindness and interest she had shown to his boy.

'But what is a lady like that doing here? On her own?'

'I didn't understand everything, Papa, but I think she has a very important brother, like a lord or a duke. Her home is a big stone house with four round towers with pointed roofs. I didn't know the word for pointed, but I knew house, and stone, and tower, and my numbers, of course.'

'So why isn't he here with her?'

'She had three ladies with her. Two got sick, and the third stayed to care for them and take them home. The lady's brother had been most insistent that she leave France, so she had come alone, expecting to be met in Harwich by some people.'

'Do you know why she had to leave France?' Perhaps she was a wanted criminal!

'I don't know, but she kept saying the word for brother, and lots or many, then a word that sounded like our word dangerous. She said it over and over again.'

Yes, she did, thought William, he had heard her and wondered at it. They arrived back for their supper red-faced and windblown. After they had washed their faces and brushed their hair, a necessity William had persuaded Sam into as they were dining with a lady, they arrived in the dining room still flushed and breathless from racing each other down the stairs. Marie-Claire was sitting, hands folded in her lap, neat and composed by the fire, in a dark red woollen gown that must have cost a good deal. The wool had the sheen of fine quality, and the dark-grey oak leaves that were applied at the hem and neck had been attached by a skilled seamstress. Despite his attempts, William felt large, coarse and dishevelled. Now she was rested he could see how tired she must have been.

The supper was good, although Marie-Claire, after taking a sip of what William thought was a reasonable red wine and nearly spitting it over his dinner, joined Sam in a small ale. He began, using any French word he could bring to mind, about her journey here. To his surprise, her eyes filled with tears as she described her terror as the boat had pitched and yawed in the heaving dark seas. She had seemed so extraordinarily composed that morning but, he now recognised, had been putting on a front in a strange and frightening place. No stars, she kept repeating. He warmed to her more than he had done. Between the three of them, they managed to convey much of what they wanted either with questions or answers.

When it was Marie-Claire's turn to interrogate them she turned to Sam and asked about his home. Sam did a reasonable job of describing the red brick and timber Tudor manor house they lived in, the pond to the side and front that had ducks on it, and the farms his father owned that lay all around. By the time she had quacked to clarify it was ducks on the pond, and not sheep or cows, and they had all fallen about laughing, the atmosphere between them was as warm as the room and their food-stuffed bodies.

When it was time to retire William was surprised by the look he intercepted from Marie-Claire. It was only a moment, but their eyes held, and he was shocked to recognise an appraising glance that was assessing him not as Sam's father (and therefore an indication of his lack of danger to her) but as a woman looking at a man she admired. His blush began low on his chest and rushed to his temples making him wonder if he was as red as the old Tudor bricks of his home! Ducking his head in an attempt to hide his reaction, he and Sam gallantly escorted Marie-Claire to her room. Her door was first, close to the stairs, and Sam gave her a grave and polite goodnight, that made William proud. Couldn't have done it better if he had stayed at Eton.

An hour after they retired Sam came and slipped in beside William and snuggling close to his warmth, fell asleep. Reserving two rooms had been a waste, but the boy was eleven, when was he going to sleep in his own bed? Would Sam have his wedding night with William next to him jammed onto the edge? Sleepless, William lay on his back with one arm under his head and the other around his boy, he gazed up at the gloom near the ceiling (the plaster cracks would have made a fair map of all the rivers in England, he reckoned) while he thought about Marjorie, his first wife.

He had known her all his life. Or perhaps, known of her would be more accurate. The final Easter of his last year at Eton the vicar, the same one now tutoring Sam, had written to him. The only useful thing he had ever done in his life, as far as William was concerned. At the Christmas break, he had known that his father had a cold but hadn't thought anything of it. Colds were as common as grey skies in winter. But the vicar wrote to say that he hadn't recovered, and the man thought perhaps William ought to come home. Surprised, and irritated, William had done just that. His mother had died two years earlier, but women often died so he hadn't thought that much of it and, in his eyes, his father was immortal. He had journeyed home in a mood of irritation, anxious to return to enjoy the summer school weeks of laughing and joking with his friends.

His father's extreme frailty had shocked some sense into him. He had set to, learning about the estate as rapidly as he could and sorting out the myriad of problems that seemed to have piled up since the previous autumn. Everything from what acres to sow and which to leave fallow, to arranging and paying for new thatch for some of the cottages that had been de-roofed in a wild storm last October. The days had been long, and as he began to learn what was required of him, increasingly frantic. His father had sunk back into his bed with clear relief to have all of the worries on his shoulders lifted, if only temporarily.

His father never rallied. His weight continued to drop until he was as light and pale as a white feather blown in the wind. The coffin had seemed obscenely large when the burial rites came. Time had then accelerated. He had been young, and although full of vigour, hadn't always known where to direct it. Some of the tenant farmers were almost three times his age, and persuading them he knew what he was doing, often when he didn't, had taken all of his courage and determination. He woke one day to the sure knowledge that all of that was past. He had grown into being Sir William without really noticing. The men who had once ribbed him and called him Young Will, now tugged their forelocks with respect and referred to him by his title. And the house was empty. He had walked the many rooms, some that had been shut up for years, in a strange mood.

A few days after that realisation he had ridden over to visit Marjorie's father and look her over. He hadn't fancied a wife far younger than himself. He wasn't sure he had the patience to gentle a chit who needed some years to grow into herself. Marjorie was about the same age as him and, he supposed, considered on the shelf. She was as he remembered, mostly, tall and big-boned. As he was a large man himself, he liked the idea that when they bedded, she would be able to take his weight. She had accepted his marriage proposal calmly. The banns had been called, and after the service, he carried her home in his new carriage, bought with matrimony in mind.

He knew he was a virgin, and assumed she was too. Who were they supposed to have practised on? They had slept next to each other, each in their neck-to-toe nightgowns for over a fortnight without touching until one night with an attitude of impatience after standing beside the bed with her hands on her hips she whipped off her nightgown. Standing naked she said,

'You married a wife, not a housekeeper. Time to get to it.'

He'd looked across the darkened room and admitted, 'I don't know what to do.'

She had retorted, 'Well, the bull and the stallion do, and you look big enough to be either!'

He had laughed out loud at that, and the ice had been broken. He wasn't sure he loved her, but he did know he missed her exceedingly when she died. Sam had been so small, and of necessity in the care of others. His life had instantly become cold and lonely and the bed far too large without her. He missed her solid good sense and her matter-of-fact approach to life and considered he could never have picked a better wife and never expected to replace her.

Chapter 5

Sam longed to go back to the harbour. Marie-Claire wanted to write to the couple, a Lord and Lady something she had been supposed to meet in Harwich, and William was content to enjoy his unaccustomed holiday for a day or two longer. So they all headed for the harbour while it was early to spy on all of the activity, watching ship repairs, fish being unloaded, and merchants furious about their cargo arriving spoiled with sea water. They returned for lunch, put their heads together to compose a legible letter to the Lord and Lady Marie-Claire's brother had entrusted her to, then headed out into the byways around the town. The air was still sharp, but the sky was a brilliant blue with huge white clouds rushing about. When the sun broke through it was warm and cheering.

After supper, they chatted in a mood of contentment and discussed Marie-Claire's predicament. Should she travel to Harwich, when the couple meeting her might not be there, wait here in Plymouth, or perhaps go to London and find a hotel to wait in until they found her? William didn't like any of the options but said little. Eventually, they played a game of dominoes, and they all cheated as much as possible to much laughter. Marie-Claire's English was improving rapidly. Eton had beaten most of his west country accent out of his speech, usually literally, but William knew that he still spoke more slowly than some, a fact that when commented upon by his schoolmates, had resulted in him forcing a few of their teeth down their throats. It seemed Marie-Claire found slow steady speech easier to understand than the various accents shot out at speed she had heard on the boat, and that was why she had convinced herself she could not speak the language. Now, with their gentle encouragement, she was proving herself remarkably fluent. With Sam and William's knowledge of French, they enjoyed a conversation that sat firmly mid-Channel.

One question that gave William pause was when Marie-Claire asked, 'When did Samuel not have his mother?'

He sat back in his chair, unpicking the question. Eventually, he said, 'Child bed.'

'Ah, I am desolated. That must have been hard. You did not marry to give Samuel a mother?'

William shook his head. 'No. Never crossed my mind. After we lost her, the house seemed to fill with women without me doing anything. There was always someone with him on her knee or in her arms. The years flew by.'

He was lost in the past for a while, remembering coming in and asking for the lad and always finding him contented with someone minding him. The local farmers' wives had simply taken both of them over. As he shook off his memories, he caught a gleam in Marie-Claire's eyes. Clearly, there had been an undercurrent to the question, but for the life of him, he couldn't tell what it was.

At bedtime, William and Sam again escorted Marie-Claire to her room, but she insisted on seeing Sam to his, to Sam's clear delight. Perhaps that means he will stay in it, William wondered to himself. This meant William had to walk Marie-Claire back to her room along the dark corridor. The sound of revelry below made William nervous about leaving her undefended and he shot a frowning glance down the stairs as shouts and laughter rose up to them.

As they reached the door, Marie-Claire turned to smile up at him but as her eyes met his, her smile slowly faded. In the gloom of the corridor, they remained frozen, until driven by who knows what, William bent down slightly, and Marie-Claire reached up slightly. The kiss began with a soft pressure of lips. A nothing. A bagatelle. But like a bonfire that starts so slowly, it appears it will go out again before surprising everyone by leaping into vigorous flames, heat roared between them. William was lost, all sense gone. His mouth ravished hers, his hands had minds of their own, now on the back of her head, now on her buttocks, now her breast. Her hands roamed anxiously under his coat, stroking his chest, winding around him. They drew apart panting. Without a word she pulled away and vanished into her room, shutting the door with a firm click. William returned to his room mind blank. Probably with shock, he thought later.

At breakfast, Marie-Claire behaved as though nothing had happened, which was a great relief to William who had rehearsed apologies until the early hours. Her demeanour allowed no room for any comment by him. They all decided to take the carriage out along the west road and visit a village for lunch and walk along the cliff paths a little. They all lived far from any coast and, now Marie-Claire was on dry land, she was also keen to see a little more of the sea. The next day William and Sam needed to return home. William still had not resolved what he thought Marie-Claire should do and it bothered him greatly.

Nothing was said over dinner, or in the companionable hour afterwards, and Sam's presence prevented William from expressing his concerns. He didn't want Sam to realise how vulnerable Marie-Claire was out in the world on her own, but perhaps her travelling companions might turn up in a day or two. Or even in the morning. That night they repeated tucking Sam up before walking back down the corridor to her door. William's heart was beating so loud he thought the people in the next house might hear it, and he felt confused and utterly out of his depth. She was much younger than he, and lovely, and clearly well-to-do, whereas he was a small landowner, with coarse and clumsy manners. The kiss last night should never have happened. She clearly didn't agree. At her door, she reached up and slipped her hands around his neck. Utterly lost, he bent to kiss her mouth, fighting to keep it gentle and respectful.

'We will marry, *oui*?' she asked.

'Yes,' he whispered, hardly able to think.

She took his hand and opening her door, pulled him gently inside. Only one candle was burning throwing a soft, but fairly inadequate light over the room. She tugged at his coat and his necktie and then he helped her down to her chemise. She removed it and standing naked before him, and without any hint of shyness, helped him finish undressing. They clambered into her bed without any haste or hesitation. Her calm manner had led him to believe she was experienced, so it was with concern he felt her stiffen and struggle when he first tried to enter her. He gentled her softly and slowed everything down. When they did join, he kept it slow and steady, and short. Afterwards, she curled into him much as Sam always did and he lay awake again, but this time for far different reasons. It seemed he was to marry again. To a woman, he didn't know. Well, no change there then. He wondered if this sense of floating, which he identified as happiness, would last until the banns were all called.

Sam woke them. He bounced into the room completely unabashed. 'When I saw your bed wasn't slept in, I thought you would be here,' he announced.

William had a brief thought about a chat about privacy, but he was too drifting in contentment to bother. Sam climbed in between them, his frozen feet making them both laugh until Marie-Claire instigated a tickling fight to warm him up.

'Are you to be my new mama?' Sam asked.

'Yes,' said Marie-Claire.

Well, it is done, thought William and, reaching behind Sam, he found Marie-Claire's hand and dropped a kiss into her palm before folding her fingers over.

Breakfast was a happy affair, with Samuel starting on teaching Marie-Claire English idioms. Her, 'Why skin cats! I like cats!' had Samuel laughing without pause.

William wanted to go out without Sam. Could he leave his boy with the woman? If he didn't trust her, why was he saying he would marry her? His head felt as if it was somersaulting. Marriage and trust were two different things. Had he been gulled? Led by his prick? The tavern keeper had told him what he needed to know. After fretting quietly, he rose and placed his hand on Sam's shoulder.

'I have to go out for a while. Will you wait here for me with Marie-Claire?'

The loving trust in the boy's eyes nearly unmanned him. Could he leave the most precious thing in his life with this woman he had known only a couple of days? As if she could read his mind, Marie-Claire touched his arm lightly and said, 'We will be 'ere, I promise, *je te promis*.'

William left, still fretting. As he sought the man he needed, he continued to worry. Was she really a Plymouth whore who was a first-class actress? Well, if she was, she hadn't robbed him yet. His coin was thrust deep under Samuel's mattress. He knew he was naïve compared to most men. He had always lived quietly, and contentedly on his acres. Eton was the only experience of outside life he knew, and he was even more green then. He sighed, still doubting himself, and her, but reminding himself that he constantly had to judge men when he bargained with them over the sale of his crops and cattle, and he seemed to do well there. But he felt in his bones, that judging a woman, especially a clever one, was different.

He found the Bishop of Exeter exactly where the tavern keeper had said he would be. The man was clearly highly irritated at being bothered by a man he judged well below himself in social standing. Thin and weasel-faced, and without any apparent godly consideration, William sighed at being at the man's mercy. He had little time for religion and considered his monthly visit to the local church as useful time to consider and plan in what order he should do the numerous tasks that faced him around the estate. And the time after the service was even more valuable as it gave him a regular chance to catch up with his neighbours.

He sighed as the Bishop prated on about how valuable his time was. The man could have done as requested in the time he had been spitting abuse at William! Finally, William had had enough. In exasperation, he shoved his hands on his hips and leant forward towards the prating man. William was large. Very large. Both the bishop and his clerk were small by comparison. The bishop suddenly stopped rabbiting on and sat with his mouth open, his eyes wide.

'Now then,' William said, 'you may have all day to waste but I haven't. According to St Paul it is better to marry than to burn, well I am about to fornicate with a woman tonight and I reckon the church and I are in agreement, the woman should have my ring on her finger before that happens. Now, are we also in agreement?'

William walked out a few minutes later with a special licence in his pocket and a smile on his face. Perhaps that useless vicar's Sunday sermons could be useful occasionally. Now all he needed was a local vicar and a church.

He had spotted a small church now lost up a side street as Plymouth had grown large around it, absorbing it into its by-ways and ally-ways. Inside it was surprisingly pleasant, with white-washed walls and one pretty colourful window of St Brendon, patron saint of navigators, and plain light oak pews beautifully carved with various sailing craft and sea creatures. He ran his hand lightly over a salmon leaping towards the altar at the end of a row and breathed in the sense of peace the quiet and calm of the place gave him.

He found the vicar out cold behind the altar, a gin bottle in his hand. They came to an agreement. The man would be sober at four of the clock and William would pay the man the extortionate fee of a guinea to perform the service and provide proof of a wedding. Outside, the calm of the lovely little church didn't last long. He watched a pretty girl with a square basket on her hip full of clean laundry being eyed up by a strapping lad with a hunk of wood over his shoulder and, in her turn, flirt a little with a flash of laughing eyes. William stood for a moment watching a wide smile spread across the lad's face before he hefted his load and continued on his way. Why was marriage so easy when one was young? And so hard for him to consider now? All of his misgivings rushed back. No one found a bride stranded on the harbour at Plymouth, did they? His life at home was like the pond that sat to the left of the front of his house, deep and still, and he was about to throw a huge rock into its centre.

He comforted himself that it was still right and proper for a man to beat a wife if she needed it. He could almost feel Marjorie's spirit hit him over the head as he thought it.

As he neared the tavern his thoughts began to whirl again. The London papers had mentioned some political upheaval in France but had suggested the authorities would bring matters to rights soon. What on earth would make a man send his sister to another country? With only female companions for support and protection? How could she be telling the truth? Was the letter she had sent, who was it to now, ah yes, an Earl of Ringshall, real? Or an elaborate hoax? What kind of hoax would want him as its target? He was too ordinary for words! Not rich, not good-looking, not powerful, not anything. His thoughts were exhausting him. And then, had she really been a virgin? Or again, was she just a clever actress? But then again, why?

By the time he entered the tavern he felt sick to his guts with his exhausting, whirling, thoughts. He entered the small parlour to find, to his relief, both Sam and Marie-Claire waiting for him, as she had promised. Relief turned to concern as he took in their anxious faces. Instantly, his protective instincts rose.

'What is wrong?' he asked, keeping his voice low so as not to increase their worry by snapping at them.

'Papa,' Sam began, glancing at Marie-Claire for permission and receiving a small nod, 'did you notice the grey man? He was dressed all in grey and had two lovely dappled grey horses in the stables. We joked about him yesterday. Because of the grey?' Sam's voice was rushed and anxious.

'I do,' William replied, remembering the man clearly. He hadn't liked him and had not known why, even though they had merely exchanged common courtesies. He had sensed the man sneering at him and Marie-Claire. She, of course, had sailed by with her small nose in the air. It seemed it was difficult to sneer at Marie-Claire and he admired her for it.

'What has happened?'

'What is a 'shot', apart from the sort that comes out of a gun?'

'It is what people often call a bill, or money owing.'

'Well, we heard the tavern keeper raging that the man hadn't paid him, and had stayed a whole week and had two horses fed as well in all that time. His wife had red eyes!' Sam's voice was still anxious and concerned. 'Isn't that stealing?'

'Yes son, it is.' William sat down heavily.

'Will they go after the man?'

'Probably not. He looked like an aristocrat, all that lace and fancy waistcoat, and those greys were expensive horse flesh.'

'He will not pay?' Marie-Claire asked.

'No, we hang starving children for stealing a loaf, but don't hang aristocrats for anything. It is just the way the world is.'

Marie-Claire made a 'bof' sound that felt impossibly French and muttered something about home. William had no idea if she was suggesting France ran things better, or worse, and he was not about to enter into a discussion on the legal and political frameworks in each of their countries with his meagre grasp of her language. It did occur to him, that when being told about the man, his flare of anxiety had been as much for Marie-Claire as for his son.

'I have news,' he said, changing the subject, and placed the special licence on the table.

'What is it?' Sam asked.

'If Marie-Claire would like, we are able to marry this afternoon. It means eating some lunch and then heading out to buy her a ring. And then we can go and marry. Would you be Marie-Claire's escort, Sam?'

'So, she really is to be my mama?' Sam's face was alight.

William looked across to Marie-Claire. She could be pregnant. He needed to put his life in order, but did she really want him? To his surprise, Marie-Claire's eyes filled with tears and she gave him a huge smile. '*Oui*,' she whispered. So, they went ring shopping.

Neither William nor Marie-Claire had eaten much luncheon, but had both watched with amusement as Samuel had tucked in despite all three of them having eaten large breakfasts.

'Fills from his ankles upwards,' William muttered and was met with a laughing glance from Marie-Claire.

Now, as they hunted down a decent jeweller, he thought perhaps he ought to have eaten more. His guts seemed to have settled now he was back with Marie-Claire. She was anchored at his side, her arm resting lightly on his, and he felt oddly proud to be walking with such a beautiful woman.

At the jeweller's Marie-Claire picked out the thinnest, cheapest gold ring there was.

'Why that one?' he asked.

She went bright pink and whispered, 'You 'ad not the intention to marry.' Her eyes looked up at his and he saw anxiety there, which surprised him.

'I am proud to marry you,' he murmured into her hair, and she relaxed a little. She had seemed so abnormally confident last night in the darkened room.

William looked around for himself, no longer trusting her choice. He spotted a wide gold band with a green stone embedded in the centre.

'Is that an emerald or a piece of glass?' he asked the jeweller.

'This is a jewellers! Not a street stall!' the man replied sharply.

William gave him a long look. 'And you haven't answered my question,' he said softly.

The man went red and assured him it was a genuine emerald, not large, but beautifully coloured. William liked the green. It was the colour he had first seen Marie-Claire in and he thought the ring would suit her.

'See if it fits.'

She shot him a brief glance from under her bonnet rim then slid it onto her finger. It was too large.

'Can you have that sized down by six o'clock?' he asked the jeweller.

'Oh no,' blurted the man. 'We need a day to make such a change.'

'Pity,' said William, 'I like the ring. Do you?' he asked Marie-Claire quietly, receiving a small nod and a little smile. 'Come, we will find another jeweller. One who can work more quickly.'

'Wait!' the jeweller blurted out, 'I could probably get it done. If I close the shop now and start immediately!'

'Well? Can do, or probably do?'

'Can do,' said the man.

'I will pay half now,' William told him, 'and borrow the thin ring. You will have both the borrowed ring and the rest of the money back at six of the clock. But for now, I need a ring to marry with.'

He lifted a leather money bag out of an inside pocked and tipped gold coins onto the counter. He pushed the amount required towards the man. As they left, they heard the bolts on the door be pushed closed.

'William, he has closed his shop!' Marie-Claire told him, 'He will make no more money today!'

William smiled down at her anxious face just as a horizontal slap of icy, salty, rain hit them all in the face.

'And how many jewels is he going to sell late in the afternoon on such a miserable day? He would have to close soon anyway. Now, do you really like the ring, or must I return and demand my coin back?'

'*Qu'elle est belle!* It is beautiful,' she whispered so quietly, he had to read her lips to make out her answer.

He patted the hand that lay so trusting on his left arm.

'I liked it too!' piped up Samuel, 'I love the green stone! It will always remind us of how we rescued Marie-Claire from the harbour side. As if she were a mermaid!'

With a lovely woman walking demurely on his left, and Samuel hopping like a cricket on his right, William strode off to be married.

The vicar was sober enough to muddle through the service, and so William paid him and they began the hike back to the tavern for dinner and a warm through. Halfway back the rain came on in force, driving in to smash them about with no regard for the importance of their persons. They ended up running and gasping into the tavern with much laughter.

The rain was still coming down when they had dried and warmed themselves as much as they could. As six o'clock drew near, William rose and began to struggle into his greatcoat to go and collect the altered ring. Both Marie-Claire and Samuel rose at the same time.

'Nay! It is still fairly foul out, you both stay here in the warm,' William protested.

But they were not to be deterred. Marie-Claire was insistent that her finger was required to confirm the jeweller had done his job properly, and Samuel, quite rightly declared that he could not be left in the tavern on his own. When William told him he could lock him in his room for safety, he grinned a huge grin back. William shook his head; he would never have cheeked his own father like that.

'You need discipline, boy,' he told him in his gruffest voice, but Sam managed to widen his grin even more.

The ring was perfect, the deal concluded, and dinner was a warm and happy affair. William went to settle with the tavern keeper as he was planning an early start in the morning. Wiltshire was a long way away, and it would take at least three or four days to get back home, even pushing the horses as much as they could. The keeper seemed almost tearfully relieved that someone at least was paying his shot, and William gave him a tip mostly out of sympathy but also because the service the man had given, let alone the excellent food, had been appreciated. In return, the man promised a packed hamper for their journey and warm bricks for their feet. William walked away thinking that his tip had been well worthwhile!

That night he dragged two of their trunks in front of the door. There were marks in the wood where a bolt had once been attached, but it had clearly been missing for a while. The trunks, already packed for the morning were heavy.

'Samuel?' Marie-Claire whispered.

'Or any bugger else,' William muttered to himself.

They curled together under the eiderdown and William allowed his hands to roam gently over the unbelievable warm soft skin that was next to him. Marie-Claire framed his face with her hands and pulled his face towards hers. Expecting to meet her mouth with his, he leant forward, but instead of meeting his lips, she feathered his face with small light kisses. It was gentle and, he felt, affectionate.

'I 'ad dreams of you,' she whispered.

'Me?' William didn't consider himself the kind of man women dreamed about. He was big and rough and preferred to get his hands worn out around his acres than sit like a lord in his house. He couldn't think of anything more dull.

'One day soon, I will tell you my *histoire*, but not this night. But truly, I 'ad dreams of you. Of a big man, with wide shoulders,' she ran her small hands across him, 'and a chest *énorme avec un grand coeur*. You do 'ave a big heart, I think.' She stayed with her palm flat against his chest. 'And I dreamed of a home, and a family, perhaps children. You have a house, *oui*?'

'It's old and draughty,' he told her, 'built when Good Queen Bess was a lass.'

'Ah, *mais* what is this droofty?' she asked.

'Draughty,' he told her, slowing the word as it left his mouth. 'Means the wind blows through sometimes.'

'Ah, you should try a chateau, built when your King Richard was a boy! All cold, cold stone.' And she gave a soft laugh.

He rested on his side and let his hand roam again, exploring her. Then he curled his hand and let his knuckles run softly from between her breasts to her navel, and beyond. He rubbed his knuckles oh so gently over the soft curls he found, left to right. He felt her stiffen and wasn't sure why. Then she relaxed and rose to meet his hand, increasing the pressure. She gave a small gasp, and William thought that even if she never gasped like that again, he would die a happy man to have wrung it from her once. Her own hand sought downwards and grasped him, and to his surprise, it was his turn to breathe out sharply.

Afterwards, she curled into him, still naked, and whispered to him in French, until she drifted off to sleep. William lay and stared upwards as he held her, and thought about Margorie. She had been a good woman, the best. But she had ruled him with a rod of iron. It wasn't long before they had somehow been coupling just once or twice a month. She never refused him, but he was let know when his ministrations would be acceptable. He hadn't thought he was hard-done-by, some men muttered about once a year when there was a Z in the month. She had always given him a small pat on his shoulder afterwards. It had always felt somewhat patronising as if he had performed acceptably. She certainly wasn't into what she called, 'messing about'. She liked it quick and fast and always, after the pat, pulled her nightgown down and rolled over to go to sleep. He had a feeling it wasn't going to be at all like that with Marie-Claire. Perhaps this second marriage wasn't such a bad idea after all.

The carriage ride home was hard. The roads were mired in mud and rutted, and the horses tired with the extra effort. And, of course, they now had the extra weight of Marie-Claire and her trunks. He had paid a carter to bring some of their luggage after, as his poor horses wouldn't have coped with the whole of the extra load. Half of his and Samuel's belongings were now risked onto the road with a man who, for all William knew, might take the lot and vanish. Late afternoons were the worst. Everyone was worn out with the shaking about a carriage ride always gave a body, and the light would be gloomy even though the nights were drawing out. Invariably, William would move to face forward beside Marie-Claire, and they would lift the boy onto the facing seat to lie curled up and then cover him with a rug. Marie-Claire would then settle into William and doze the last couple of hours of the journey in his arms. William would close his eyes and wonder about his new wife, his rescued mermaid, and about where she had come from, how it was that she had washed up into his arms, and what kind of life she had been living. And also, whether he was being every kind of fool.

Samuel seemed to be coping well with the rigours of the journey. William still hadn't got over the sight of his poor boy, so frail and seeming nearer death than life when he had collected him from Eton. Despite Sam's recovery, he still watched keenly for any sign of a decline. He would have to go back, of course. This autumn, he thought. The boy needed to be toughened up and Eton school was what his family had always relied upon for that job. He told himself that Sam wouldn't break this time, he was far stronger nowadays.

He and Marie-Claire spent most of the time improving his French and her English, though to be fair, there wasn't much wrong with Marie-Claire's command of the language when she was feeling confident and people spoke clearly to her. He despised himself, but he had watched her closely to see if her affection for the lad seemed at all false. He still fretted that he had been gulled in some way. It seemed too unreal that a woman like her would want him. They had written to some Earl of Ringshall from the tavern, giving his home as a return address in an effort to find out if they had made it to Harwich, and let them know that Marie-Claire was safe. Perhaps they might have a reply in a day or so?

They arrived at Causton Manor, his home, late one afternoon, exhausted from being rattled around and worn out from the long journey. William hurried them all into the house and called for hot food and warm beds. Tomorrow would be plenty of time to introduce everyone and show Marie-Claire her new home.

To his surprise, Marie-Claire slid into his home without a ripple. Oh, there was gossip, the county was rife with it, where had she come from, who was she, oh my goodness, she was French, who were her family, the noise was loud in the lanes and byways, but it was, and this surprised him, good-natured. The women, whom he feared the most, competed to make her acquaintance, the men nudged him good-heartedly as a sly dog to do his courting so quietly. He gave daily thanks that everyone assumed his trip to Plymouth had been a marriage trip where they could enjoy the beginning of their partnership in privacy, and Sam's presence seemed to confirm this! Of course, he would want his new wife and his heir to become acquainted out of sight of prying eyes. The wedding ring on Marie-Claire's finger confirmed all of their assumptions. The idea that he had met and married in about four days never seemed to cross anyone's mind. Not for the first time, William marvelled at the ability of people to invent something and then believe in it. He kept his mouth still and nodded. It seemed to do the trick.

Marie-Claire was extraordinary. Instead of trying to apologise or hide that she was French, well that would have been hard with her thick French-accented English, she presented it, to the women especially, as a handicap. Oh, my dear, how is that done? Arranging flowers, well how could a silly foreigner do that properly? Run a home, oh, all advice was appreciated and grateful, fulsome thanks given. Meanwhile, she carried on within the Manor in her own sweet way. To the men she smiled sweetly, misunderstood what they said and, he noticed, kept close to him. She seemed wary of men and when in mixed company constantly sought the assurance of his monitoring presence. He would have died for her, but doubts continued to rise.

If she were an aristocrat, how was it she knew how the kitchen ran? Or the laundry? Or was willing to work hard around the house? He had come home last week to find her wrapped in a huge apron polishing the spindles on the stairs with beeswax and lavender, the maid of all work, Joan, helping her. And then Sam told him a story, his face full of glee. Sam had been under the huge table in the kitchen. It was hot and the door stood propped open to let sunlight and air in. He had scrambled under the table to share a crust of bread with one of the older dogs who was sheltering from the heat on the flagstones. Marie-Claire had come in and shushed cook, who was taking a nap by the range. In a spirit of mischief, Sam had stayed quiet. Marie-Claire had begun crushing sugar in the pestle, then sieving flour, causing soft clouds of white to drift down in the sun shafts. Warm, and full of his lunch, Sam had drifted off to sleep with his head on the dog and his flank cool on the stone floor. He awoke to a delicious smell and rubbed his eyes as Marie-Claire held a small cake out to him.

'If you don't take it, the dog will 'av it,' she told him.

Sam said it was the loveliest cake he had ever eaten, and he was highly amused that Marie-Claire had known he was there all along. It did not add up to an aristocrat.

Eventually, it burst from him. They were in bed, lying quiet in warm companionship, no desire that night driving them together. In the light of the one candle still burning William could live with it no longer. He didn't care where his wife came from, he just wanted to *know*. His whirling mind must have shown itself, as she stroked the side of his face and whispered, 'What is it my William? What is troubling you?'

The words didn't come out with any grace, 'Lass, were you really a virgin that first night?'

'Does that give you problems?'

'Only that I have so many questions about you in my mind. I want to feel comfortable with you, but thoughts flap around, like bats in my head, and I want them gone. I want to know who you are and how at the age of twenty-seven, you came to be my wife.'

'I was a virgin, but only barely, as I will tell you. Find our nightgowns, and we will sit up and be comfortable.'

Her voice sounded calm, but William thought, 'nightgowns!' and hoped he hadn't ruined their habit of sleeping nude. To lie against the warm skin of his sweet wife was one of his greatest pleasures. Perhaps, as Marjorie had done, she was about to set out new rules. Not feeling at all confident, he helped her into her gown and yanked his over his head.

'My father is a duke, brother of Louis, King of France. Much of his land is in Aquitaine.'

William didn't know where Ak-it-ten was but vaguely wondered if it had anything to do with Eleanor, wife of the second Henry.

'I was the last of my mother's children, *numéro quatorze*, fourteen, and she died soon after my birth.' She gave a small shrug, 'I am surprised she could manage so long,' she said, 'but many babies died. I have two sisters, much older but rarely have I seen, who are married and live in other parts, and a brother, who again, I saw but rarely. In fact, when any of them visited, which was not often, they put me in my room as I was not mannered enough to be in their company, being still young. I would escape, of course, and peep at them from high windows, and marvel at the beauty of their clothes. Oh, how I longed for satin and lace. I was very young and very, very foolish.'

William considered a young girl longing for pretty dresses to be completely normal, not foolish but remained quiet. Marie-Claire continued,

'When I was fourteen, I was quite tall for my age, you always say how tiny I am, but that is mostly because you are so large, *mon* William. *Mon père*, my father arrived one day and called for me. He told my nurse that I was, how you say, acceptable, and she must pack my things. It seemed I was going to court. I travelled alone with a new maid, who until then I had never seen. She did not speak to me and I was afraid of her. We arrived at Versailles and they took us to our rooms. She was furious, and yelled a lot, very loudly, because they gave her a very small room next to mine, while I had a bedroom very big and also a *salon*. It was clear she had not chosen to be my maid!

'For three days and nights, they dressed me in as much silk, satin, lace, and brocade, as any girl could ever have wished for. I learned quickly how to stand for hours in the hall of mirrors and not move when the king was present. If I became *fatiguée* then the mirrors gave me away and my father would give me a pinch hard. Other times I paraded around the rooms by my father's side. Women wearing much make-up and *parfum* would come and pinch my cheek and tell my father, never me, how pretty I was. Men, the age of my father would stand too close and look down my bodice. As I was quite small, I wished them luck of that. I met the king and found *incroyable* that I could call him uncle! He seemed so grand and important and 'ad a very silly huge wig.'

This made William snort with laughter. He had never heard a king put down so well. He wondered what Marie-Claire would make of their George. At this, Marie-Claire giggled, and the atmosphere between them became more comfortable.

'The fourth night,' she continued, 'the maid woman, who was too important to be my nursemaid as she told everyone, came and with two other women and took off my clothes, dropped a nightgown over my 'ead. I don't know if it was silk or cotton, but it was so *transparent* I saw a graze on my arm that had only nearly healed through *la manche*, the sleeve. I glanced down and saw all of my body as if I was undressed *complétament.*

I was horrified. The night gown was completely *indécent.* 'Not very big for sixteen, are you,' the woman mocked, looking at my breasts. When I protested that I was fourteen, she slapped my cheek and told me not to lie, to the point that I wondered if indeed I had mistaken my own age.

'They brushed my hair down my back, which was indeed a relief. Hairstyles at court were intricate, took so long to do, and were so forced into forms that hurt the head. Then they walked me down long, empty corridors, *totalament vides.* The floors were cold, and my slippers too thin, and although the corridors were free of the court, they were not *libres* of guards. They lined the route, and I watched as they stood with their noses straight but they let their eyes see me on one side, and then follow me to the other. I was paraded past a dozen men who were permitted to gape at my naked body. There were even more guards as we approached the rooms of the king. I was living *un cauchemar*, a nightmare, and couldn't wake, and felt so, so cold. The room was empty when they forced me into it. I could not understand, it was not as large as our great hall at home, but it was large enough and full of fabrics and furniture and a bed, covered with brocades and silks *luxurieuses*. Then the king entered. He stood on the other side of the room and smiled a horrid smile and gazed at me. Then he came to me and began to stroke me through the nightgown. His arm ran across my shoulder, then down my arm, and held my breast. So I vomited on his shoes.'

William gave an enormous yelp of surprised laughter. 'You did what?'

'I emptied my over-rich dinner onto his feet. He stayed very calm, 'e stamped his heel on the floor and a servant appeared and I was taken away *brusquement*. The king clicked his fingers and I was removed, back along the long cold corridors, this time smelling disgusting as my nightgown was splattered *avec* the contents of my stomach. There was one guard, a big man with blond hair peeking out of his helmet; his eyes met mine and he looked so sympathetic. He didn't insult me with his eyes, he saw me as a frightened girl and I have never forgotten him. Perhaps that is why I used to dream of a big husband and why I was so attracted to you when we met.'

'My hair is not blond.'

'No, it is a lovely rich *noix* brown,' she said, reaching out to stroke it and place a kiss on his cheek.

'What happened then?' he asked.

'My father came to the room and beat me with his hands. I was sent home the next day alone in the coach with two men on the reins and two outriders, and he seemed to forget about me. Perhaps he did because when I met my brother, he said my father's mind was gone a long time before he died *finalement*. I lived at the chateau and kept well away when he or anyone else visited, which was not often. Being forgotten about was *ennyeux*, boring. There was not much in my rooms and my nurse had been dismissed, so I began to wander around. I found my way to the kitchens. At first everyone curtsey, which was not good, but in time they got used to me. I began to join in the household tasks.' She shrugged.

'Sometimes I read in the library, and the first time that is where I nearly got into trouble. I had no idea some men had come to stay. The weather had turned bad and they had arrived at the chateau to find shelter for a night or two. Because of the storm, I had heard nothing. I was by the fire reading when a man came in. I was not worried until he began to pull at me and try to kiss me. I kicked him 'ard and ran like a *lièvre*, I think you say a hare, up to one of the towers. This is why I said I was a virgin, but only barely. I nearly wasn't that evening. Another time I was near the kitchens when a man pushed me up against a wall and tried to lift up my skirts. The serving girls told me later that when that happened, they had to stand still and take it. But I wasn't a serving girl and I had been on my way to the flower garden and had a knife in my hand. A very sharp knife. Rose stems are 'ard, you know? I stabbed him in the arm and hissed in his ear that I was niece to the king and one word from me and he would receive much more than a sore arm. This time I walked away. I was indeed niece to the king and 'ad a weapon I was not afraid to use. He did not come after me.'

William's head was spinning. Could all this be true? He didn't know what to think, this was so outside his quiet, tranquil life.

'But how is it your English is so good?' And it was, despite the heavy accent he had now become accustomed to.

'My first governess was English. My father wanted me to learn English as he said we had been at war with them since the world began, and he wanted me to learn. My brother said his idea was to marry me with an English duke and have me spy for the French.'

'He was training his daughter to be a spy?'

'Ah *oui*, yes, he had a mind very devious. I cannot write English as he said I should never write anything in that language, but if I sound out the letters I can sometimes understand written English, but it is so 'ard. After my governess left and I had been to Versailles, I found one of the servants, a girl with the name of Gail. She 'ad been married to a sailor, and when he died, found herself lost in France. She found work at the chateau and we would sometimes speak together. She always said my accent was dreadful, but we understood one another. She was from a new castle.'

William frowned, then he put it together. 'Newcastle?'

'Yes, it is near here?'

'Not much.'

No wonder Marie-Claire's English was so hard to understand, anyone born more than ten miles from Newcastle couldn't always understand the true Tyne folk. If her fledgling English had been polished by a lass from the North East, it explained a great deal!

'William, I have a secret,' Marie-Claire confessed scrambling off the bed.

She moved over to her clothes press and a small chest that stood on the top for all to view. She rummaged in a drawer for a key and then brought both to the bed. Climbing back beside him she placed the chest on her knees and unlocked it. Inside was a mess of glass.

'These are not mine, you understand,' she explained anxiously, 'my brother gave them to me for to keep safe. Some have been belonging in our family since there were only three numbers in the year.'

William frowned at that, then blinked. Before the year a thousand? Well, he had heard that some of the French aristocracy traced their linage back almost to the year dot. Perhaps it was true? He poked a finger into the heap, so Marie-Claire tipped the whole lot into her lap.

William stared. Were they real? Or some tomfoolery? The clear stones looked dirty and lumpy, but there was a blue one that caught his eye. He held it up to the candle, and the light glowed deep within, flashing as he twisted it from side to side and giving back a colour, he did not believe any glass could achieve. There was an emerald the size of a pigeon egg and a ruby in a lozenge shape the size of his thumb nail.

'These are the unwanted ones, of course.'

'Unwanted?' William asked, his eyebrows up near his hairline.

'The modern jewels were, of course, with my father in Versailles. These were left behind as they were cut in the old way still, and the settings are old-fashioned, *démodés*, but my brother thought there was perhaps some value here and he wanted them out of the country.'

A wrenching thought hit William. Had her brother really been sending his sister to England, or the jewels? He had so impressed upon her how important it was to get to England, she had travelled alone, weathered a storm, and been stranded in a foreign country with no support. They still hadn't received a reply from the Earl of Ringshall.

He picked up a brooch absentmindedly. There was a similar one on a dress in a painting in the attic, and the woman wearing that dress had lived in this house when it was new over two hundred and fifty years ago.

'What did you mean, when you met your brother?' William asked. He wasn't liking the man much at the moment.

'I was coming down the stairs and he walked in the door. I looked one time and ran for a tower to lock myself in, without the intention to come out until I believed it was safe. I had no wish to meet men in satin and lace. I had found them untrustworthy. He chased me. I was terrified. He caught up with me and grabbed my wrist and I screamed and bit him. Then he smacked me.

"Who are you?" he demanded, "you are no servant that I know? Are you a thief?"

I stopped struggling and hissed at him, "I am niece to the king and he will have your hide if you lay one more finger on me!" Then he let me go and said, "Marie-Claire? You are supposed to be dead!" We got to talking and he was so kind to me. At last, I had someone, a brother, I love him very much.

William wasn't much impressed. To his mind, Marie-Claire, unforgivably alone and unprotected, would have loved any tinker that had turned up to claim her and make her feel wanted.

Suddenly Marie-Claire slipped from the bed. 'I will return,' she smiled at him, and then she was off.

William sat against the headboard and scooped the stones until they lay cradled in his lap. He let them trickle through his fingers. Ugly stuff, to his mind. Thoughtfully, he picked each one up and settled it back into the chest. As he did so a realisation came to him that lifted a huge weight off the back of his neck. He sat up and stared at the opposite wall. He wasn't at all sure he believed all this. Marie-Claire still might be a servant who had stolen the gems and absconded. Be a thief. A body servant would know all about the family, how they behaved, and who they were. Where the valuables were kept. Who was to gainsay her? But equally, what did it matter? She was here, now. She was a warm and kind wife. His. She was genuine as far as he and Sam were concerned, and now, that was all that mattered. France was a long way-away. A foreign place with foreign habits that he wasn't interested in. Now, here and now, she was his, and she pleased him.

The door opened slowly and Marie-Claire returned, with a tray on which stood two beakers and a candle. 'Hot milk,' she told him.

William smiled and hid his opinion. He hated hot milk. Cold from the larder, in the summer, it could be wonderfully refreshing, but warm made him feel ill. But he took the beaker and smiled. Then he smelt it.

'What is in here?'

'Good French brandy, honey, nutmeg, cloves and cinnamon.'

William sipped. Nectar from the gods. He grinned at Marie-Claire and she grinned back as if she had read his mind, which she probably had, women were good like that. Milk finished Marie-Claire tugged at his nightshirt. 'You need this?'

William grinned. She was warm, she was loving, and she was his. Life was good.

The following morning the courier arrived. William had spotted him a quarter mile out and stood on his step wondering why a very dusty and travel-stained man was hurrying a horse up his drive. A good horse too, he could see that from here, expensive no doubt. Frowning slightly, he waited. In due time the man slid from his horse and peered up at William.

'I am looking for my lady,' the man said, his voice demanding.

'Now which lady might that be?' William asked, beginning to be amused.

'The French lady,' the man replied, still with an arrogant tone, and a definite French accent.

'Ah, that lady.'

William turned his head and called for Molly the maid. Gormless Moll appeared, and William sent for Marie-Claire. He remained standing on his step, in front of his open front door, and didn't move. The man similarly remained beside his horse, still looking unfriendly.

When Marie-Claire arrived at William's side she glanced up for information, but he nodded at the man with his head, directing her that way. Marie-Claire frowned at the man.

'*Vous-êtes qui?*' she asked in French, before remembering William and saying, 'Who are you?'

The man responded with a tirade in the language, but William understood enough to hear m'lady, duc, and something about grovelling apologies, and then the name Ringshall. He then bent low in a courtly bow that would have looked far more appropriate had they actually been in a court and handed a large letter to Marie-Claire that looked to be made of parchment. Marie-Claire took it looking concerned.

'Well, lad,' William said to the man, 'No doubt you have travelled far, if you walk that way you will find the kitchens and stables. One will feed you, the other the horse. Off you go.'

The furious, insulted glance the man threw at William left him smiling. This was his house, his land, and his wife. He wasn't having some stranger with no manners glare at him on his own front step.

'Looks important lass,' he told Mary-Claire.

'Will you come help me read it?'

'If you want me to?'

It was her letter. Yes, he was curious, but she would tell him what it was about if she wanted. She nodded.

In the study, they sat together while Marie-Claire broke the seal. She read for a while then turned to William, her face quite white.

'Lass, what is it? Is it bad news?'

'It is from the Earl of Ringshall, the new Earl of Ringshall. It seems this is the son, who has inherited recently the title.'

Willian frowned. What was all this with new Earls?

'It seems his mother, who was French, and his father, were travelling to Harwich to meet me. The storm that blew me to Plymouth, overturned their coach and they were both killed. He apologises for the delay in replying but he has only now discovered why they were on that road. He wishes to offer me his protection, as his father did, and if I wish he will send a carriage and outriders to collect me and take me in safety to his home. He says he has been careful not to tell anyone of my title, only that I am an important French lady.'

'And what is your title?' William asked, beginning to feel slightly anxious. Earls were powerful people. He was massively outgunned here!

'Oh, it is the most important title in the world. Very special. Very, very wonderful.' She grinned up at him, her dark eyes dancing, 'It is Lady Causton, wife of William,' she reached up and kissed him on the cheek. 'All of this,' she waved the parchment dismissively, 'it is what my brother wanted for me, or more, for our name. An important family to sponsor me, a court life here in England, no doubt a rich husband of influence. Bof!' It was such an expressive sound, so utterly dismissive. 'I belong here now, I will not leave you and Samuel, you are my 'ome!'

William dropped a kiss on her head. He wasn't sure words were needed.

Marie-Claire had written a reply to be taken back to the Earl. She had said little, simply that any responsibility for her, or to her family, was now satisfied. She would remain in Wiltshire, with her husband. Once the courier, who clearly thought his job as a lackey to an Earl put him higher on the social scale than a mere Wiltshire landowner, had left, William walked out towards the orchards, back to his original plan for the day. As he walked, he considered the huge red circle of wax that had terminated the parchment letter. It had been impressed with a massive seal, and he had seen some kind of bird on it with an open beak. A raptor of some kind. A symbol of power. Perhaps those ugly rocks *were* valuable? Perhaps he and Marie-Claire ought to find a better hiding place than in plain sight in their bedroom!

That evening he thought of another question to fret about. 'Do you consider yourself my wife?' he asked Marie-Claire. Samuel had been galloping around the estate with two other lads and having nearly fallen asleep in his plate, had been sent to bed soon after dinner.

'Have I not said so?'

'But the vicar in Plymouth, he was not Catholic, and I suppose you must be. So in law here, and in my mind you are, but what about in yours?'

She made a dismissive gesture. 'I am your wife because you and I will it. That gin-soaked man who wed us, yes, he did the paper, but I am here because I wish to be, and you also wish it.'

'But if you are the niece of a king, are you allowed to marry a small English landlord?'

'Beh! There is nothing small about you! Besides, if all of France could desert me for years in a chateau with no proper company, and forget about me so completely, why should I care what any king thinks, or anyone else? I was very lost, and very unhappy until I decided to make myself useful. I learned to live and to do what I wanted. And I dreamed. I had dreams of a big man, who could take small men who smelt of *parfum* and still stronger than me, and who 'eld me against a wall with one hand and tried to lift my skirts with another, and throw them from here to perdition.'

William had to laugh. 'So, you only married me for my bullish strength!'

'*Mais oui*,' Marie-Claire seemed totally unruffled. 'I decided I liked you, liked you very much, as we walked to the tavern. Yes, you were big and strong, but also you seemed kind, and you loved your son. That was important to me. I watched to see if you seemed mean, and you did not, I asked about your home, and you had one, and you were of a good, sensible age and you already had a son, so if I am too old to 'ave a child, you already have an heir.'

William sat back amazed. He had been thoroughly assessed! He was speechless for a moment.

'You did not think to marry,' Marie-Claire said softly as she bent over her sewing. 'Are you angry with me?' Her cheeks had gone quite pink. She shot him a small quick look.

'Best idea you ever had, lass,' he told her, with a broad smile.

Her own smile widened as she bent closer to her sewing, her cheeks now very pink.

'Feeling tired?' he asked.

She looked up with wide eyes, 'It is too early, William, you are very naughty!'

He settled back to smile into the fire. Bedtime would come soon enough.

Their first argument was a week later. William thought he had done well to get a month under his belt. Marie-Claire had taken it upon herself to sit in with Sam and the vicar during one of Sam's lessons. She came into William's study wholly indignant.

'That man, Sam knows more than him! Why is he pretending to teach? He knows nothing!'

'It doesn't matter lass, Sam will be off to Eton in the autumn. It is only for a few more weeks.'

Marie-Claire opened her mouth and stared at him wide-eyed. 'You will send him back to that place that nearly killed him!' she gasped eventually.

'He will be fine,' William said placatingly. 'He is older now by two years, and besides, I went there and so did my father. He has to go somewhere. He can't stay here. We aren't grand people, but we are large landowners. He may wish to stand for parliament, who knows, but he won't be able to do so unless he goes out into the world. Meets people, becomes a man.'

Marie-Claire erupted. The argument ended with her leaving and slamming the door. William sighed and sank back, relieved it was over, at least for now. He knew she loved the boy, but that was a problem. It wouldn't help Sam if he was molly-coddled all his life. He returned to his accounts wondering when the next salvo would be fired.

To his consternation, Marie-Claire acted as if nothing had happened. William increasingly felt he was walking on eggshells. What did happen was a flurry of letters to the Royal Academy and to Oxford University. William paid to send them off but didn't ask what they were about. At the moment he didn't like to enquire. Instead, he watched Marie-Claire with increasing nervousness and wondered if he was playing it all wrong. Perhaps he should put his foot down and demand to know what she was up to. But of course, he didn't. The revelation came in the shape of a lady of middle-age and stern countenance. She was ushered into William's study one morning and introduced as Miss Buckley. Ah, thought William, at last, we have it.

Miss Buckley, it seemed, had twin brothers who were slightly older than herself. What this had to do with anything William wasn't at all sure. The brothers hated to be parted and, when they had departed for Oxford, Miss Buckley had gone along as their housekeeper with their parents' blessing. William looked to Marie-Claire for guidance as to why this woman was sitting across his desk from him.

Marie-Claire spoke up. 'Women, they cannot attend a university, no?'

'No,' agreed William.

'But Miss Buckley has. She has discussed every night with her brothers what they learned if anything, that day. She knows as much as they do. She wishes to put that knowledge to use and teach Samuel. She can make him ready for Oxford, or Cambridge, and he will not have to go back to that horrid school. She is not stupid, like that *imbècile* vicar.'

William considered laughing. Well, she had out-manoeuvred him. What a minx! 'What if I don't want my son taught by a woman?'

Marie-Claire glared at him. 'Our son,' she stated, holding up her gold band with the emerald. 'And what our son needs, is to be taught by an intelligence, whether that intelligence is in a man or a woman.'

'Nay lass. I can't have the boy taught by a governess! He would never live it down. He has to become a man, not a gently reared young woman!'

To which, Miss Buckley gave an inelegant snort. 'Don't look to me for embroidery or pianoforte lessons, Sir William. What I offer is advanced mathematics, astronomy, physics, and geography, from the most advanced globe yet made and made entirely for me. If,' she paused, 'I take on your boy, he will arrive at university more educated than any other boy from the so-called public schools. He will have received an education few men have the opportunity to benefit from.'

William wasn't giving up. 'But the boy needs to make friends, alliances, get to know the boys that will one day run this country.'

It was Marie-Claire's turn to snort inelegantly, 'And be beaten, starved and bullied?'

'It's not always like that!' William protested, 'I had a good time there!'

'And with how many politicians do you remain in contact?' Marie-Claire demanded.

William felt a little flustered. He wasn't in contact with any of his old school companions, and he hadn't experienced any further schooling as his father had died so early in his life.

'That's not the point,' he maintained. 'Besides, I never got to university. I'd like Samuel to have that chance.'

'I can give him that chance. If he is bright enough,' interrupted Miss Buckley.

Bright enough! thought William indignantly.

'Besides,' Miss Buckley hadn't finished, 'it depends upon your son. Whatever you intend, I will not teach him if he does not want to be taught by me. I'd like to meet him now.'

William swallowed. He was slow to anger, but he could feel the stirrings now. It was time for this woman to go. But then he decided she was right. There was no way Sam would agree to a governess.

'By all means,' he said tightly, 'perhaps Marie-Claire would take you to meet him.'

After they left his anger began to grow. He wasn't sure what to do with it, so he poured himself a brandy.

Sam adored her. Of course. 'She has her own telescope!' he excitedly informed his father. 'Her brother is the Royal Astronomer and she knows all the planets and stars. She was his assistant in his research.'

William wondered whose life he was inhabiting. It certainly didn't feel like his own. First a French princess to wife and now the sister of the Royal Astronomer as tutor to his son. Was there such a title?

Miss Buckley refused accommodation at the manor with the family. She, it seemed, had independent means and wished to purchase, or have built, a small house of her own, if Sir William might assist her in finding such a property. With resignation, he rented her the Dower House. It hadn't been used in years and where it had once been isolated a mile and a half from the village, over the last hundred years or so the village had crept to meet it. When Miss Buckley exclaimed that it was far too large for her, it was Samuel who pragmatically suggested in that case, she should only use half.

Miss Buckley's response was, 'Well boy, I knew I would like you the first moment I saw you.'

Sam just grinned.

'It is very, *comment dit-on*, in pieces,' Marie-Claire fretted once she too had viewed the house.

'It is lass, but it gives me an excuse to modernise it. I have been putting off bringing in workmen for a long, long time.'

Samuel loved the house. It had a walled garden at the back full of blackberries, apple trees and darting birds, a short front garden off the lane, and ancient trees all around. Best of all for Miss Buckley, despite being private, it was only a brisk walk into the village for any provisions she might need. Marie-Claire took the opportunity to give Molly to housekeep for the new tutor. She found 'gormless Moll' irritating, preferring maids who dashed around, sang as they polished, washed or swept and were mentally acute enough to understand her heavy accent. Moll on the other hand had one speed, slow. She never stopped, was completely thorough, but moved at her own pace. Marie-Claire, who ran from dawn to dusk, found her beyond frustrating.

Sam enjoyed a blissful summer racing around either on foot or on the back of a pony with two other boys, went fishing and shooting with his father and ate everything Pells, the cook, or Marie-Claire set in front of him. 'Grows like a weed,' grumbled William proudly. His social awkwardness failed to improve, however. His extreme shyness made him dumb whenever he was faced with more than one or two people at a time. At any kind of gathering, Marie-Claire refused to let him from her side, always claiming her English was so poor she absolutely required him as her interpreter. In this way, he slowly became more comfortable with a greater number of people, but the pain of his shyness seemed more to be partially under control rather than conquered.

That autumn Miss Buckley and Sam began his academic career. She couldn't sing his praises loud enough. William continued to fret this wasn't the education his son ought to be engaged in. Samuel, however, thrived.

They had been married three years when William came home unexpectedly because he had forgotten something. He could never remember what. He had no reason to go upstairs to their bedroom, it was just that the hairs on the back of his neck felt uncomfortable when he couldn't work out where Marie-Claire was. He found her crouched on the floor heaving her guts into a chamber pot. Striding across he found a jug of water and wrung a cloth out. When she finished, he offered her a mug of water.

'Rinse your mouth, lass,' he murmured, as he wiped the sweat from her face.

Eventually, she seemed somewhat recovered so he sat her up on the bed and settled beside her with his arm around her. 'When were you going to tell me?'

When no child had come, they had both settled on the unspoken assumption that it was not going to happen. Now, it looked like they had been mistaken.

'We 'ave not eaten fish!' Marie-Claire said indignantly.

William didn't know if it was a French thing, but she put all stomach upsets down to fish. William found he was beginning to smile. It seemed he had more experience than she had.

'I don't think fish is to blame,' he murmured into her hair.

'It happened yesterday,' she complained. 'But then I felt better. Now it is back again!'

'Will probably come back for a long time to come.'

Marie-Claire frowned up at him, looking hugely put-out.

'My guess is you are with child,' he said, grinning.

For years afterwards, when his mind was wandering, it would take him back to the look of utter astonishment on her face and he would laugh softly to himself.

Samuel was entranced. He knew all about animal birth, he had grown up surrounded by it, but this was entirely new. He watched Marie-Claire like a hawk, fascinated by the changes in her and when he was encouraged to hold his hand to her and feel the baby kicking, he was in awe.

Chapter 6

Marie-Claire was about six months along when the letter came. It was delivered by a dusty carter who had obtained the missive from who knows where and didn't stay around long enough to explain. The weather was hot and so William took it up to where she was resting the afternoon away on their bed. He watched anxiously as she read it, and paled to a shocking greyish-white.

'My brother,' she whispered, 'they cut off his head. In public.'

She began to cry with huge heaving sobs. William picked her up and sat up against the headboard, holding her in his arms letting her howl her anguish out. Finally, she fell asleep in his arms. He sat there and watched the afternoon finally fade. He had tried to read the letter, but most of it defeated him. Whoever wrote it had been taking lessons from the hens in his yard. They scratched exactly like this writer.

He sat for a long while cupping her head to his shoulder in one of his large hands and her bump in the other. Even in her sleep, he wanted her to feel protected and cared for. The baby seemed to be turning summersaults at first but then settled like his, or her, mother. Eventually, he tried again to make out some words on the letter. After he had noticed that Marie-Claire stumbled over her words in the evenings, or even struggled completely to find one, he had begun to realise how hard it was for her to think and speak constantly in a second language. From then on, from when the plates met the table for dinner, they all spoke French, much to Marie-Claire and Sam's amusement. It had taken him ages, but gradually his spoken French had become reasonably fluent. And it had been fun and brought them together. But this chicken scratch letter was beyond him.

When Marie-Claire finally awoke, it was clear that at first, she didn't know where she was. William was still concerned the shock might bring the baby on, but she seemed at least partially recovered.

'Aren't you stiff?' she asked him.

'As a board.'

'Oh, you old fool. Walk. Walk around!'

Smiling he did so. If she was slandering him then they were fine. 'Do we tell Sam?' he asked, 'Or the baby one day?'

Marie-Claire was determined. 'Never. What if they come for him, or this babe? Who knows who will have the power? If my brother is such an enemy of France, then I am too, and possibly my children also. Even if one day it seems safe, there did not seem to be danger immediately before all this began to happen. No, no one needs to know where I come from. I am just a little piece of French flotsam you gave a home to.'

William was quiet for a long while as he chewed it over. He remembered how at first, he had wondered if Marie-Claire was spinning a tale and she was in truth merely a lady's maid with dreams of grandeur. After all, Marie-Claire had arrived without escort or servants. If it hadn't been for the coloured rocks, now well hidden, and the letter Marie-Claire had read to him, he would always have secretly wondered if she was who she said she was. He was a down-to-earth plodding man, neither princesses nor mermaids were likely to fall into his lap!

'Ringshall knows,' he said at last.

'*Bah*! He has no more interest in me. He is, how you say, off the hook.'

'True. But I don't like telling lies,' he said, scrubbing the back of his neck with his hand.

'Sins of omission,' Marie-Claire said. 'You are too honest for me. I corrupt you.'

'It's not that lass. It is only that untruths when they come out later, make people feel they have been betrayed. But you are right, I won't have Sam, or our babe, be put in harm.'

'But seriously, William, do you have enough money? We could sell the stones. They are now yours to do with as you wish.'

'Keep your stones, lass. We have plenty. The estate is still doing us proud. You can have as many new bonnets as you want.'

She nodded, clearly reassured, he knew very well she wasn't a woman to fret for fribbles.

'You might one day want to claim a French inheritance.'

'Never. All I want is to be your wife and live here, nothing more. I am happy for France to be the past.'

William turned to leave her, but as he went for the door, she couldn't help herself, 'William,' she called softly, 'you do love me?'

He paused and looked over his shoulder, then crossed back, sat beside her and gathered her into his arms. He knew a lot about women with babies in their guts, so he rocked her for a moment then took her hand and placed a kiss on her palm. Curling her fingers over he brought her hand to rest against the centre of his chest.

'See here lass, right in my centre, the core of my soul, there is a small flame burning. That is you, buried deep in me. That flame will never go out, not ever. You are a part of me, in my very bones, don't you know that? People love kittens and puppies, what I feel for you is part of the essence of me. That word just isn't sufficient.' He looked down at her and wiped the lone tear as it slid slowly down her cheek. 'Is that good enough?' She nodded, and he kissed her lightly. 'Now, I need to find you something hot to drink. You have had a bad shock and still feel cold to me. I will be back in a moment.' This time she let him go.

William called for a jug of mulled wine, with a lot of honey and spice. Marie-Claire was still dismissive of the wine he had in his cellar, but if it was hot and sweet, he reckoned it would do her a power of good. As he waited for the maid he leant against the bannisters, his hands gripping the rail as he gazed down at the hall with its worn flagstones, hanging weapons and heavy dark chests. He was running through in his mind everyone who might be able to guess, or who actually knew, who Marie-Claire was. Despite everything, it was quite a list, and the brother remained an enigma. Marie-Claire said that when he had come home to the chateau, he had claimed he was sick of Versailles. Despite letters from the king insisting he return he had remained at the chateau. Each time their priest, the man who had written Marie-Claire's letter, had written back falsely explaining that the man was too ill for the rigours of court life.

The brother had taken Marie-Claire under his wing, and she had thrived on his care and companionship, but the fact that he had pressed Marie-Claire to continue improving her English made him suspicious. What was behind her brother's insistence? William suspected that like his father, he saw Marie-Claire, once married off to an English aristocrat, as a future spy for France. Why else would he send her so precipitously with only female servants to a family she did not know? What defence would Marie-Claire have had against a brother she thought loved her? And might someone else come for her in the future once France settled down? The London papers were full of debates, riots and revolutionary behaviour in the Paris streets. There had been riots in England too, and it was clear that anyone who had something to lose was worrying about revolution crossing the narrow sea to their own shores. He wasn't at all keen on international politics crossing into his quiet patch of Wiltshire either.

Well, he had a decent rifle. Guns, however, were unreliable and took an age to load. As he gazed at the wall opposite where a pattern of swords and lances decorated it, he considered the crossbow of his youth. He had found it in the attics, worked out how to use it, and practised shooting bolts into the trees around the edge of the pond until his father, annoyed with the damage he was doing, took him out hunting deer with it. He could load it far faster than he could load his rifle, it was more accurate, and a bolt could pass through a silver birch tree of reasonable size, so would make short work of a man. He nodded to himself; anyone coming here with ill intent would have to get past him first. He was well prepared to protect his own.

A few nights later, William called for his horse and headed down to the local inn. He had drunk there often as a lad and then again after his father had died and left him to take over the estate years before he had expected to. Once married to Marjorie however, it had been a rare night he had ventured out. She had seemed to enjoy his company of the evening, though he had always felt she preferred him out of the house during the daylight hours, not least as she always made sure he had a bite of lunch in his saddlebag each morning when he left home.

As he rode down the darkening lanes, he remembered the night after he had lost Marjorie. He had stood late that afternoon gazing at her new grave; his neighbours having finally left him to his grief. He had laid her beside their three dead infants. He had stood until he had realised it was dark, thinking about the four souls in front of him and of God and his mysterious ways. Two different influenza attacks had taken two of the mites, and measles the third. Life had taken a turn for the better when Sam was born, and they had enjoyed watching him thrive and then begin to stumble around holding onto a finger or two. When the next measles outbreak hit the village, they had been silent with fear. Apart from a few spots, Sam had sailed through the disease and they had breathed deeply with relief.

Six months later a fever had laid Marjorie low and she had slipped away within days. William turned to look at the church, now fading away into the gathering darkness and decided if there was a god, he didn't much like him. A god who killed off little babies and loving wives wasn't a god he had much time for, he decided. The thought had been extraordinarily liberating. If there was an afterlife, well, he would cross that bridge when he had to. Until then he would get on with coping with life, as best he could by using his own resources. Clearly calling on the supernatural for help was a waste of time and he couldn't be bothered with it all. Nothing since had changed his mind.

That night, grieving, he had walked from the churchyard straight to the tavern. It had fallen silent as he walked towards the bar. The last time he had come in regularly he had still been 'Young Will', a lanky youth, and now he was Sir William. He had thrown his money purse on the counter and quietly asked for some ale. The landlord, a man he had known since boyhood, had gently pushed the purse back to him, gripped his shoulder, and gone to fetch him his drink. William found a seat well back from the fire. It was the only warmth some of the older ones would know that night and he left them to it, though his very bones felt made of ice.

At some point, he had slumped unconscious in his seat. He woke in his own bed, his boots set neatly at the side. Mrs Pells told him he had been brought home in a cart with his horse tied behind. He had frequented the tavern a lot after that until Sam had come home from Eton in such a poor state and he hadn't wanted to leave him at night.

Now, he had a question in his head, and if he didn't ask it, he thought he might explode. As before, his unaccustomed presence brought quiet to the place. He strode to the bar and Frederick, the keeper, gave him a keen look and asked quietly, 'Lady Causton?'

'All fine, thanks Fred, all fine. I've come to speak to the lads.'

He turned and addressed everyone in the room, 'You all know who I am, and I am landlord to most of you.' Actually, all, if his eyes didn't play him false. 'Now, I am no doubt a madman, but there are riots in London and some other places, and over in France, a lot more than riots. The people there are cutting the heads off people like me, landlords. What I want to know is, do you want to cut my head off? I'd rather you told me than snuck up on me one night.'

There was a general laugh at that one, and then they all went quiet again.

'Anyone got anything to say?' he pressed.

One man called out, 'I'd like to own my own land like you do, Sir William, but that ain't going to happen, so I reckon a decent landlord is the next best thing. I love my farm as if it were my own, and if tradition holds true, my son can inherit it if he wishes. To me, living here is as good as me owning the place myself. My father and his farmed the same bit of land I do, and if my roof blows off, 'tis you who will have the cost of replacing it!'

There was wide laughter at that, and it broke the ice. William sat down and listened, and was surprised at what he missed sometimes about what was going on around the estate.

One of his oldest tenants came to sit opposite him once everyone seemed to have had their say. William asked for paper and a quill to write down all the promises he was making. Seemed there were some blocked ditches he hadn't known about and a couple of roofs that needed seeing to. He had begun to think he needed to come down for an ale more often. The old man didn't bother to speak until William seemed to be let alone at last.

'This revolution,' he said.

William frowned, 'Yes?'

'It ain't goin' away, the man commented, sucking on the stem of his pipe.

William waited.

'Seems like we been at war with the Frenchies pretty much non-stop, and I reckon there is another one in the offing.'

William nodded, 'You could be right.' He saw nothing to disagree with.

The old man went on, 'We will have the recruiting sergeants round soon enough, and a lot of the young men will want to go.'

'I can't stop them.'

'No,' the old man sighed. 'An' I have two hulking grandsons who will be itching to go.' He pointed with his pipe stem across the room. 'My Rob there, he longs to work with horses, any chance you have something for him?'

'Yes.' If he didn't, he would find something. 'What about the other lad?'

The old man chortled, 'Oh, give it enough time and he should tie himself up right and proper. He has been lifting the skirts of a lass called Lottie, baker's daughter. Once she catches in the family way her da will have him pinned down and no arguments.'

William had to laugh, 'Well, I hope you are right. War isn't a place for a good Wiltshire lad, but farming isn't for all of them.'

'No,' the old man sighed.

They both sat quietly drawing on their pipes and supping their ale and musing on the daftness of youth.

Samuel was entranced by his baby brother. His father had been beyond distraction while Marie-Claire had been in labour. It had taken three days, but mother and baby had survived the experience. William marginally less so. Sam had gazed down at the small body curled in his arm, at the eyelashes lying fanned on the cheeks and the small pink damp mouth and fallen as deeply in love as had his father. He had remained fascinated as the small curled creature had grown plump and sturdy, then rolled over, then crawled. He was amused by the baby's noisy demands and helped in the night as much as the nurse did.

'He is so brave!' he observed, 'There he is so small and vulnerable and yet he bosses us all about!'

He was the one who held the small hands for hours so the baby could begin to walk, chatting to him all the time about what Miss Buckley was teaching him. William reckoned that the baby would be ready for university at the same time Samuel was.

They eventually named him Lucien. William had dithered and refused to come to a decision about a name. Marie-Claire had watched him and finally decided that it was fear. William thought that the baby couldn't die without a name, so if he didn't name him, he couldn't die. He had buried three little ones and the grief still ate at him, so she murmured 'Lucien' to the baby so he would know his name and by the time William agreed to consider a name, it was too late. If he minded, he didn't let on. They agreed to a christening because they didn't think any of the local girls would marry him if he remained so outside of the Church. Sam scratched the back of his neck and wondered at the intelligence of adults. Fancy worrying about marrying the lad off when he was still crawling all over the place.

When Lucien was a furiously active three and a sister, Chantel, a determined one-year-old, Sam rode off to university. Two other lads from the area were also going up at the same time and they all seemed to be looking forward to the experience. Sam carried a number of introductory letters from Miss Buckley that he wasn't sure he would ever use and at seventeen, was the youngest, but was unusually confident that he was ready.

University suited him, and he found his way home often, mostly so he could come and play with Lucien. He was utterly fascinated by the child's rapid development. He seemed far more confident in himself but was still painfully shy in company. For his part, Lucien adored his big brother and hung out the windows if he thought he might be arriving home. Sam finished his undergraduate career and came home finally to help his father on the estate. That Christmas he was twenty, Luc was five, his sister was three and there was a third on the way. Samuel couldn't be happier to finally be home, to be with his family, and be able to settle into his adult life at last.

He still stayed close to Marie-Claire at any social gathering. Over-tall and gangly, with too many wrists and ankles, he had a tendency to knock things over or break them. His shoulders seemed too wide for his body and he blushed furiously and stuttered when anywhere near a female who wasn't his mother, his sister, or one of the house servants who had known him all his life. He was still pale, even more so after so much book work, with rather lank almost-white hair. He considered himself deeply unattractive, especially as his skin still erupted into spots without warning and they showed up brutally clear on his pale complexion.

Marie-Claire allowed him to cling to her and smiled complacently when she regarded him. She watched as some of the local young ladies tried to capture his interest. They might not consider him good-looking, but he was heir to a decent-sized estate. What increased her amusement was that Sam was utterly oblivious to his financial charms and the wiles of the daughters or their mothers. It simply never crossed his mind that a girl might be making eyes at him, so he sailed along blind to all blandishments. Marie-Claire wasn't worried. She knew he would grow into his shoulders one day, the spots would vanish, and whoever caught her wonderful, kind and loving son would have a loyal husband. And she was perfectly happy for that not to be for a year or ten. She sometimes thought of Marjorie, his first mother, and hoped she could see how well he was turning out.

The years slipped by. Sam took on more and more of the estate duties, while William, with the war well underway, sought out lucrative grain and meat contracts with the army and now made regular trips to Bristol. Miss Buckley, now Lucien was older, having had what she considered a too-long rest, was back teaching. She frequently commented on how different Luc was from Samuel. Where Samuel had soaked up knowledge like a sponge, Luc would slip out of the window if she left the room and would not be found for hours. He reduced her name to Miss B and refused to call her anything else. She found she didn't mind. He had adopted her into the family with the renaming, especially when it caught on. However, he was such a handful he was summarily packed off the Eton, where like his father before him, he thrived. His sister, Chantel slid into his place with no one really noticing. She was reading at four and naming the planets and stars by six. Miss Buckley was happy and Chantel thrived, glad to be away from her younger brother, James, who was at the screaming and demanding stage.

PART THREE

Two lives collide.

'Marriage is the mathematics of joining two to make one that is stronger.'

Chapter 7

Once he returned from university, Sam pretty much ran the estate, with his father concentrating on the marketing side. Blocked wells and blown roofs were now his sole responsibility. He considered himself too busy to be lonely, and still avoided social occasions, mostly because he became bored at them. He still found Miss Buckley the most stimulating company he knew and enjoyed keeping up with her vigorous correspondence with academics from all over the country.

He would have been amazed at the wistfulness he brought to many a now-matronly breast. More than one of the girls who had attempted to catch his attention now watched from the safety of her parlour window as Sam, tall, confident, lithe, a significant contrast to their rather portly husbands, sped his long-legged way across their yards, coat tails flying and a broad smile across his weathered and handsome face. As Marie-Claire had predicted, he had grown into both his looks and his status. Now he avoided single women as he found them dull and lacking in conversation, not because he was uncertain of his looks. He no longer blushed in company but was secure in his position in the world. He had a quiet, confident manner, and was usually to be found with a half-smile on his face. He had become the kind of man who spoke rarely, but when he did, was listened to. Securing him for a dinner was considered a coup, and more than one lady wondered that if one day a hayrick were to fall on her husband, whether she might have a better chance a second time around. For his part, Sam enjoyed his neighbours, but in small doses.

It was a blustery windy day, and he was on his way home. The light was fading but the horse knew the lane as well as he did. Sam was tired, but not terribly so, however, a warm fire would be more than welcome once he arrived under cover. He didn't see her, but his horse, Greystoke, did and shied, doing a small skip to the right. Sam reined in, not sure what had startled the horse, and turned in the saddle. There was something in the hedge, a bundle of cloth he thought. He paused, uncertain. Then, deciding he would regret not taking a look, with a soft sigh slid from the saddle and secured the horse. They were so near to home if he didn't the dammed thing might head for its stable and supper.

He walked back a dozen steps and even after he bent forward, he wasn't sure what he was looking at as the shadows were so deep at the bottom of the hedge. To his shock, he realised it was a woman. At first, he assumed she was dead, she was so still and cold, but there was enough warmth in her cheek to suggest she might be alive. Then, as he rolled her, she groaned, but still appeared unconscious. There was a brown leather valise beside her, so he shoved it deeper into the hedge next to his horse. He tried to raise her and then realised she was heavily pregnant. He ran back to his horse and stood for a moment undecided. Without the belly, he would have slung her up over the horse and climbed up to hold her in place in a more comfortable position, but there was no way he could lift a woman in that condition, hold her, and then climb up himself. Could he get her up and then lead the horse? Finally, he decided that wasn't an option either. Securing Greystoke more firmly, he strode back to the woman and lifted her into his arms. She wasn't that heavy, but any load became heavier the longer it was carried. Sighting a light in the distance he headed out diagonally across some newly ploughed fields. He had about a mile and a quarter to cover.

He arrived at Miss Buckley's door in full dark and struggling, mostly because of the mud that had held onto him with every step. The woman had not come to, and he wasn't confident she hadn't died on him as he carried her onwards. His arms were in agony. Miss Buckley rose to the occasion, as he knew she would. She paused as she took in the scene, then turned and yelled for Molly,

'Take her straight upstairs. Put her in a bed.'

'She is pregnant.'

'All the more reason to tuck her up and get her warm.'

Sam regarded the stairs with distaste, then, taking a breath, carried the woman upwards clumping clods of mud everywhere. A fire had been lit recently in the hearth, but so recently it gave out little warmth.

'Make yourself useful,' instructed Miss Buckley to Sam, 'see if you can stir some heat out of that.'

She and Molly were busy stripping the damp outer clothes from the woman. Without the cape and jacket, her pregnancy was even more obvious. The woman seemed totally unconscious, but then her features contorted and she grunted. Her eyes opened, but she appeared to see nothing. Molly was picking the laces of the woman's boots undone and Miss Buckley had her hands on the woman's stomach. She said quietly, 'I believe she may be in labour.'

'Is there a midwife near?'

Molly and Miss Buckley both turned blank faces to him. 'Not a creature either of us has had need of,' Miss B said dryly.

'Mrs Plumton is the nearest mother,' Molly said, 'I could run and ask who she uses.'

At which point the woman hauled herself up on her elbows as if she would crunch in two and screamed.

'Not sure we have time for that,' Miss B muttered.

'I've delivered foals, lambs and puppies.' Sam was thoughtful.

'Well, you are about to add human babies to your list.'

The labour progressed fast.

'Not her first,' said Molly.

Within two hours Sam cupped a head in his hand and helped a small and greasy body out into the world. She was quite blue. Sam bent his head intending to blow softly into the small mouth, but his fingers, wrapped around the tiny mite, were telling him another story. Slowly he explored the fragile rib cage with his fingertips. All of one side was stove in, and the arm on that side was clearly broken. He gave a grunt of shock. The baby had been dead for a while, he suspected. He met Miss B's eyes and she left the woman to be bathed by Molly and came to see. She said nothing but met his shocked eyes with hers.

The woman had sunk back into unconsciousness and they left her sleeping with Molly to watch over her and took the tiny wrapped parcel downstairs. They placed the baby in a basket and set her in the cellar where it was cool. Neither of them had a better idea. They sat facing each other on either side of the sitting room fire. There didn't seem to be much to say until Miss B asked, 'How did you come to find her?'

'I nearly didn't. Greystoke, my horse, shied. Her skirts must have been caught by the wind and flapped and she stepped sideways. I went to see what had startled him and found her.'

'Where was that?'

'Pool Lane. I couldn't see how to get her up onto the horse, so carried her here as yours was the nearest house. I could see the light, if it hadn't been for that it would have taken me even longer. There is not much moon tonight and it is black as pitch at times.'

'Where is the horse?'

'Tied to a hedge.'

'Might he get stolen?'

Sam laughed, 'My biggest fear is that someone will find him and take him home and I will have to walk back across the field and then walk home too!'

'Take my cart.'

'No. I shall get off in a moment.' He paused, then said, 'That child is badly damaged. I wonder if we should keep quiet about your guest until we know more. A boot tip might explain the shape those ribs were shoved into, and why would a heavily pregnant woman be walking alone when dark is coming on in a deserted lane? There isn't a cottage in Pool Lane anywhere along it.'

It was Miss B's turn to go quiet. 'I agree. I'd like to know more before I give her location away. There might be someone who wears boots looking for her. I will have a word with Molly.'

Miss B had offered Sam a bed for the night, but he had wordlessly shaken his head, kissed her cheek and set off back across the sea of mud he had already traversed once that night. She hadn't made any comment upon his wordlessness; perhaps she hadn't noticed. He rather hoped not.

The mud was no less clinging, but this time he had no candle-lit window to guide him. The clouds that had scudded across the sky when he had carried the woman, chased by the wind that had whipped his greatcoat around his knees, had paused in front of the moon. It was a dark and bitter night, and he was exhausted. He couldn't remember ever feeling so tired before. He stumbled often, but did not curse; he hadn't the energy. With every step, his boots collected more mud and became ever heavier. Just as he had with the woman in his arms, he plodded on. He longed for one thing. To throw himself at his father and mother and demand comfort for the trials of the night.

It took him perhaps far longer than an hour to cross the field, he suspected. He clambered through the hedge to the lane some yards from his horse and tried to loosen the clods from his feet as he stomped towards his mount, thankfully still tied to the branch where he had left her. On reaching her he smoothed down her nose with his hand and nuzzled her cheek. To have his hands sliding along something warm and alive was infinitely comforting.

Greystoke trudged home, and all Sam could do was slump on her back. He rode slowly into the yard, but the noise of hooves on cobbles was impossible to dampen. As he slid off the horse's back a dog barked and then a sleepy stable lad appeared. Sam sighed as guilt hit him. It was the early hours of the morning and the lad would have been sound asleep.

'Is that you Daniel? Go back to your rest. I will see to her.'

Daniel ran into the light from the lantern Sam had lit to light the stable.

'No, Mr Sam. It is my job, and I'll do it. Sides, you look worn out.'

Sam shook his head. 'You have the right of it Dan, lad. I will let you overrule me. She is cold and hungry, I am afraid, but she has been good as gold for me.'

'Don't you worry none. She is a darling. I'll look after her, won't I lass.'

The last was directed at Greystoke and after watching Daniel stroke her nose with care and affection, Sam dragged himself into the house with a settled mind, at least as far as the care of his horse was concerned.

The kitchen door always scraped, but it was a soft noise, surely it wouldn't disturb anyone? A huge cauldron always stood at one side of the vast brick range keeping water tepid, so boiling water was not such a long-winded process as heating it straight from the pump. He dipped two large cans into the depths knowing that cook would see the level had dipped substantially and be cross. With one in each hand, he crossed in his stockinged feet to the stairs.

The air in his room struck cold, and there would be no coals to warm the sheets. None of it affected him. He stripped rapidly and filled his smaller jug with water from one of the cans. Pouring it over his head he soaped his hair and rinsed it. Then attacked his face and neck and began to methodically scrub every inch of his skin. Then he stood shivering violently as he scraped beneath his fingernails of one hand with a nail from the other, then repeated the process until he began to think his hands might be clean. Then, throwing the water out the window onto the garden below, he shoved the window closed again and once more scrubbed his hands and arms. Eventually, he pulled his nightshirt over his head, thick knitted socks on his feet, and for once, a warm cap for his head. Sliding between the icy sheets he lay and stared up at the canopy above his head.

His hands still felt besmirched. Closing his eyes could not shut out the vision of the woman, back arched backwards, knees bent, screaming with the pain of the birthing. Nor of the tiny mite he had held in his cupped hands, so small, so perfect, with bones so fine like a little bird's. And the broken right arm. And the damage to the right shoulder. And the lack of life or breath.

The little body was warm, but from her mother's warmth, not from her own heartbeat. She had begun to cool even as he held her, safe in his large warm hands. But no, not safe. She would never gurgle, as babies should, smile, or learn to run. Those little arms would never wind about a neck and inform someone special that she loved them; no mother, sister, father or brother would hear those precious childish whispers. He could still feel the softness of the shawl he had been passed to wrap her in. See the weave of the wicker basket that became her bed. Smell the potatoes and beet and hanging fowl when he had laid her in the cool dark of the cellar. Tomorrow he and B would need to discuss what they needed to do next. Call on a magistrate? But why was the child dead? And why was her heavily pregnant mother alone in a lane as dark drew on?

Sam identified himself as a farmer. He had helped deliver countless animals. As his father's heir he had never sat around waiting to inherit but had dug in to learn everything he could about the estate from its crops, to its woodlands, to its farms and their people. There was nothing he hadn't done from ditch digging to hauling foals from a mare struggling to deliver. And death was part of the whole circle. But nothing had ever felt like that tiny, greasy, blue little body as it had rested against his skin. Nothing had ever felt so precious or so fragile.

Never had grief hit him so unexpectedly. The bed refused to warm, so he lay and shivered and let the dark scratch at his eyes.

In the morning he found his way down to breakfast. As he lounged in his chair down the table a few seats away from his siblings and parents, their laughter and warmth felt like a thousand miles away.

'You were in late, lad,' his father commented.

His mother looked over at him with laughing eyes.

Sam nodded, 'Stayed late at B's.'

His father nodded back and turned to answer a question of Luc's. He slipped from the room as soon as he decently could. Food sat poorly on a gut full of secrets.

The weather had worsened and it suited his mood. Icy rain shot him in the face and the wind seemed determined to unseat him. Greystoke was skittish and kept tossing her head not enjoying the weather either. When he had ridden this way late the previous night, he admitted that his instinct was to throw himself on his father's shoulder; bury himself in his mother's embrace. Like a child! Like a limp weakling! This morning, watching his family tease and laugh over toast and eggs and bacon, he had known that he could do no such thing. An instinct he hadn't expected had risen up and, whatever the cost to himself, he knew he wanted to shield them from what he had gone through. It was his burden to bear. It was time he left home. He had been floating day by day ever since he had returned from university, but this had brought him up hard; it was time he became independent. He would think about it. Marriage was the obvious answer. Unfortunately, the woman he might marry was not so obvious. It was time he grew up.

He crept into B's house as quietly as he could. B was sitting in a wrap in her drawing room gazing morosely out of the glazed doors and out into the garden. Sam walked up to her in his stockinged feet and kissed her on her cheek. She reached up and caught at his hand.

'How are you?' he asked.

'Shocked. Sick.' Her voice was low.

Sam settled on the footstool at her feet. 'Do we know who she is or how she came to be here?'

'Yes and no. She whispered her name Louisa to Molly but apart from that she has slept.'

'Did you see the bruises?'

B breathed deep. 'On her body. Yes. She has been badly beaten. I find women in her condition, with child, somewhat revolting, but how someone could do that I have no idea.'

Sam couldn't help his smile. 'Revolting?'

B gave a theatrical shudder, 'Too fecund by half.'

Sam lifted her hand and held it against his cheek. 'It is a good thing I know you well.'

He left then and continued with his day. He was supposed to be helping with a roof, but in this weather, none of them would want to continue with the task. His thoughts became busy with alternative uses for his time, and the problem of the woman and her dead child was shelved for the time being. At least he told himself that. In fact, it never really left his mind. But until they could question her there was no point in calling in the magistrate.

He called in at B's on his way back home for his supper.

'She were running from 'er 'usband,' Molly grunted. ''Tis the second babe he has kicked out of 'er.'

Molly's Wiltshire accent was thicker than normal. It was the only indication of how much the events had affected her. Sam found that unbearably moving. Molly was an imperturbable rock. She wasn't supposed to have emotions to feel.

'Well,' Sam began, 'we are the only three that know what happened. What are we going to do? Are we going to call on the magistrate?'

The two women spoke in unison and the response was an emphatic, 'No.'

'I agree. Molly, can you find me a spade?' Sam asked.

'What are you going to do?' B asked as Molly left the room.

'Dig as deep a hole as I am able in the orchard. Every spring the apple blossom will be pink and white like her cheeks should have been.' His voice was flat, but he had no doubts now.

He stood waiting, his hands thrust into his pockets until Molly returned. As he took the spade he glanced at B and was surprised to see her eyes were a little too bright.

'Might have been nice to have a little one running around,' she murmured.

'So you could teach her how to use an astrolabe?'

'Ha! You do know me too well!'

The wind and rain had eased off a little, but the ground was full of tree roots. Sam bent his back to the task and strained his shoulders and arms to dig as deep as he could. His coat ended up hung on a tree along with his jacket as he chopped into the ground with all his strength. He used his knife at times to hack through roots the spade couldn't break and knew the blade would never be the same, but still, he kept digging. The moon sailed free of a cloud cluster and the light brightened as the hour passed. And all the while he grieved for the little girl and wondered what kind of man could harm a baby even before she was born, let alone his woman. His disgust and anger fuelled his efforts.

He wouldn't let the women come to the little grave side. He wanted the crime to be as much his alone as possible. He laid the wicker basket gently into the earth, but throwing the first clods of earth on top seemed as huge a sin as a man could commit.

Delivering a human baby had taken more out of him than he realised! He had tensed with every one of the woman's contractions and had been more worried than he had let on that he might do something wrong and either hurt the baby or the woman. If it went wrong with a horse, you shot it. He was quite sure that option hadn't been open to him in this case. He had been more than a little anxious that the woman might have died in the night. How would he have explained that to a magistrate?

As it was, she was still sleeping. He crept up and took a look at her, for no reason other than curiosity. Molly was dozing beside the fire and looked up as he went in, as silently as possible. She just nodded a greeting and closed her eyes again. He stood and looked at the woman for a while, before creeping downstairs again. She looked white-faced and thin. Miss B met him with a pot of tea.

When they had drunk it, they stood together outside the front door. Sam shoved his hands in his pockets and tipped back to stare at the sky, which was as grey as ever. 'What to do, B?'

'I suggest nothing. Molly is good with her, and she is malnourished and clearly almost insane with grief. She needs peace and time to heal.'

'But we should be informing both the magistrate and the vicar.' He was saying it out loud to see how it felt.

Miss B made a snorting sound. 'Well, neither of us cares for that limp vicar. I am not a believer in sacred ground; that child is as well tucked up in the orchard as in a churchyard. No god worth his salt would mind. And as for Blackwell, after he has hung that child accused of stealing bread without even asking the child's name, I suspect he would hang Louisa for murdering her baby, and totally ignore the fact that she had been kicked to pieces by some ignorant man.'

'I know you are right, but if we are found out, we might hang as dead as that child.'

'I am too old to care. They can hang me all they like. And you have enough consequence not to be hung at all. Besides, I would deny you had any knowledge of anything.'

'What about Molly?'

'Molly's great talent is love. Louisa needs exactly that. I am too independent for our Molly, but Louisa needs all the care she can pour into her. Molly has taken the poor girl under her wing, and will probably take anyone apart with her bare hands if they threaten her. She will not give us away.'

'I have never understood how you put up with Molly. Ma and Pa always called her gormless!'

'Indeed, both I and Molly know that. She isn't academically clever like you, but she can sum up a person with withering accuracy, and her work is immaculate. She is clever in a different way. I like having her around. We deal well together. She finds me acceptable; I keep regular hours, never tell her what to do and am either at my books or out walking leaving her in peace. Your mother drove her mad as she was constantly on the go.'

Sam laughed, 'Oh, yes! One of Pa's names for her is 'Wren', as he says she flits about non-stop just like a wren in a hedge.'

'Suits her,' Miss B commented dryly.

'She had a valise. I left it in a hedge. I will head that way now and bring it back. It might tell us who she is,' and with that Sam took his leave.

It didn't. Inside Molly said she had found a few female undergarments, a solitary lightweight dress, a hairbrush and a few hairpins. Nothing else. Except for a few baby clothes.

As he finally left, he turned and called back quietly, 'B? If she doesn't remember, don't tell her I delivered the baby. Let her believe you and Molly did it if you can.'

Miss B nodded and then went back indoors. Sam got on with his day, but it was a long time before he got the sound of that howl of pain out of his ears. He was worried too, about what might happen to them all if the local magistrate, Blackwell, discovered what they had done. He was only the local magistrate because William refused the job. And Blackwell seemed to hate the whole world. He had recently hung a nine-year-old runaway boy who had stolen some bread because he was hungry. No one liked thieves, but the rapidity with which Blackwell had strung the rope shocked the whole area. He hadn't bothered to find out the boy's name, where he came from, or why he was roaming one of the local villages. Both mothers and fathers of boys much the same age were unsettled and upset. The idea that one of their own could, after a family row, not an unusual occurrence with boys at that sometimes-awkward age, might head off and before anything could be mended, be swinging from a rope didn't sit well with them. Possibly also because crime of any kind was rare in the area. William had received a delegation of local men asking him to investigate, and hopefully, tone Blackwell down and William had asked Sam's advice. In the end, they did nothing, and now it bothered Sam whether they had made the correct decision. On the other hand, the less Blackwell thought about or resented Sam, the better.

As it was, he was so busy for a few days that he didn't exactly forget about the stray woman, he simply had too much else on his mind. His father was once again in Bristol arranging grain contracts and so all of the problems on the estate fell onto his shoulders. They were still as close as father and son could be but lived very separate lives. William was particularly busy because he had three younger children now, none of whom seemed to be taking an easy route in life. Lucien was headstrong and listened to no one. The only reason William thought he wouldn't end up at the end of a rope was that he would run too fast. Chantel was not nearly as headstrong but had her mother's direct manner, which tended to disconcert adults who found her disturbingly perceptive, and James was a bull of a child who appeared to have come out of the womb determined to kill someone. He was obsessed with swords and every other weapon and as soon as he could talk told anyone who would listen that he was going to be a soldier. Samuel was of the opinion that where he had gone to Eton and been horribly bullied, it was James nowadays who might be the bully. He secretly cheered the boy on and felt somewhat guilty about thinking that way.

It was quite a few days before he once again knocked on Miss B's door. He greeted her with a kiss on the cheek. 'Are we still agreed we aren't going to the vicar or the magistrate?'

'Don't ask daft questions,' was B's sharp retort. 'What good would either of them do?'

'Ah,' Sam thought, so we are to continue as partners in crime.

Miss B grunted as if she could read his thoughts, as she probably could. 'I will go and get her. I will tell her you won't eat her and she needs to thank you. She would be dead but for your intervention.'

Clicking her teeth in impatience, she went up the stairs as Sam found his way into the parlour and settled into his usual chair.

His first thought on getting a proper look at the woman was how gaunt she was with the pallor of a cell inmate. She stood with her back to the door as if she lacked the strength to stand. B snapped at her, 'Thank the man, girl! Without him, you would be a corpse.'

The woman gave Sam a small nod and turned and left the room. On the other side of the door, they could hear Molly scolding her for being up and about. B made a sound remarkably like a snort.

'Give her time, B.'

'Well, how long is she going to stay?'

'Be a nice B,' Sam advised with a chuckle. He wasn't sure he knew the curse word she threw after him as he left. Something in Latin he suspected. Or Greek?

Eventually, Louisa gained sufficient strength to rise and spend her days sitting in the parlour. Mostly she sat silently regarding the garden through the tall glass doors, gazing towards the apple orchard. One day, she asked if she might see Sam. On the odd occasion he had called since their first brief meeting, she had never been up and around.

Sam entered B's parlour rather dreading the meeting. The woman was wearing a loose green dress the colour of oak leaves and staring out into the garden. She turned as she heard him enter. B and Molly had made themselves scarce. She was still pale, but her hair was groomed and her clothes tidy. She wasn't a particularly attractive woman, he thought.

'Ma'am, how do you do?' he began.

'Poorly,' she commented, rather brusquely.

Sam couldn't help his half smile. 'Indeed,' he said. 'Well, not one to beat about the bush then!'

'I am grateful to you for finding me, Mr Causton.' Her voice remained brisk. It didn't sound like thanks, more like an aggressive attack.

'Indeed,' he repeated.

'I'd like you to show me where you buried my daughter.'

Sam took a moment to look at her carefully. But she seemed to mean what she said. 'Of course,' he said quietly.

He opened the glazed doors and they made their way down the flagged path to the orchard. When they reached the spot Sam simply drew her attention to the disturbed and heaped soil.

'Only the four of us know she is there,' he told her, 'I thought she might like to lie under the apple trees. There will be sweet blossom in the spring and fragrant apples in the autumn.'

She gave him a sharp look, and Sam returned her gaze evenly. He had a little sister. And younger brother. He knew small children. He had done what had seemed right to him, and she had not been in any state to express a view. For the first time, she showed some emotion. Her eyes were too bright and she had to swallow twice before she offered huskily,

'Thank you.'

They walked back into the house in silence. As he was fastening the doors she said softly, so softly he wasn't sure he was supposed to hear, 'My mother and father are buried in a beautiful place too, high in the mountains between Portugal and Spain in the Peninsula.'

Sam took the conversational opening and ran with it. 'Do you have any relatives you can go and stay with?'

She turned and gave him a hard look. 'No. My only relative by law is my husband.'

Sam had no answer to that. He wondered what she intended to do with her future. Return to the man? Or find work? He had no idea what work she might be able to find, but it seemed a bleak future. He had never met anyone who seemed so alone.

He rode away thoughtfully. He supposed he had expected weeping and grief, not that iron-hard self-control. And when she had mentioned her husband, the bitterness had rolled off her in waves. He could feel it even across the width of the room. Would she go back to him? He wasn't sure he didn't feel sorry for the man! And what a woman! She had stood rigid, hands fisted at her side, chin high. Like some kind of war goddess and very different from the corpse-like woman, he had first glimpsed. She was tall, and he guessed, no man's fool. He gave an involuntary bark of laughter. He wasn't sure Greystoke hadn't bucked him and he was about to hit the moon with his arse! He wasn't sure he liked her, but she was the first woman to stir his blood for as long as he could remember. He determined to put her firmly out of his mind.

Chapter 8

So that was Samuel Causton. Louisa stood by the glazed doors into the garden and frowned out at the light rain that had come on. The lawn near-to was ragged and gleaming with the moisture, causing the apple trees towards the bottom of the garden to appear brown and dreary by contrast. She had summed Samuel up in moments. She knew she had lived an unusual life. Men and women rarely spent time together. Amongst the lower orders, men worked outside and spent their evenings in the tavern and women worked inside. Even paid work for women was usually from the hearth; spinning, weaving, lace making, keeping hens and the like. And amongst the higher orders, men escorted women places, then left them to amuse themselves with other women. They certainly didn't sit at their own hearth sides of an evening, being more likely to hie off to drink and carouse with other male friends.

But Louisa knew men. From birth she had mixed with men, running through their legs as a child and as a young woman watching her father interact with them. She had watched them in all their shades wait for battle, some looking sick, some desperate to begin, some wild with eagerness to prove themselves, all of them afraid. She knew exactly how variable the grim reaper could be, some taking an agonisingly long time to breathe their last as she had trickled water into their dry throats and held their hands and others going as quickly as her mother had, simply lying down and being gone, with no warning. She had stood in the shadows behind her father time and time again as he had ordered, chastised and praised. Oh yes, she knew men.

And now she felt she knew Samuel Causton. He was not physically attractive to her. He was too tall and too pale, despite the wind scorch on his cheeks and nose. His height appeared the more extreme as he was so thin. He reminded her of a stork or heron, long and thin and light against the dark afternoon. His hands were nice, though, beautifully shaped with long elegant fingers and hard calloused palms. The hands and face declared a love of the outdoors and of making things work by his own efforts. But what she had especially noticed, was that he was a blithe man. His pale blue eyes sparkled with merriment and intelligence, while his mouth enjoyed two emphatic small crescent creases, one on each side that, along with the lines radiating from his eyes, proclaimed here was a man well used to smiling and even laughing. A merry man. A man of humour. And probably as deep as a dish of tea.

Sam had intended to stay away from Miss B's house for a good length of time. He couldn't see that he could help the woman, Louisa, and not telling his father about what had occurred weighed heavily on his mind. It seemed best to keep some distance at the moment. He was about as far on the estate as he could be from home and Miss B's when the gossip reached him. He had been wondering whether to ask for a bed for the night as it was far later than he intended and the cold had bitten hard into to ground over the last night or two. Winter was swishing her skirts. It had always amazed him that the post was so slow, and gossip so fast. Gossip seemed to cover miles a minute! He was disturbed to hear that Miss B had driven her cart into the village, as usual, but on stepping down had collapsed and landed face first on the ground. Everyone who saw her rushed to her aid and, as she appeared to be out of her wits, someone had tied his horse to the back of the cart and having settled her back in, had driven the cart back to her house and handed her over to Molly.

'Poor woman,' said the wife who was over-excited to be the bearer of news, 'that maid hasn't got the sense of a flea.'

Sam listened without comment, it was an opinion widely held in his family. However, he had seen Molly's instinctive care for Louisa and had been impressed with how she had been entrusted with Louisa's secrets. He no longer thought of Molly as 'gormless', and had begun to wonder if it wasn't a bit of an act so that Molly was left in peace.

He left immediately, no doubt to Greystoke's disgust as she had been happily munching hay in a warm stable. It was wretchedly cold, and for the first time, Sam seriously wondered if he should consider employing a manager to help him. His father wasn't getting any younger and was nowadays away much more with arranging contracts for the sale of their produce. By the time he arrived at Miss B's his face was rigid with cold and he had lost all feeling in his hands and feet. It was Molly who answered his rapid blows upon the door, which didn't calm his worry as Miss B liked to answer it herself if she was around.

'Is the news right,' he demanded. 'Has B had an accident?'

Molly let him in, tutting as mud from his boots and coat fell on her spotless flags. 'Come and see for yourself,' she told him, ushering him into the warm parlour.

B was sitting with a leg raised, and one arm in a sling. When she turned, he could see one side of her face was badly grazed. His hands, face and feet were screaming as the warmth began to restore circulation but he ignored it and in two strides was crouched by her side.

'What happened,' he asked softly, taking her good hand.

B sighed and shook her head, 'I was too efficient.'

'Efficient?' It wasn't a word Sam expected to hear.

'I planned to fall from my cart, but my foot caught in my skirt and I went truly flying. I hadn't intended to do quite so much damage.'

'You planned to hurt yourself?'

'Mm.'

He stared at her. 'Am I allowed to ask why?'

'Because I am widely seen as a stubborn old bat who refuses help of all kind. The fact that Molly takes care of me alone is often commented on, and the fact that I do all the vegetable growing, and some of the cooking and cleaning, are seen as indications of my ridiculous independence. If I am to suddenly require a companion, eyebrows would be raised.'

Sam was stumped. 'A companion?'

'Louisa of course. I need to explain why I am suddenly in need of another lady to live with me. Louisa will take the name of Buckley, and I will put out that she is a young cousin of mine, recently widowed and so has come to assist me in my declining years.'

'Declining years, my foot!' declared Sam, standing to take in Louisa sitting quietly across the room. Then he turned on B, 'How could you do anything so foolish? I have been worried out of my mind wondering what could have happened.' He reached over and stroked her cheek, 'Don't you know there are only three women in my life and you are one of them.'

Sam was persuaded to stay for dinner. It was a cordial affair and Sam found himself glancing repeatedly at Louisa. She was looking a little better, though that wasn't saying much. She had decent enough manners however, and she could certainly pass as a cousin of B's. B meanwhile spotted his glances and simply kept her smile to herself.

Much later, as the three women sat by the fire, listening to Sam's horse as it clattered out of the yard, Louisa asked, 'Who are the other two women?'

B didn't pretend to misunderstand her, 'His mother and sister.' Molly, B was pleased to note, kept her head down over her darning.

Sam became a regular guest at B's dinner table. He argued that B had given him such a fright he needed to keep a closer eye on her. Certainly, B ruefully admitted it had taken her longer to recover from her fall than she intended. Louisa became a five-day wonder in the area as far as gossip was concerned. Once everyone who wanted to had gained a look at her, and once everyone interested had discussed her deportment, her clothes, her likely story, she became invisible, just another face that appeared in the village on occasion. Sam listened to the various stories going around about her: she was still desperately in love with her dead husband; her parents had cut her off without a penny; she had once been on the stage; he had to raise his eyebrows at that one. It seemed local imagination was perfectly capable of making up a decent story if a real one was unavailable.

He called round one morning some months after Louisa's arrival. He had rarely spoken to her in particular, only over the dinner table or over a game of cards that also included B and Molly, but this morning, unknown to him, both B and Molly were away from home. Louisa let him in, her hair looked tousled and her cheeks ruddy. It was almost summer and the glazed doors from the parlour were open to let the sunshine and sunlit air in. She had clearly been working in the garden and was breathless from rushing to answer the door. She looked windblown and more like his war goddess than ever. Sam found his breath leave his body but schooled his reaction. The last thing this woman needed was a man interested in her.

Louisa found a jug of cold water and some glasses, so they sat inside the parlour in the shade with the glass doors open in front of them. Louisa suddenly blushed a warm rose and said crisply, 'Mr Causton, you are staring at me.'

Sam grinned, 'Yes, I was. I am sorry if I made you uncomfortable.

It is that it has suddenly occurred to me how very well you look.'

Louisa flashed him a glance and said thank you in a low voice.

They sat in silence for a while then Sam said, 'I'd like us to be friends if that is possible. And friends know about each other. I thought if I told you about myself…' he let the comment hang.

'Then I might tell you about myself,' Louisa said quietly.

'Exactly. I am mortally curious.' He shot her a wide and wicked grin.

She gave a small smile in return, 'Mortally?' she queried.

'Absolutely!'

She ducked her head with a small smile, 'In that case,' she said, 'off you go. I should hate to have your mortal remains on my hands.'

His grin widened. 'I assume B has told you something about my family?'

'Not really, your B is very discreet.'

'Well, there is Pa, Sir William, Ma, my second mother.' He paused deliberately.

'Your second mother,' Louisa echoed.

'Indeed. But I chose this one.' His broad grin drew a small smile from Louisa. 'Do I go on?'

'Indeed,' she offered.

'I don't really remember my first mother. I have vague recollections of the smell of fresh bread and a warm lap, but that could have been Mrs Pells the cook for all I know.' Sam gazed out to the garden, hazy in the sunshine and fairly mad with bees. 'Pa and I were in Plymouth; I have never got around to asking why. We were staying in a tavern for a few days, and there was a ferocious storm. We heard about the havoc at the harbour at breakfast, so walked down to see what was going on. The storm had swept a number of ships off-course and they had had to make it to whatever harbour they could. One ship had been intending to land at Harwich on the East coast but had been swept so far off-course it had ended up in the south, at Plymouth. It wasn't alone, and the scene was one of chaos.'

He turned to smile at Louisa with the memory so bright in his mind. 'A woman was standing with her luggage, and she looked so proper, with her back so straight, all the stevedores were walking around her carefully, whereas I think anyone else would have been swept out of the way with all the work that was going on. She was speaking French to the captain, and he was clearly frustrated with not understanding her. The vicar had been tutoring me and I had picked up a little, so being a nosy child, I insisted on helping.'

'All children are curious,' Louisa said softly.

'Anyway, we walked her back to our tavern and procured her a room. All of her servants had deserted her. We spent two days together, and I already adored her. I had decided that I wanted her for my mother.'

'How old were you?' This time Louisa sounded genuinely interested.

Sam shrugged, 'About eleven. On the second night, I let them put me to bed then crept out and hid in the shadows. I think I had intended to ask Pa if he liked her. Then I saw them talk in the darkness, and go into her room, so I decided he must like her and went back to bed feeling hopeful.' He started to laugh. 'Oh, my goodness!' he exclaimed, 'I have never before spoken about that night. I have always seen it through the eyes of an eleven-year-old. Now I can see he never had a chance!'

'What do you mean?'

'When I saw her reach up to him, I thought she wanted to whisper in his ear so as not to wake me. Now I can see that she kissed him. Poor Pa. He would never have laid a finger on her, let alone kiss her if she hadn't started it. I can see that now. She was a vulnerable woman, he wouldn't have dreamt of making any kind of assumptions, but when she kissed him, he was lost. Clever Ma! She had him wrapped around her finger from day one.' Sam shook his head.

'Are they happy together?'

'Oh yes. Pa adores the very ground she walks on, and Ma's eyes still light up when he walks into the room. She has been the best mother I could have chosen,' and he laughed softly.

'My parents were in love.'

Sam turned to look at her. 'What happened to them?'

'Father was an army major, and my mother and I followed the drum. We lodged wherever he was. I was an only child, and we were close. I adored them both. Then mother became ill and died suddenly. Father was desolate. Soon after he went out one night and was found dead the following morning. He had fallen into a stream. I was seventeen.'

'Good heavens, what happened to you?'

'He had left a will making another major my guardian, but he too had died since my father made the arrangement and the papers hadn't been updated. The colonel decided I should become a ward of the regiment, and so I was married off to any man who wished to claim me.'

'Was he the one…?' Sam didn't know how to ask the question.

'Oh yes. His name is Lieutenant Colonel Lord Rupert Douglas McCloud. To this day I don't know why he did it. The first time I became pregnant I was so happy. I longed for someone to love, who would love me. He came home drunk and out of sorts and kicked me around the room, literally. I went into labour and about three days later gave birth to a boy. He was dead, of course. The midwife took him away and I never saw him. I swore that I had slipped and fallen down stairs, and everyone went along with the story for a quiet life. Army regiments really do close ranks to protect their own, and if I had said a word I would have been totally shut out, and I knew it. The attitude was that if a woman deserved a slap, she should take it.'

'Hell Louisa, that was more than a slap.' Sam felt sick with outrage.

'When I became pregnant a second time, I hid the fact. He didn't often look at me so it wasn't hard. I had begun to squirrel small sums of coin away, though I had no plan. Now, I am so grateful my second child is buried in such a beautiful place as B's orchard. I have no idea what happened to my son, and I never shall.'

After a silent while, Sam said, 'What is his name again?' Louisa told him. 'Almost long enough to hang him by,' Sam muttered.

Louisa, to her surprise, gave a cough of a laugh. Anyone in the area with a name like that would cause gossip, and he knew from plenty of experience how fast gossip moved. If the man came sniffing around here, he would know soon enough. They sat quietly again and watched a cloud of comma butterflies drifting over the heads of the flowers; their cut-out wings fascinating them both.

Eventually, he said, 'You are an impressive woman, Louisa.'

She swung to look at his face, her own expressing amazement. 'I'm in no way impressive! Why ever would you say that? I am just a frightened woman, how on earth can that be impressive?'

Sam held her eyes, 'If you were lying in bed with smelling salts beside you, I would not blame you. And you say you are afraid, but all I see is courage. I admire you.'

Louisa found she was blushing. His approbation mattered and she wasn't sure why but, suddenly feeling self-conscious, she dropped her gaze.

'I am an army brat,' she said. 'I followed the drum alongside my mother. I have carried water to soldiers whose mouths were parched with gunpowder mid-battle, crawling by dead bodies to find the live. I have bandaged and aided men where possible after every battle. I have walked for days to reach the next battlefield, struggling through the mud the army waggons have churned up. Women with the army do not only sit and wait. Either we cope, or we have to leave. It is a simple code. Besides, I have examined the field you carried me across, Molly knew the place where you found me. That was impressive, in my eyes. It must be well over a mile. To carry anyone that long is a huge effort, I know, let alone a woman heavy with child. So, I think we are square.' She turned to look at him again and realised for the first time how even when his face was still, his eyes laughed. Suddenly, she liked that. He wasn't a man full of demons, he was too busy being amused by his fellow man. 'Tell me more about your family,' she pressed.

'There are four of us,' he began. 'Lucien is the first of my siblings. I was totally besotted by him when he was tiny, but am less enamoured now he is a schoolboy. He put a mountain of frogspawn in my bed last week. He has tight black curls and vivid dark eyes and is never still. If there is mischief, then he will find it. I worried when he went to Eton as I had hated it, but he thrives there. I missed him, and the house felt horribly empty and quiet without him. Now when he comes home, I count the days until he goes back. Then comes Chantel, called by all Tilly or Tills. She has had some tuition from Miss Buckley but Ma has found a school for her for later. She is too bright and independent to simply sit at home, and she is lonely too. She needs some girls for friends that are as clever as she is. There is a school in Bath and she will board there eventually.'

'Does your father allow her to study as much as you did? I cannot imagine Miss B teaching deportment, needlework or water colour painting.'

That did make him laugh. 'Precisely. According to Miss B, she fares well to be a better mathematician than all of her brothers. Don't try arguing with her, she gets like a dog with a bone and will wriggle her arguments into all kinds of shapes to prove she is right and you are wrong. She has the same colouring as Luc, but her hair seems more out of control and is the bane of her life. Generally, she seems to pile it up onto her head and shove a stick through it to hold it in place. Ma is always buying her hair ornaments, but she loses them before she is down the stairs.

'The youngest is James, and he takes after father, with brown straightish hair and blue eyes. He is fierce. Already he has decided to be a soldier, and none of us knows where he gets that conviction from. He was recently given a set of toy soldiers and you are likely to find them to step on all over the house. His favourite possession, however, is his wooden sword, and I am constantly being challenged to duels.' He grinned widely.

At that point, Miss B came in along with Molly. 'Ah, Samuel, are you staying for tea? I am desperately thirsty,' was her greeting.

Sam rose and kissed her cheek, 'No B dear, I am off now Louisa has company again.'

'Come to dinner tomorrow,' B invited.

'Thank you, I will.' With that, Sam turned on his heel and was gone.

Later, after the tea, B asked in her blunt fashion, 'What did you and young Sam find to talk about?'

Louisa smiled, 'He told me about his family. They sound wonderful, and very close.'

'Yes, they are that. I only intended to come for a while, I thought I might stay a few years, see young Sam off to Oxford, and then find another project. It was his mother who sought me out. She is a woman after my own heart. Doesn't mince her words. Says exactly what she means. However, the years have slipped by and I am happy here, so I have stayed. I am honoured to be considered family by them. It would be hard to leave now.'

Louisa went back out into the garden then. She found some overgrown bushes that needed a trim and went slowly and methodically about the work. Something had awoken in her, and she wasn't sure what. But she welcomed it. She would be blowed if she would let that brute Rupert destroy her. She had found a haven, and despite what Miss B said, she was becoming frail. She had a role here. Miss B might not admit it, but she did indeed need a companion. She would do everything she could to deserve and earn her place in this house.

Sam spent the day with half of his mind on his work, and half on the way the light shining behind Louisa had highlighted the soft wildness of her windblown hair. And the curve of her cheek. And the way she blushed. And much more. He had always thought she was pleasant, but having spent some time alone with her, he had been intrigued. At last, he had begun to gain a glimpse of the real woman, not the façade she hid behind so skilfully. She fascinated him, and she was in his mind far more than made sense.

The weeks slipped by and a warm spring began to mature into a hot summer. Crops were ripening faster than expected and Sam was working from dawn to dusk to ensure every farm that needed labour was, as far as possible, getting it and at the right time. His father had suggested they start a tannery and siting and planning it was proving harder than expected. Miss B and Louisa occasionally dined at the Hall with Molly happily ensconced in the kitchen, and once or twice William and Marie-Claire came to the Dower House. Miss B had also accepted one or two other invitations, and Louisa found she was beginning to settle into the area and feel accepted. Her quiet and reserved manner was looked upon with favour by the women and respected by their menfolk. When she ventured into the village or encountered anyone while walking, she was greeted cordially and ignored in the way that everyone else was. She slowly stopped jumping at shadows and began to feel that Rupert wasn't hunting for her. After all, if he was, surely, he would have found her by now?

On another day when Sam caught Louisa alone, something he always hoped for without admitting the hope to himself, Louisa was in a pensive mood.

'You are troubled?' he challenged.

'I have been thinking about my husband.'

Sam felt as though a wind had dashed iced water at him. 'Are you going back to him?'

Louisa turned and gave him a warm smile that dried him out instantly. 'No. Though I never intended to leave him forever. Not at the time. I only wanted my baby safe. Rupert never meant to harm me, you see?'

Sam didn't. He wasn't sure he believed in evil, but surely what that man had done was as close to it as humanly possible. He tucked his tongue behind his teeth and kept mumchance.

Louisa took a breath, 'Rupert was the third son and had no choice but to join the army. He was commissioned to the regiment when he was fifteen. Rupert wasn't a deep thinker. He was more than a little bovine.' She flashed a quick smile to Sam. 'But he did have emotions. I once asked one of his sergeants what his men thought of him. He answered, "It is like this ma'am. His lordship don't like losing men, and the men don't like being lost. So, they likes him well enough." And then I understood. The night he kicked my first baby out of me, he had lost forty-two men in a skirmish. He was very drunk, and he was a man who could drink any other man under the table. Rupert hated the army. But he had no choice. He would have loved your life. Being out of doors, working with his hands, being on the back of his horse. He was as trapped as I was. I began to realise that he had married me because the whisky he drank every night was no longer bringing him the sleep he so desperately craved. He wanted a woman because he knew that afterwards,' she paused, then continued, 'well, afterwards, he always fell asleep.'

She could feel the heat in her face, like a fire banked with logs late at night, but would not look away. The attraction between them sang in the air. When Sam grazed an accidental touch her whole body reacted and vibrated. She fell asleep every night hoping he would call the next day or evening. If he had a disgust of her, better to face it now. She looked him directly in his eyes, and realised with a shock that they were not blue as she had thought, but pale green, like opals. Sam gazed back just as directly. He did not look disgusted. She swallowed and continued.

'Purely by chance Rupert was called home to Scotland. We had to cross the Peninsula to reach Oporto. There was always the risk of local bandits. Rupert's valet did not anticipate that the journey would take so long and we ran out of whisky. I suspect it was the first time Rupert had been partially sober in years. In Oporto he was a different man and, for the first time, I began to believe our marriage had the chance of some mutual contentment. But then he was violently sea sick for the whole of the crossing. As soon as we reached port he downed as much whisky as he could lay his hands on. I had already decided to run away until my baby was safely in my arms, but he caught me coming up to the deck and kicked out at me to emphasise I should stay below. And then you found me.'

'So, you really didn't mean to leave him permanently?'

'No. He is my husband. In law and in truth. So, no.'

Neither of them spoke for long moments as they each absorbed what had been said. It was Louisa who broke the silence.

'But now I am free of him, I cannot go back. While I was living that life, I could cope. Now I am free of it, I cannot face it.' She watched his face keenly. How would he judge her?

All he said was a quiet, 'Good,' and then what felt like their stolen time together was broken with the opening of the front door and B chastising Molly for some misdemeanour the other was volubly disputing. 'Time to go,' Sam offered quietly, and rose. Louisa watched him leave and wondered what he was really thinking. Thinking about her, was what she meant.

Without noticing it the days when Sam did not appear began to feel empty and lonely for Louisa, and the days or evenings when he did felt brighter. Her heart seemed to beat faster when he was around and he seemed to enjoy her company, she hoped. The quiet evenings in the Dower house sped by when they talked together late into the evening as Miss B snored softly and Molly sewed slowly and with what appeared to be total absorption. On the evenings he visited, Louisa had begun to be the one to escort him to the door. She would wait then until Greystoke's hooves clattered out of the yard and she knew he had really gone.

One night they both ventured beyond the main outer door and stood gazing at the swathe of stars that washed across the night sky. A patchy breeze cooled the warmth of the summer night, while the almost full moon cast its silver shadows out over the flagstones on the path. Sam was leaning back on his heels, hands thrust in his pockets, head tilted back to the heavens. In a purely conversational tone he asked,

'Have you a complete distaste of men? What would you think if a man was interested in you?'

Louisa's heart caught in her chest and she felt as if her insides were being squeezed. 'Interested?'

Sam turned to gaze at her and said softly, 'Yes, interested.'

Louisa swallowed and taking all of her courage in her hands replied as softly, 'It would depend upon who it was, but if it was you, I would be pleased.' Her throat was so dry and her voice didn't sound quite her own, but what on earth did she have to lose?

He gave her a smile so brilliant she could see it in the dark, and strode off towards the stable not even offering her a 'goodnight'.

For a moment Louisa stood in shock. Then a roar of anger swept through her as Greystoke clattered away in the distance. How dare he? Furious and raging she stormed inside and shot up the stairs as if rapid movement might help. She didn't sleep for a long, long time.

The following night Sam knocked as he so often did. As Molly showed him into the parlour Louisa bade him a civil 'good evening', and concentrated on her sewing, refusing to look up. Her anger had seethed all day and she was boiling to spill it all out, but absolutely not in front of Miss B and Molly. Sam sat for a quarter of an hour and asked with concern about Miss B's health. She batted back his concern stating that she was as hale and hearty as ever. After a couple of comments to Molly, Sam stood and asked if Louisa would mind showing him out. Louisa almost threw down her sewing. Oh yes, this was definitely something she wanted to do. For good if possible!

As they stood on the flags outside the door Louisa spun on him. 'What did you mean by last night? You left me feeling insulted and as if you had peeled a layer of skin off me! How dare you ask a woman such a question and when she reveals herself simply walk away! You didn't even say goodnight!' She was so angry her voice was uneven and she was close to furious tears.

Sam reached out, pulled her close, and dropped his head to hers. 'Oh sweetheart, I am sorry,' and then his mouth found hers, so softly and gently it was almost not there. He gradually deepened the kiss until the longing rose raw between them. He eased away a little and his warm breath cooled her wet mouth, 'Did you think I could do this and walk away? It was late. It was late as I had been gathering my courage all evening in order to ask you.' His long, lean body had tucked her against his. 'Now, it is early, and there are two blankets in the hay loft. Shall we go and see how comfortable they are?'

'I hate you!' she said.

'No doubt I deserve it, but what about the hayloft?'

And she found herself giving an uneven laugh. Taking her hand in his he tugged her gently across the cobbles towards the stable. His hand was warm and hard, with callouses from hours of riding and working that rubbed into her softer skin. It felt wonderful.

In the hayloft Sam threw a blanket down with another at the side. It was still light, with the yard outside half lit with late summer light like another world. Sam's boots came off first, as Louisa kicked off her slippers. She reached for his neckcloth as his fingers fumbled with her buttons. She had wanted to be close to him for so long, and at last her hungry hands could roam and explore. Rupert had just rammed into her, so to be naked beside a man who was simply lying beside her, kissing her, stroking and holding her, felt amazing.

'I didn't know skin could feel so wonderful,' she whispered.

'Nor I!' was his laughing response. Eventually he rose above her, taking his weight on his elbows. His words whispered in her ear, 'There is something I need to tell you, I am a virgin.'

Louisa pulled away slightly, 'In truth?' His answer was a low hum of confirmation. 'Well, that is not a problem, I am not and know what goes where,' she told him. He laughed again, and she could see his teeth white in the fragile light that filtered in from the outside. She couldn't help saying, 'I was afraid for a moment you would say you were married. One of us in that state is quite sufficient.'

It had never occurred to her that this act could be accompanied with laughter and good humour.

When Sam settled himself and began to edge towards her, she felt herself stiffen. Rupert had been fast and brutal, and memories of pain and revulsion for a moment flooded her mind. But the fact that Sam had never done this with another woman suddenly filled her with tenderness, and the warmth from that feeling seeped into her rigid body and softened it and made it welcoming. Once he was in, he rested, his head dropped down to hers,

'Bloody hell,' he said. And Louisa laughed, and then they kissed, and then it all went very well indeed.

They lay heated and content for a moment, and then Sam pushed up on one elbow and began to run his hand over her breasts, one after the other. He tested their weight, ran a finger around her nipple, then drifted down over her ribs to make a circular motion over her stomach.

'What are you doing?' she whispered.

'Learning you. Studying you.'

Louisa had wanted Sam's lovemaking in a rather mild way. She cared deeply for him, might even love him, but had not, deep inside, expected to enjoy the experience. But it had been lovely. Feeling him deep inside her had felt good and holding him in her arms and thighs wonderful. Now something strange was happening. Her blood was heating and an ache was growing between her legs. She wriggled her hips up and down, trying to rub against a yearning that was growing.

'Sam,' was all her mind could manage.

His hand had reached her curls. He began to explore tenderly, the tips of his fingers probing.

'Sam!'

'What is it love?'

'I don't know.' Surely her body didn't want more; she wanted to keep tonight a lovely memory, not have it spoiled.

Now he pushed her thighs apart and once more gently edged inside. Louisa's mind had gone blank, her body had taken over. She lifted her hips to take more of him in. This time he moved slowly. Agonisingly slowly. He reached down and nuzzled her neck, licking and kissing her skin. A part of Louisa sat outside herself, aware in some part of her mind that she was writhing like a mad thing and straining for more. Always more. This time it lasted far longer and when they collapsed, spent and sweating, they both simply held each other close and dozed.

She came to, to find Sam leaning over her, blocking out the moonlight, just a dark shape above her. His mouth found hers and the kiss was deep and long, and then he rolled to one side, snuggling her in close.

'Why was I the first?' she asked softly.

'No real reason. I was a gawky youth, all wrists, ankles and horrific spots.'

'Spots? You have lovely skin.'

'Don't forget the shyness. I hated being in company. Oh, I fancied many girls, but hid behind Ma's skirts rather than actually talk to them. They all seemed so confident and, frankly, terrified me. Some of those same girls are now married and I have to be very careful not to be compromised. You wouldn't believe the number of wives who think they have rot in the timbers above their beds and, of course, mention it only when their husbands are away.'

'Rot in the timbers?'

'Mm. Unimaginative, but to the point, I suppose.'

It was Louisa's turn to push up on one elbow. She poked him in the chest, hard. 'Well, tell them that you are taken. Or I will rip their eyes out of their sockets.'

'Ah, I had no idea you were so bloodthirsty. I approve.' And with a laugh he lifted her and set her above him, straddling his stomach. 'If it can be done one way, I assume it can be done another. You do ride, don't you?'

It seemed she did.

Sam made it home for breakfast. He slunk up the backstairs, shaved, then ate silently as Chantel kept everyone in stitches with tales of what her pet hedgehog had been up to in the night. When his plate was empty, he sat lounging in his seat, his face turned slightly down and away from everyone else, and wished himself back in a hayloft with straw poking him in the back. He managed to make it out for the day without saying a word to anyone. He didn't feel up to normal conversation.

The day went badly, and it was his fault. He couldn't concentrate and found that he was extraordinarily clumsy, as if he were a gangly boy again. He knew why. He didn't want to be there. It took what felt like a super-human effort to pull himself together and concentrate on estate business. He had a job to do, and needed to get on with it. But oh, it was hard in a way he had never envisaged. By six o'clock he had hidden Greystoke once more where he could leave without crossing the cobbled yard, and therefore informing anyone for a half mile where he was with hoof clatter. Louisa arrived scrambling up the ladder at half past emerging from the yard and threw herself into his arms.

'I missed you,' he said against her mouth when he had the chance. Her answer was to rip at his clothing. It was fast, desperate, and frantic. Then they lay and cooled and murmured together as the light faded. At this time of year, it was still light until nearly ten, but hidden up in the dust and straw of the hayloft they had their own world. Louisa had explored his frame with her hands, learning the corded muscles of a man who worked with his body as well as his mind.

'I can't believe you were still innocent.'

'Weren't you when you married?'

'Yes, but isn't it different for men?'

'I suppose so. But it didn't happen for me. The last time I seriously lusted after a woman I was sixteen or so. She was called Sarah and was a maid. I spent hours lingering in rooms and wandering corridors in order to catch a glimpse of her.' He gave a low laugh, 'I thought I was invisible and my feelings a total secret. Looking back, she must have known. Sarah had a rather secretive smile and whisked her backside when she knew I was watching, and she had an admirer somewhere. By the time I came home for Christmas after my first term at Oxford she had married and moved away.'

'And no one else?'

'Oxford was a revelation. I was dropped into a world I had never imagined and thrived in it. I spent all my time either reading or debating. I was soaking up knowledge as fast as I could. I was intoxicated with learning. Then I came home and all of the local girls were busy pairing off and there was I, able to discuss Astronomy and Aristotelian thought, and as tongue-tied as a lad could be when faced with a pretty smile. I was still gawky and blushed as soon as thought.'

'Well, you aren't gawky now, and I think you are the most beautiful man I have ever seen.'

'Men aren't beautiful. You should say ravishingly handsome,' he told her as he rolled her under him and began to kiss her collar bone.

They had nearly three weeks, and the nights were slowly drawing in, when a voice called from the bottom of the steps.

'Time to come down, you two, Molly is making tea.'

It was Miss B and Sam's smile split his face. Louisa had gone bright red and punched him lightly.

'Come on,' he said, 'I am not ashamed of loving you.' They helped each other dress and descended to enter the parlour and face the music.

Miss B was pouring tea as if nothing unusual was happening. Molly was nowhere to be seen.

'You cannot go on like this,' Miss B began. 'Once autumn arrives you will freeze to death.'

'We will cope,' Sam said. He still had a huge grin as if he were a boy caught scrumping apples. Louisa couldn't supress her guilty blush. 'I can't marry her, B, so what do I do about the husband with the too-long name?'

That killed Louisa's blush. She opened her mouth but no sound came out.

'Do I go looking for him, and if I find him, what do I do? He is a professional soldier and I am a farmer. Do I challenge him to a duel, or sneak poison into his favourite tipple, as a divorce is out of the question? I hope you have a suggestion because I have been going mad trying to decide what I should do.'

Louisa leaned away from him and stared with her mouth still slightly open. She had had no idea he had been thinking like this! Sam turned and smiled gently at Louisa. Turning to B he said softly, 'I'd marry her in a heartbeat, B.'

'I know,' she said just as softly, 'so we had better come up with a plan.'

In the end it was simple, there was plenty of room in the house so they would move into the half that wasn't used. Neither B nor Molly was concerned with morality. Sam would simply rise a little earlier than usual each morning and be home at the Manor in time for breakfast. He already led a reasonably separate life to his siblings and parents, which included staying overnight at various farms now and then. He would simply say nothing and carry on. Louisa decided to brazen it out. To her surprise, it worked. She had expected to be spat at in the street, or some such, but it never happened. Oh, there were some sly looks, but those she just smiled at and continued on her quiet way. It seemed Sam was too important to challenge; he was heir to every scrap of land for miles around. Besides, he was generally liked. And Louisa was clearly genteel and kept herself to herself. Miss B was a known eccentric, and Louisa was simply lumped into the same category. If the household wished to be unconventional, there wasn't anyone around who felt in a position to complain. Besides, they were doing no one any harm. It wasn't long before their strange relationship was simply part of the local scenery. As for Lieutenant Colonel Lord Rupert Douglas McCloud, he was ignored and forgotten about. A fact that would have irritated him no end.

Chapter 9

Sam and Louisa had been living together as invisibly as possible for a month or more when one afternoon his father brought matters to a head. It was late afternoon and autumn was coming on. They were headed home after a day spent together, something that happened rarely these days. They had been riding along easily, not talking, when William brought his horse to a halt, swung down, and tied it up. Then he walked a few paces and stood with his hands thrust in his trouser pockets. Sam stayed astride for a few minutes, then, realising his father intended to stay for a while, followed his lead. He walked over to stand beside him. They were on a small hill, looking down over a long valley covered in the vivid green of an early Wiltshire autumn, with touches of gold in the trees that promised a change in the weather was to come. There was a wind, and it had an edge to it, but the late sunshine made it pleasant rather than something to avoid. They stood in silence for a while, shoulder to shoulder, then William took out his pipe and peered at it, and Sam knew that this pause in their day was no accident.

'Your mother and I,' William began, 'well, our first question is, is it a man or a woman?'

Sam swung a shocked look at his father, who was intent on scratching out his pipe bowl. He took a deep breath and echoed, 'A man or a woman?'

William nodded, 'You know about Oak Farm now, don't you?'

Sam nodded back, 'Yes. I have always wondered why you tolerate it.'

'Don't do any harm, always pay their rent on time, keep the land in good heart, what is there not to tolerate?'

'Blackwell would horsewhip them if they were tenants on his land.'

'Aye well, Jack Blackwell's lad is one, that is why he has to come across as so vehement.'

'I didn't know that.'

'His mother reckons the lad has gone to be a Catholic curate in Ireland, Marie-Claire got it out of her. She wanted to pick Marie-Claire's brains about Catholicism.'

'I didn't know that either.'

'Aye, I think the lad is a clever one. He is burying himself amongst other single men who aren't allowed to marry. If he went for the Church of England, even curates are expected to marry and clearly the lad couldn't face that.'

'Well, it isn't a man.'

'Well, there are another two options. One is that you have discovered whores, but neither of us think that is the case. Luc now, that boy is going to rut like a stag.' William shook his head slowly, 'I can see it coming already. If the boy isn't careful, he will rot his prick off, but there will be no telling him.'

Sam nearly choked. That his parents discussed matters such as this had taken him entirely unawares.

'So, then there is the question of many lasses, or one,' continued William. 'I don't take you for a flirt, leading a number of girls on, though there are many you could.' Sam found this surprising, but William hadn't finished. 'So that leaves the idea that there is just the one. Now, you haven't said a word to either of us, and no reason why you should, you are a man grown, but we trust that if you cared for anyone you would bring her home to meet us. We would want to meet her; if you care for her, then so will we. But you haven't. And you are spending less and less time in your own bed, so we think it is serious.'

Sam swallowed and found he was struck dumb.

'So, that leaves a woman who, for some reason, you can't bring home openly. So most likely a married one. Are we right?' Sam nodded. 'Now, there could be a husband somewhere around,' he turned and met Sam's eyes, 'but neither of us could believe that of you, so we guess the reclusive companion of Miss Buckley, Louisa. Is she married?' Sam nodded. 'And you care for her?' Sam nodded again.

They stood in silence for a long while gazing down at the valley as the cloud shadows raced across the bright green of the grassland.

'She is a lovely, lovely lass, that one,' said William. 'If she ran away, she had no choice. If the husband comes sniffing around lad, you let me know, right? Your mother and I, we think if you make breakfast now and then the young'uns will never notice.'

With that he returned his pipe to his pocket and turned to find his horse. As Sam mounted his, he rested his head against the polished saddle for a moment. He didn't think he had ever loved his father more than he did at that moment.

Sam was horribly jealous of Louisa's husband. It wasn't rational. It wasn't sensible. But there it was. The only way he felt he could exorcise the man was to learn about him, so he asked. Louisa's surprise was immediately evident. 'Why on earth do you want to know about him?'

Sam shrugged, then went for honesty. 'I can't stop wondering about him.'

'Are you jealous?'

He took in a deep breath. 'No,' he said slowly, 'not jealous, just bothered. I can't explain it any better.'

To his surprise she reached across and kissed his cheek softly. 'Then I shall tell you,' she said, before taking a deep breath. 'Have you heard the word, bedevilled? Because Rupert was bedevilled. He had been bought a commission when he reached sixteen. When he married me, he was thirty-eight and he had been fighting for twenty years. He had buried close friends, men he admired, and men he respected. He had lost count of the number of men he had killed. Everyone saw him as this huge, tough, man who was the epitome of the first-class warrior. What they didn't see was that he needed brandy or whisky simply to get himself going in the mornings. He lived with nightmares not just at night, but in the day. He married me because the one way he believed he could sleep was after bedding a woman. The bedding seemed to settle him. That was what I was for. He often hit me, but often didn't know it was me he was hitting, his nightmares were so real to him. I believe he had become fond of me because I never gave away his secrets and acted as if nothing was amiss in public. I helped him hide how damaged he was.

'In one way he was a total pig and I hated that I was his to own, but in another it broke my heart to see how hard it was for him to live up to his image. No one is all black or all white, and Rupert was a mass of contradictions. When we crossed the mountains to reach Oporto to sail back to England, we became almost friends. I didn't leave him intending to stay away forever, at the time I only wanted to have my baby safely. But when he killed her, and I was free of him, I couldn't bring myself to go back. And then I fell in love with you.'

Sam took her in his arms. 'Better?' she asked.

And he nodded. He felt far more settled in his own mind. It was more comfortable to feel sorry for the man than hate him.

Louisa wasn't surprised when she fell pregnant. But she was terrified. She tried to hide it, but so was Sam. He couldn't hide his anxiety, and when quizzed, admitted his fear.

'Louisa is pregnant,' he told his father. 'Women die in childbirth.' He knew all about the three tiny plots that lay beside his first mother's grave.

William sucked on his pipe. 'Aye, and they live.' He thumped Sam on the shoulder harder than he might have. 'I am to be a granddad! Your mother will be that thrilled. And that insulted. Doesn't see herself as a granny just yet.'

With that he remounted his horse and the two of them continued on their way. All Sam could think was that he had wasted months worrying and he could have seduced Louisa far earlier than he had!

Louisa welcomed the nausea. In her eyes, and from what she had seen and been told by the army women she had grown up with, it meant the baby was growing well. Why they had to inflict vomiting on their loving mothers, no one could explain, but generally it was considered a good sign. Molly said nothing but provided weak tea and dry toast each morning. Both she and Miss B kept their thoughts to themselves but kept keen eyes on her. Louisa found she was permanently tearful with gratitude for their constant silent support. The baby was definitely making her emotional. And the love that Sam poured into her. The last two times she had felt totally alone, and the gruff matter-or-fact support of the women around her had felt cold and indifferent. Losing babies when on the march or after gruelling journeys following their husbands was not unusual, and often welcomed. Louisa's ignorance had felt like a sea she was drowning in. At least now she knew the process and could monitor herself, more or less.

The first time she ventured into the village knowing she was beginning to show she had her heart in her mouth. She could cope with whatever was thrown at her but her child, if it lived, would grow up here. She desperately wanted her child to be welcomed. Her condition was noticed, but her unofficial 'marriage' to Sam was old news. They were totally discreet in public, acting as friendly acquaintances and no more, and the sight of her becoming ungainly was news, but no surprise. Marriage in the army had been a fluid thing. When a man died, for whatever reason, one of his mates would take on his woman and children and everyone around them simply accepted the new state of affairs. There was rarely time for the formality of a legal wedding. The system worked, more or less, as 'poaching' another man's wife, whether she was legal or otherwise, was frowned upon. Any man found sniffing around the wrong woman's skirts could well find himself in a dark corner with more than a few serious bruises, if not broken bones.

It was somewhat different for officers, of course. Standards were far stricter, and a kept woman who was not legal, had to remain very much in the background and received significant social ostracism. Louisa, however, had been married by the regiment chaplain, and escorted to her groom by the Regimental Colonel. She therefore felt she had good reason to consider herself very much legally her husband's chattel, despite having nothing to prove such a thing. Therefore, if her child were a boy, he would be her husband's heir, and that didn't bear thinking about. The idea of Rupert, or his father, arriving to remove her son to train him to take over the Douglas McCloud estates, made her blood run cold. She had no legal rights over her children, and she prayed to a god she didn't think she believed in nightly to keep her safely hidden from her old world.

So, it wasn't helped when Sir William arrived one day asking to speak to her. She received him alone in the part of the house she and Sam considered theirs. Then, when he took out his pipe and began peering into the bowl, she really began to worry. Her father had always done that when he was about to say something he knew she wouldn't like.

'Now then lass,' he began. 'Seems like my first grandchild is on the way.'

Louisa swallowed. Would he ask her to give up Sam? Let him marry someone more suitable? Forget the 'more', just suitable would be a reasonable request.

'This fool husband of yours. He is, I understand, a soldier?'

Oh, Louisa loved that, Rupert would have gone apoplectic to be dismissed as both a fool and a mere 'soldier'. He had loved all of his many titles.

'Yes.'

'Well, from the amount of grain and boot leather the army are buying off me, seems they are busy.' Louisa nodded. 'Any chance the idiot is dead?'

Louisa nearly stopped breathing. She had been living with the fear that Rupert would find her for what felt like forever. The thought that he might no longer be around to terrorise her hadn't occurred to her. She had no idea why, he was a soldier, after all.

'I don't know.'

'Any way we can find out? I'd like to dandle my grandbabies in public, not only in private.'

'You don't mind?'

'Oh, I mind. I'd like the lad to have what he wants, and that is his ring on your hand, not some other charlie's. On the other hand, it sort of suits him, this being the way things are. Always been a private soul, our Sam, quite happy to be away on his own with his thoughts. Not like his brother Lucien now. That one is right in your face every instant. I have hopes the school might beat some manners into him, but I am not holding my breath. No, for our Sam, he would have hated to wait before an altar with the whole place staring at him. Not his thing at all. A drunken parson married me and Marie-Claire on the quiet during a rainstorm and that has suited us for all these years. She sends her best wishes, by the way. Nay lass, I'd like to be able to claim you as one of our own, which indeed you are.'

'I do love him,' Louisa said softly, 'so very much.'

'Never doubted it for a minute lass, not for a minute.' With that he stood to leave. 'Give some thought to what I have said. If the man is dead, then we can dance on his grave. Good day now.' And with that he was gone, leaving Louisa to think.

Miss Buckley took on the task. She hounded Louisa for every

regiment officer's name she could remember, and sent a list of them to one of her brothers. Months later, Louisa was pacing in the kitchen getting in Molly's way when the letter came. Rupert, it seemed, was alive and kicking, probably literally, and in Portugal. Louisa went into labour that day with two reasons for a string of expletives in her mind.

Sam was beside himself. William tried to keep him company but ended up leaving him to it. There was no easy way to get through the next hours, neither for Sam nor Louisa, so he took himself off to do something useful. Sam had never admitted he had delivered Louisa's dead baby girl, and now he wished he had so it was him upstairs in the bedchamber, not the very skilled mid-wife the stable lad had fetched. Miss B sat writing letters in the window, and pressing whisky, which he loathed, on him.

They called her Elena. When William returned and opened the bedroom door, Sam was on the bed, propped up, with his arm around Louisa and the baby. They were all fast asleep. William left them to it and went to inform Marie-Claire that all was well.

When Elena was toddling Sam came in, his face full of laughter. Louisa looked at him and her heart filled with love, so much so she was sure it would flood the room and they would all drown.

'What is it?' she asked.

'Pa has been offered a peerage. He is to be a lord.'

'Why?' Louisa hoped that didn't sound rude. William suited being a Sir, but she couldn't imagine him strutting around as a 'Lord'. And in her mind, lords were full of their own self-importance, and that just wasn't William.

'Services to the Army. I have never seen him so cross! He is charging around as if he has thrust his head into a bee hive! He reckons it is because they hope they can blackmail him into lowering his grain and leather prices. And, of course, he will have to go to London, a place he has never had time for. Let alone the new wardrobe he will have to be fitted for. He is as mad as a cat with cutlery tied to its tail.'

Louisa sent her congratulations and carried on sewing. Her daughter was growing like a weed. So, it seemed she might have a title once more. If she and Sam ever did manage to marry. She looked over at Elena. She was already clearly going to be tall, and had her father's pale blonde hair, except where Sam's was straight and tended to look lank, Elena's had a wave. She was the apple of her father's, and her grandfather's, eyes. As the granddaughter or possibly daughter of a Lord, she should make a good marriage. Louisa frowned and continued to sew. What defined a 'good' marriage was up for debate, in her opinion.

Time slipped by, and afterwards, in Louisa's mind it was full of golden light. It all went so wrong so suddenly. She was once more pregnant, her belly beginning to swell. Elena had found her feet, and was charging around and telling her mother what to do. Her favourite word was, 'no'. The house was full of activity and laughter. Now Lucien and James were both at Eton, Sam made little pretence that he lived anywhere but at the Dower House with Louisa and Miss B. Chantel had gone to a girls' boarding school in Bath, and was thriving. She loved, it seemed, being with other girls, and Miss B had approved the place as it gave girls the chance to study mathematics if they so wished.

She had been making her way up to the bedchamber, when she had realised that Molly was working in the kitchen. As it was nearly midnight, she was puzzled. The stairs were full of the scent of savoury steam. Louisa pushed the kitchen door open gently. Molly was chopping root vegetables finely, and dropping handfuls into a large saucepan.

'What on earth are you doing at this time of night?' she asked. 'Are you getting a start on tomorrow's chores?'

'I'm going to be leaving, Mrs Sam,' was Molly's quiet response.

'What do you mean 'leaving'?' she asked, frowning. She couldn't imagine this house without Molly's dour solid presence. She was backbone of this home in so many ways.

'None of you has noticed,' Molly said firmly, 'and I reckon I can handle it best.'

'Noted what, Molly? What are you telling me?'

'Mrs Will,' was the unhelpful reply.

'Marie-Claire, what about her?' Louisa was more puzzled than ever.

'Dyin' ain't she.'

Louisa frowned, 'What are you talking about? Lady Causton is fine. I saw her this morning when she came to visit.'

'Weren't visitin', were saying goodbye to you and the little lass.'

'Molly, please, what are you talking about?'

Molly looked straight at her with both her good and her wonky eye. 'You saw her you say, but you didn't look. I did.'

Louisa pulled out a chair from under the table and sat down. She respected Molly, and trusted her. Might even love her, a little. If Molly had seen something, there was every chance she was right.

'Please Molly, please explain it to me.'

Molly was throwing a handful of chopped herbs and another of barley into the broth. From the bones and scent it was a chicken being boiled up. Molly always made chicken broth when there was serious illness around.

'Like I said, dyin' she be. I'm going to the manor tomora to nurse her.'

Louisa left her to it. But fell asleep worrying and wishing Sam was with her. He was spending a rare night away from home.

Marie-Claire had endured the usual number of illnesses in her life. However ill she had felt, she had always got better in time. In a way, now, she didn't feel ill at all. It was odd. But she knew at some level she had never before experienced that something was very wrong with her body. Most days she felt quite well, but on others, sometimes for only an hour, the pain in her abdomen was so extreme it brought her to her knees. Her clothes were beginning to hang loose on her and her appetite had faded to almost nothing. And then suddenly she would be hungry. But mostly, she tired easily. Whenever William was near, she smiled and hid her fear. Not for herself, for him. She loved him far too much to leave him alone.

The morning Molly arrived she had stayed in bed. William had left early, and she had acted as if she was about to rise, but instead she had sunk back into the mattress and fallen back into an exhausted sleep. Hiding that something was wrong with her was becoming increasingly difficult. Thank heavens all of the children were away at school. When she awoke, Molly was sitting beside the bed. Marie-Claire frowned. She didn't only dislike Molly's looks, with her eyes that looked in two different directions, but the girl, now a woman, had always worked at what she thought needed doing not what Marie-Claire had directed her to, and her pace was so slow to be stationary. So, she wasn't filled with delight to see her.

'I've made you soup,' Molly announced. 'You won't be able to eat much more than that, I reckon.'

'How did you know?' Marie-Claire asked.

'Seen it before. You's quite a long way along.' Molly's tone was matter-of-fact.

'How long have I got?' Marie-Claire couldn't help asking.

Molly shrugged, and took the lid off an earthenware pot. Marie-Claire found, to her surprise, it smelt appetising. 'Wore yourself out yesterday, didn't you.' Molly stated. 'Wanted to see the little moppet.'

Marie-Claire sighed and accepted a spoonful of the very good soup.

'A day of rest, and you might be fine tomorrow,' Molly informed her.

To her surprise, Marie-Claire felt tears prickle her throat. It had become so hard to pretend she was well. It was such a relief to give up for a while and let someone else take control.

When William strode in to his hall that evening, he saw the two newest maids huddled together over their bags. The housekeeper, Mrs Munster, was checking them over and seemed to be giving them instructions. Her face, when she turned it to him, made him frown. Something wasn't right. The girls nodded and passed him bobbing curtsies, and he heard a cart pulling up at the front.

'Mrs Munster?' William's voice was interrogatory.

She hurried over. 'Lady Causton is unwell,' she said, looking flustered. 'Molly has arrived to nurse her and those two,' she nodded after the girls who were leaving, 'are going to the Dower House to take her place.'

The fact that it needed two girls to replace Molly sailed by him. All he cared about was the news that Marie-Claire was ill. She had seemed to be struggling recently, but he thought she was still trying to throw off a cold. He took the stairs two at a time. The room was darkened by the drawn curtains and he walked as softly as he could towards the bed.

'What is wrong?' he said, too urgently, too loudly.

'William, I am just a bit tired,' Marie-Claire insisted, reaching up to kiss him.

But he could see it was more than that. She hadn't been that unwell yesterday, had she? She had visited Louisa and little Elena. She had retired early, but he hadn't thought anything of it. He glanced across the bed and realised Molly was sitting in the shadows. 'Why is Molly here?'

'Because I know how to look after her,' replied Molly.

'Look after her?' he felt as if he had been swiped around the head, he couldn't get his mind around what was going on.

'She has been ill a long time,' Molly said, 'she needs to rest.'

William opened his mouth and then shut it again. What had he missed? How could he have missed the fact that his beloved wife was so ill?

'What have I done?' he whispered.

'Nothing, *mon cher*, I was hiding it from you,' Marie-Claire whispered back. He heard the click of the door as Molly left.

'You don't even like her,' he said.

'She is not so bad. And she is gentle, and seems to understand without being told what I need her to do. We are getting on well, I promise. I just woke up today too tired to fight any more. I only need to rest a while.'

William sat on the bed and held her. He stared away at the wall for a long, long, time.

William arrived before Sam headed out for his day's work. He sat down heavily, and told them both how ill Marie-Claire was. Except he didn't really know. Clearly something was wrong, but he was hoping whatever it was would clear itself. Molly was being marvellous; he had never realised what a good nurse she was. This morning Marie-Claire was up and dressed, but now he was paying attention, he could see that she had lost weight and looked permanently tired. Louisa thought he had aged ten years overnight. He was trying to sound positive, but it was clear he was desperately worried.

Sam kissed her, and left, leaving Louisa worried and not sure what she could do to help. She wasn't officially in the family. The younger children never visited the Dower House. As far as they were concerned, she was simply Miss Buckley's companion. The appearance of a little girl on the premises had passed them by. She held her swelling abdomen and hoped Marie-Claire would be well when her second grand-child made an appearance.

She was larger still when the letter arrived. One of Miss B's brothers had received a correspondence from someone he knew, whom he probably wouldn't admit to knowing. Mathematicians were frequently used by certain people for codes, and there was, after all, a war on. In any case, Lieutenant Colonel Lord Rupert Douglas McCloud was dead. Sam was often over at the Manor with his father, being ripped into two with his beloved adopted mother clearly now frailer than ever. Louisa couldn't tell him about the letter until the morning. She had been sound asleep when he had slipped in beside her, frozen and exhausted.

They sat up against the pillows while he too read the letter.

'Can we trust it?' Louisa asked.

'I don't see why not. B's brother says the news is cast iron. In which case, will you marry me, Lady Louisa? Will you reduce yourself to being the wife of a mere farmer?'

Louisa gave him a laughing deep kiss. 'How quickly can it be done?'

'I will take that as a yes, and ride over to the vicar this very morning to ask for the banns to be read.' He hugged her close, 'I hope Ma is still with us for the wedding. Pa said she was up and walking in the garden yesterday berating him for not having the borders properly tidied for the winter. If she is nagging him, maybe she is on the mend?'

Louisa held her peace. She had spoken to Molly, and Molly seemed very confident that she knew the path the disease would take. But there was always hope.

Sam went off straight after breakfast. He gave her a long kiss and whispered, 'Mrs Causton, hey?'

He went off with a smile and his eyes laughing as they hadn't since Marie-Claire had become ill. He was going to the Manor afterwards, as William had signed two new contracts with the army. The tannery was doing great business, and two shoemakers, who spoke no English had arrived from Flanders on the strength of gossip about the place. There were now faces in the high street she didn't recognise, and it was clear to Louisa that their village was rapidly becoming a town. When Sam didn't come in that night, she was concerned, but she was sure he would appear for breakfast. Perhaps he had spent the night at the Manor, celebrating the new business and the fact that they could finally marry. The baby had been active all night, and when she finally rose she felt as if she had been in a boxing bout.

When Sam didn't arrive for breakfast, she really began to worry. It was so unlike him, and surely he would want to come and tell her that he had ordered the banns? She pulled on a heavy shawl and wandered out into the yard. The two new maids were perfectly able to keep Elena amused. She really must learn their names, but her mind felt like fog sometimes with this baby. She drifted to the edge of the yard and looked out across the field that led to the parsonage and the church. She could clearly see the steeple in the distance.

The ground was frozen solid and glazed with frost. A weak sun was attempting to warm the air, but failing miserably. The bitter air felt good after her restless night, and her breath danced out in front of her like a dragon's and she puffed it out just for fun. There was a footpath leading from the yard, diagonally across the first field towards the church that generations of people living at the Dower House or nearby had used every Sunday. She began to follow it slowly, gaining pace a little as she settled into a rhythm, not that she had much pace with this lump inside her! The baby seemed to like being walked and had ceased turning somersaults and kicking. With one hand resting on her bump. Louisa decided to walk to the first hedge. Clearly, this ramble was doing both her and the baby good.

She didn't intend to go far in case she missed Sam, but he would find her easily in this field. At the stile she stepped up to gaze at the sun as it glimmered over the far steeple. Something moved in the distance. Whatever it was, it wasn't in the next field, but the one after. A head came up. Not a man's, a horse's. The head vanished behind the hedge again and all was still. Had she imagined it? She turned to look back at the house, so large and solid behind her where all was still. Perhaps someone was working in that field? But she knew that shouldn't be the case because three weeks earlier the staff had all returned from church complaining bitterly that they were all caked in mud to the knees. The ploughman who had done that field had churned the footpath in as well as the weeds, and later rain had turned the route to a heavy muddy mess. So, the field was set for the winter; there was no work left to do.

The horse's head had looked light-coloured. Like a grey. Like Greystoke. Louisa began to walk slowly and carefully across the second field. At the next stile she climbed up again and looked forward. She was as far from home as she wanted to be in her condition, and no one knew she was here. It was a horse, and it did look very like Greystoke. And then the horse moved around, lifted its head and whinnied. And now Louisa could see a man lying on the ground under the horse's hooves. She hauled herself over the stile and began to run, except she couldn't, she could only frantically stumble. Time beat against her like a physical force as she propelled her cumbersome body forward.

He was as covered with frost as the churned frigid ground beneath him. He lay on his back, with one knee bent so his foot was flat on the ground, as if he had begun to rise and failed. Greystoke nuzzled her hair as she reached for Sam, but she pushed the horse away. The horror of what she was looking at hit at her as if a stone building had fallen on her. Gasping, she fell to her knees. Greystoke nuzzled her again. She was trembling. Louisa rose and regarded her. She was a huge grey, which was what Sam with his long, long legs had needed, and the saddle was so unbelievably high as she gazed at it.

She and the horse regarded each other for a while. Then Louisa reached for the reins and tugged. Slowly they crossed the field again towards the far gate. Louisa was pulling on the reigns far more than was kind in order to keep herself going and upright, but Greystoke seemed to take it. She was as exhausted and cold as Louisa. There was a stile beside the gate. Louisa shoved the horse where she wanted her and told her to stay still. She wasn't sure she knew how Sam had instructed her, but she didn't move once in position. Climbing onto the top of the stile she balanced precariously and hauled herself across the horse, finally swinging a leg over. She lay forward on her arms panting and rested. There was no hurry. They had all the time in the world.

The fact that she was putting both herself and her unborn child at risk by mounting a horse from a four-inch piece of wood set high in the air never entered her head, and if it had, well, she didn't care. Not anymore.

Louisa clopped into the yard at the Manor as the sun finally broke through properly to gleam a winter light on the cobbles. As it happened, Birch the head of the stables was in the yard as she arrived. He rushed over to her.

'Mrs Sam, whatever are you doing up there?' He was a big man with arms like tree trunks and Louisa looked at him and then slid sideways knowing he would take her weight easily and get her onto the ground. Her legs gave way as she touched earth.

'Sam,' she said, 'Hook Field. He needs to be warm.' She gazed up at his face frowning. 'He is so cold. Someone must make him warm.'

Birch's face went rigid. He took Louisa's head in one of his big hands and pressing his palm against her ear, pulled her head into his chest, as he began bellowing orders. As he did so Louisa felt her legs, stockings and boots become wet and warm.

'It's too early,' she said, frowning even more, 'much too early.'

Birch looked down and saw that the front of his boot that had been under Louisa's skirts was newly wet.

Two of the maids had come running, more out of curiosity than because they thought they might be useful but one gave Louisa a keen look and told Birch, 'I'll get my boots and run for the midwife. Where should she go, here or the Dower House?'

Louisa suddenly came to, 'Home! I want to go home!' she tried to shout, but her voice was weak.

'Very well, we will get the coach. We will have you home in a trice.'

Birch was in charge and Louisa didn't care. The world wasn't a place she wished to be in. The baby took a long while to appear. Louisa didn't care. The pain seemed appropriate and she didn't fight it. Eventually a little girl was placed in her arms. A second live daughter. Louisa gazed at her with indifference and went to sleep.

Susan, one of the new maids, took over looking after Louisa and the new baby, while her sister Christine saw to little Elena. Louisa's milk came in. It soaked her front. There was plenty of it, but she just sat staring at the wall. If Susan unbuttoned her and put the baby to her, she held it and let it feed, but was equally as likely to loosen her arms and let the baby fall if Susan wasn't quick enough. It was clear the baby could sense the milk and would scream her head off in frustration as

Louisa sat indifferent to her noise. Susan went to see Miss B.

'We need a wet nurse,' she told B.

B had learned more about babies when Elena had been born than she had ever wished to know, and now she was being tasked with finding a human dairy. She was not at all amused.

B's trap and pony were well known around Causton. She had no real idea of where to go, but, was determined to give the problem her best effort. The memory of that other little baby, so blue and broken, still haunted her at times, and she had no wish to repeat such an experience. One dead little girl in her orchard was quite enough.

She was returning from visiting a second farm where a mother had recently birthed. Neither woman had felt she could leave her other children, her husband's demands, or her household tasks to come to The Dower House for an indefinite period. This wasn't the city. Almost every child was born into a family. There simply weren't single mothers around who were desperate for a home and work. B was fretting over the problem, but had decided to return home and regroup when movement caught her eye. There was a cottage set back from the road, with a long straight front path. B glanced that way, to see a girl shoved out the door. A man followed her and pulling back his arm gave her a massive smack to her face. The girl fell, twisting like a cat to land flat on her back. Shocked, B jerked on the reins and pulled the trap to a stop as the girl hit the ground with her head giving an audible thud as she landed. B had never been backward in coming forward.

'Girl!' she yelled.

The girl was getting awkwardly to her feet, using only one arm. She seemed, not surprisingly, stunned. B yelled again, 'Girl, get over here.'

Slowly the girl covered the fifty or so feet to the road and stood looking up at B. Her face was set and sullen. B wasn't in a position to object. 'Is that a baby?' she asked referring to the bundle in the girl's arm. The girl gave a tiny nod.

'Is it yours?'

Again, a glare and a nod.

'You feeding it yourself?'

'It's a boy. Not an it.'

So, the girl could talk. 'If you think you can feed two, get in. I need a wet-nurse. I will feed and house you both and give you a sovereign in a year. Interested?'

The girl stood still glowering, but eventually responded with, 'I'll take your sovereign.'

Neither of them said a word until they reached the yard of The Dower House. As B drew the trap to a halt and the stable lad ran towards them to grab the pony she said, 'Was it your father who hit you?' The girl glared even harder. 'Hmm,' said B, having received her answer.

Louisa didn't even seem to notice the new face in front of her. The girl didn't give her name but settled her own baby in a nest made out of her cloak on the floor and took Louisa's little mite into her arms. Her face softened. She undid the front of her dress and settled Louisa's baby to her, before accepting her own little boy from Susan and settling him to her other side. B made a hasty exit. As did Susan, who expressed her preference for not caring for small babies by setting to and scrubbing the flagstones in the entrance hall with enthusiasm. She had B's sympathy.

When William came to see Louisa, she frowned slightly as if she might know him, but other than that stared at the wall and said nothing. As he looked at least twice the age he had been a few days ago B thought that might be part of the reason. She took William downstairs to sit in the parlour. It was an overcast day, the clouds low and any sunlight fitful. Despite the glass doors, the room was gloomy, which suited their mood.

William asked, 'Is she always like that?'

'Hasn't changed since she was brought home after finding Sam. It's as if her mind has shut down. I can't say I blame her. I can barely think straight with knowing I won't see him again.' Her old eyes glazed with unshed tears. 'I loved him, you know?'

'Ah B, I thought I had finished burying my children. I never thought he would go before me. Let alone so sudden.' He swallowed loudly and stared away out towards the garden. B left him to his pain. He was losing a wife slowly, and had lost a son suddenly. Goodness only knew the agony he faced each morning when he awoke. Assuming he could sleep, that was. They sat in silence for a long time. Fate was a wicked bitch sometimes and there was no gainsaying her, and they were both long enough in the tooth to understand that. For the moment B was simply glad to have his company.

Eventually William said, 'The funeral is tomorrow.'

'I don't think Louisa will know,' B said.

There was a soft knock and Elena was ushered in. She spotted William and ran over to him, resting her little hands on his knees. William looked down at her indulgently. 'If Marie-Claire was well I'd take this little one home.' He lifted her and sat holding the little girl for a while, letting her pull his beard and sort through his pockets, finding his watch and his pipe, all the while chattering softly to herself. 'In fact, shall I take her anyway? Molly is still with us, and we can find a girl to take care of her. It might cheer Marie-Claire up to watch her run around.'

'She will cry for her mother,' B warned.

'Doesn't she anyway? Her mother can hardly be said to be aware of her.'

B sighed. 'It would be a weight off my mind. How is Lady Causton?'

'Much the same. She has good days and bad. Sam going has hit her hard, but she is determined to be at the church service for him.'

Juggling the child William rummaged in one of his huge jacket pockets took out a folded piece of paper he held it out to B. 'Have you seen this?' he asked.

'What is it?'

'Read it.'

B took the letter, written by her own brother, detailing regimental losses.

'So, he is dead. That explains why Sam was in Hook Field. It is directly between here and the church,' said B thoughtfully.

'I think he was heading to have the banns called,' William said. 'She could have been my daughter in truth. No more hiding. I could have claimed this little one as my own.' He stroked Elena's hair, 'Heard her call me granddad out loud.' He gave a deep sigh. 'But she is mine, all of them are. I am writing to the bank in Bristol this afternoon. The estate will pay Louisa and the girls a pension. As Sam's wife she would have received at least that much. Sam has brought home to me how perilous life is. I am afraid for their futures, and I want to do all I can to keep them safe.'

'I don't think she will stay as she is, Louisa I mean,' B told him. 'I think finding him like that, then the baby coming early, I just think it is all too much for her. I honestly believe she will come back to us one day.'

'I hope so,' William said sadly. 'But call on me for anything you need, more staff, or supplies, anything at all. Your household is growing.'

'As I am aware,' muttered B. The days of her and Molly jogging along seemed a long, long way away.

The pall of Sam's sudden death hung over the Causton estate. William's smiles came infrequently, and Miss B found that where she had believed she was too old to cry, tears could lay heavy on her chest, making breathing difficult. Miss B visited Marie-Claire regularly, but the woman was clearly ill. Where she had smiled, even when looking pale and drawn, and swore that she would be 'better tomorrow', losing Sam seemed to have ripped away the energy she needed to make lies appear facts. No one sang as they worked in the house any more, and the men of the estate seemed weighed down. Sam had been both liked and admired, and his loss rippled through everything. He had been the heir, and William's shoulders no longer looked firm. People began to worry.

The winter drew its wearying way on, the grey skies appearing far worse than the biting cold that seemed unwilling to give way to change. Finally, snowdrops appeared, then the delicate bells of the narcissus, and finally the haze of bluebells blowing gently in the soft spring breezes. At long last a day appeared that where as long as you sat in the sun, it felt warm enough to be outside and not moving vigorously. Susan had helped Louisa dress and led her gently down the garden to sit in a sheltered spot. She felt sorry for the poor lady who had lost her mind. She was as easy to care for as a biddable child. The wet-nurse, Julie, saw to the two babies, and little Elena remained up at the Manor, being brought to visit once or twice a week, though perhaps that might stop soon as it upset the little mite to have her mother so indifferent to her.

Louisa was vaguely aware of the sun on her face, and the white blossom in the heavily thorned hedge that outlined the garden. She was down at the end of the lawns, the orchard and vegetable plots beyond. Vaguely she could hear a baby cry and be soothed, and it scratched at her mind as if it was something she ought to pay attention to. Suddenly a huge man appeared from amongst the apple trees, the blossom falling like snow onto his wide shoulders. He was moving fast, striding out, and his face was contorted with anger. Louisa stood, frowning. As the man drew closer, she could see his red face, the vein pulsing at his temple and his clenched fists. Shock and fear pulsed through her and for the first time in months her mind cleared. Memories came back with a flood. She spun around and ran, heading for her baby. Julie was nursing one child, the other in a basket at her feet. As Louisa drew closer, she yelled, 'Run!' and reached down to grab the basket. The two women spun around and turned to the wide-open glazed door to the parlour.

'No!' shouted the man, 'Stop!'

Louisa and Julie turned frightened faces to the man, who was so close they could touch him. He must have moved like lightning! B appeared in the doorway, leaning on the silver headed stick she now used for much of the time.

'Julie,' the man said, 'will you marry me?'

Julie's mouth hung open. 'Jeff?' she said. 'Why are you here?'

The man rubbed his forehead with his hand, and his skinned and bloody knuckles were plain to see, as was the fact that his shirt was torn and his waistcoat had lost most of its buttons. He was breathing loud and hard. 'I only now found out,' he said. 'I just beat him to within an inch of his life.'

Julie had gone a bright red.

'Why didn't you tell anyone?' he asked, 'Why didn't you say?' His voice was anguished.

Julie lifted her chin a little, 'I did,' she said. 'I told my Pa.'

Humph, thought B; she had seen how that turned out. Julie's face had taken two weeks to clear of its bruising.

'Why on earth are you asking me to marry you?'

The fascinated onlookers now turned to look at her as one. So, perhaps this wasn't the father of her little one. They all turned to look at the man, still breathing hard, who was facing them. 'I am serious,' he insisted.

'But you'd be raising another man's child. And he is a boy.' Julie's voice was puzzled.

'I know. But if you marry me, he will be mine. And…' he seemed to be struggling for thought, 'Giles is my cousin, so he will be blood anyway. I won't ever blame the boy. This isn't his fault.'

Julie seemed close to tears. 'But you don't have to pay for Giles' crime?'

Ah, thought B, so she was forced. She had wondered. The girl had seemed almost as traumatized as Louisa.

'Julie, I have watched you since I was a boy. You are so pretty and delicate. I knew I didn't stand a chance. I am only a lump of muscle who humps barrels around for my father who is a mere tavern keeper. I always knew you could do better.'

Susan, who was one of the fascinated faces watching from the side-lines, let her gaze run appraisingly over those muscles and hummed softly.

'Oh Jeff, you are a fool,' was Julie's unromantic response.

'Ah, so you don't want me,' he looked so crestfallen.

Julie smiled such a sweet smile suddenly everyone could see the pretty young girl she had been before she had been assaulted so wickedly. 'Did you hurt him a lot?' she asked.

'Busted ribs and a leg. Kicked him in the guts. Some teeth came out. Didn't kill him though I wanted to. I'd hang for that and I want to be around to thump him again when he recovers.' Jeff's voice left none of them in any doubt that he was serious.

B's eyebrows raised. Perhaps she should have a chat with him about his approach to anger, on the other hand, she gave a satisfied sigh, if she couldn't meet out such punishment, she was oh so glad someone could. Perhaps she was best leaving Jeff with his anger.

'Would you like to meet the baby?' Julie asked. 'You ought to see what you might be getting into.' She took the baby from Louisa's arms and handed him to Jeff.

'Ale,' said B. 'And tea.'

The shock of being faced with a violent man had brought Louisa back to the land of the living with a crash. Her milk had dried up weeks ago, and her little daughter was holding up her head and trying to crawl. Julie had overnight turned into a different person. She smiled constantly, and sung softly to both of the babies. When William was sure Louisa was strong enough, he brought Elena back and gradually she and her mother began to rebuild their fences. Jeff came every afternoon, as he worked mornings brewing and evenings hauling barrels for the tavern, courting Julie and getting to know the baby, whom they had decided together to call Thomas.

Then came a further stunning blow, one none of them had expected nor knew how to cope with. Life had truly changed again, and for the worse. William had dropped dead in front of young Lucien, and Marie-Claire had only lasted the following night. Louisa and B were too shocked to cry. They simply sat white-faced and unmoving for what felt like days until Molly returned. Then they both broke down. So-called gormless Moll was their rock, and it was on her shoulders they spent their tears.

At first nothing much altered publicly for Louisa. Shock and grief kept life at bay for almost a year, along with two growing small children, one running everywhere and one hauling herself up on furniture with legs desperate to follow. It was only gradually, as the local populace began to realise that the Caustons really had deserted Causton Manor and the growing town, that resentment, and judgement, began to assert itself. Lord William and Mr Sam had been respected and, in part, feared. But now as one incompetent manager after another arrived to run the estate the goodwill that had existed for generations began to erode.

It was in the local haberdasher's that it really came home to her. As she waited, wishing to buy some ribbons for her girls, she became slowly aware that she was not being served. As new customers arrived, they were immediately seen to and Louisa was left standing in the shadows. Louisa looked around her with a frown. She had always adopted a reserved persona in Causton and nothing had happened to cause her to be more intimate with anyone in the village. First there had been the fear of Rupert, and then the knowledge that she was living with the heir to the estate out of wedlock, and then worse, had borne him two children. Now as she gazed around the interior of the shop and took in how modern it now looked with its polished wooden counters and extensive stock, it hit her quite suddenly that Causton was rapidly becoming a sizable town and that she had no protection from anyone. 'They look at me and see a whore', she thought. Without buying the ribbons she slipped out of the shop and walked home burning from shame. Not an emotion she believed she had ever felt before. Not one person she passed acknowledged her polite 'Good mornings'. She may as well have been invisible.

'I have to move,' she told B.

'Thought so,' was the crisp reply. There didn't seem to be anything more to discuss. Clearly, she had been living in a dream while B had been aware of how untenable her situation was becoming. She settled on Bristol. It was near the bank that was paying her the pension William had, far-sightedly, set up and it was a bustling and growing port city in which a widow on a low income might hide. The awful thing was that she was genuinely a widow now, and her improved marital status didn't help her one bit. She had no idea what kind of response she might receive from Rupert's family if she used her legitimate title. Always at the back of her mind was the dread of some kind of reprisal for deserting him and the terror that his family might take her girls away from her. If a Lady Douglas McCloud suddenly appeared out of the woodwork, the family would surely come to investigate in order to evaluate if she were an imposter. Pretending to an aristocratic title was an offence that carried a jail sentence or even a hanging. She had no proof of who she was. Becoming Mrs Bland, especially while the girls were so young, seemed a far better idea.

Chapter 10

Miss B proved a loyal and regular correspondent to Louisa. This surprised Louisa, somewhat. Certainly, B had taken her in and allowed her to stay, but on the other hand, B herself had no real claim on the Dower House, especially once all the Causton children outgrew her tutoring as, as far as Louisa was aware, she had never been required to pay rent. Also, she clearly was perfectly happy with her own company with only the maid Molly to care for her and the house. When the girls had been very small, it had been clear she had no time for babies or inarticulate small people, and had only taken an interest in them once they could ask a question. There had been a mellowing in her distaste for children then, as B had become intrigued once their favourite word was 'Why?', and seemed to enjoy the challenge of explaining the 'Why?' in a language they could understand. Louisa sometimes wondered if Elena even at her tender age didn't have a far better vocabulary than she did herself, after hours of chatting to the older lady. However, she had always worried that she and the girls had been a trial that B had to put up with because, well, she had to.

Miss B's letters had always been quite impersonal, passing on local news she had gleaned from Molly and from occasionally dining with the various families around the area, so it was with some surprise she received a deeply affectionate letter, wrapped within another one.

My dearest Louisa,

If you are reading this, then I am no more. Doctor Melton has been keeping this letter for some time, ever since I realised that, sadly, I cannot live forever. Both of my brothers have left this life, so it is now for me to also discover whether there is what the Vicar promises or no.

You were the kind of woman I had dreamed Sam might find, but the boy seemed an utter slow-top until you fell into his lap. My life would have been far poorer if you had not arrived in such a shattering way, and the girls, once they could lisp their questions, fascinated me. To watch how they learned about life was a treasure. Thank you for sharing them with me.

Molly has no one to turn to, so I have bought her a little cottage. Like me, she now feels the weight of years in her joints. What is left over, is yours.

I never told you how much you and your wonderful daughters have enriched my life. I loved Sam as a son, or beloved nephew, and when I saw how smitten he was with you, I was glad. You were exactly what I wanted for him.

Good bye, my beloved girl.

Louisa was in tears before she reached the end. Wrapped around, was another letter from a Doctor Melton, telling her when the funeral was to be. Louisa had never hired a coach on her own, and she was terrified. The world suddenly seemed emptier and she even more defenceless. There was no man she could turn to when she felt overwhelmed, and with Miss B gone, there was not even a friend who she could tell herself was somewhere in the world and on her side. The first inn, where she had enquired about hiring a coach and a man to handle it, had been brusque and insulting. Both the man who ran it and his wife had clearly thought she was some kind of light-skirt. 'Well, I am, I suppose,' she thought, and felt no stronger for the admission.

The second landlord was far kinder. He took her inside, sat her down with a pot of tea in the front parlour, and told her, 'Rest your bones, my love. Funeral, is it? Now, you need a trustworthy man to see you there and back, and I reckon I know just the chap.' Louisa did rest her bones, feeling tears hanging around her heart, and sipped the tea. But she was still terrified. She was planning on placing her and her daughters' lives in the hands of a total stranger, who would carry the three of them miles across the country and then back again. They would be totally at his mercy. Anything might happen.

The man the landlord brought to see her was sturdy with longish light-coloured hair, streaked with grey. 'Now, I have known George since we were nippers,' the landlord told her, 'I would trust him with my own wife and daughter, so don't you worry now.'

Louisa looked into the man's clear blue eyes, and decided she had no choice. If they were to travel to Causton, then she would have to put her trust in someone. And then she felt like laughing; a touch of hysteria, no doubt. The new man, a Mr Jobbings, quoted a price, and the landlord immediately began to knock him down. A fair argument ensued, before they shook hands and turned to Louisa to see if she was content with the agreement. Louisa nodded; what else could she do?

'I'll be bringing my son,' Jobbings told her. 'Time he travelled a bit.

He ain't never been to Wiltshire, and with three ladies, two men be best.'

Louisa returned home, feeling that perhaps it was going to be alright.

In the end, it took three days to reach Causton. It rained solidly for two, and parts of the road simply turned to bog. At one point, late on the first afternoon, as Louisa and Samantha climbed out to lighten the load, Elena skipped to the back and put her slight shoulder to the rear of the carriage to help push. Elena's help, which was no doubt no help at all, had warmed the carriage man's heart and caused his big stolid son to admire her with blushing admiration, and from then on Mr Jobbings argued with the inn keepers when they needed to stop and ensured that his 'three ladies' were well looked after. 'Or it will be me and my Jack they will be answering to!' he insisted.

For the first time since Sam's death, Louisa relaxed gratefully into a man's care. Normally she did not feel a lack, but being knocked about with grief, and having two young girls to protect, she was deeply grateful.

Miss B's funeral was well attended. Louisa and her girls stood and ignored the rain sheeting off their cloaks and the winter's gloom that hung around the leafless trees, as most of the people of Causton ignored them. Perhaps they didn't recognise her, Louisa thought, but she doubted it and felt bitter. Families she had passed the time of day with on the streets and shared family concerns with in the shops, now openly snubbed her. It hurt. She hadn't changed and if Sam had lived just one more month, they would now be crowding around her, asking after her health and admiring her girls. She would have been Mrs Causton, the squire's eldest son's widow, and someone whose friendship was worth courting. But Sam's death four weeks early had turned her into a whore. Fury rose within her. She put an arm around each of her daughters and lifted her chin in defiance. Her girls were wonderful. How dare these people judge them!

Mr Jobbings and his son found the rooms above the stables at the Dower House well aired and set out with clean linen on the beds. They were content, and happily spent time in the local inn over their meals and ale. Doctor Melton, who had handed over the keys, had ensured that the house was clean and that food was simmering on the stove. Molly, it seemed, was laid up with a winter illness and so had missed the funeral. As she couldn't come and care for them, the doctor's own maid came over each day to cook. After the behaviour of people at the church, Louisa was glad that she also did not need to eat at the inn. She was too unhappy to cope with what she saw as blatant hypocrisy.

They stayed three days. Louisa spent longer than she should standing in the orchard over her little daughter who lay cold in the ground beneath the apple trees. She had no more tears, instead, a stone sat hard in her chest. Her baby was here, Sam was in the churchyard beside his parents, and now Miss B was there too. Lucien was notable for his absence, and Doctor Melton said he had never met him, having only arrived in the town recently.

Miss B's accounts showed that her outgoings almost exactly matched her income until a few years ago, when she had begun to draw down on her capital. Prices had soared with the war, and simple foodstuffs such as bread had become expensive. There was a sum of four hundred pounds for Louisa to claim. Molly's cottage had cost twenty, so Louisa certainly didn't begrudge her that. The money would make the next few years easier, certainly, the girls were growing out of their boots and clothes almost weekly, it seemed, and they needed meat to grow well, and that could be expensive. Cheap cuts cost the earth in fuel to make edible and the more expensive cost a premium. 'I lose both ways,' Louisa thought glumly.

Time passed and Elena grew lanky and her white blonde hair did not darken, as children's hair usually did. She had high cheekbones and a firm chin and was the image of her father. Samantha, the one named for her posthumous father, took after Louisa with her non-descript dark-blonde hair and hazel eyes. Clearly, she had made a mistake with their naming! The bitterness that she had felt at B's funeral remained lodged deep inside like the stone inside a cherry and all ties with Sam now seemed rubbed out. The army had been a family, the Caustons had accepted her, so now her state of utter friendlessness hurt. Bristol was full of women widowed by the war, but she seemed unable to find any to feel comfortable with, even with the fear of Rupert finding her now gone. There was still, after all, his family out there somewhere. A family who might make some claim on her girls, or wish to punish her, or them, for bearing them while still legally his wife. To go to them for help might one day be necessary, but to do so she would have to accept the title of mistress, or worse. What if they called her whore in front of her beloved daughters?

Remembering the women in Portugal, Louisa supplemented her income with embroidery. A local seamstress cut out the gowns and passed them to Louisa who decorated bodices, hems, cuffs or collars with winding trails of the flowers found in the nearby hedgerows. The seamstress never revealed who her talented embroiderer was and Louisa assiduously avoided any fame that might have come her way.

Sewing for a living was hard and often strained her eyes, but she had no other skill. The long dark nights of winter were the worst. When the girls were asleep, she would lie awake beside them and remember a time when Sam had run his rough hands over her and just having him close had made her complete. She was raw with missing him, but life was so hard and so exhausting her memories were fading, and the pain of acknowledging that was almost as bad as finding him frozen to the ground. And then at other times her mind cycled endlessly with anger and recriminations. How dare he leave her! How dare he die so young! Only when her mind became completely exhausted did she then fall asleep, to awake feeling dull and once more aware of how alone she was. Fuelling herself with anger, she forced the girls into their routines and attacked the world with fine needles and pretty yarns.

Then the Causton estate pension stopped. The bank, where she had drawn funds once a quarter did not know why, and Louisa did not know who else to ask. For a year life was possible, but gradually it became a case of endurance. Miss B's money had gone and the girls would not stop growing, shoe repair became impossible as those they had fell to pieces, their lessons were now being rendered as charity, and meat became first a weekly and then a monthly treat. Embroidery could not pay for food, lodgings, and three hungry women.

When she had her interview at the bank, the man there pointed out that Chantel, Sam's little sister, had grown up enough to marry a duke. Louisa had been shocked and surprised by the news. It frightened her. Was this another high-ranking person who could claim her daughters? She lost sleep worrying about what to do, but as she listened to Samantha cry quietly with hunger, she came to a decision. A week later, Louisa left her home with her rent overdue and whatever the three of them could carry and began to walk. She knew which county, and the home of a duke was never a secret, so they simply followed a road out of Bristol and headed north. It was amazing how, faced with starvation for the three of them, losing her girls seemed a small matter. At least the souls she loved more than life itself wouldn't cry themselves to sleep because of hunger any longer if she could help it. She was now prepared to beg.

PART FOUR

'Sorry is the hardest word.'

Chapter 11

Xavier rode up the drive to Daughton Court, the main residence of the dukedom, with his guts in knots. He found his emotional situation amusing. From the age of twelve the fear that had stalked the back of his mind had been that once under fire, he might disintegrate and prove himself a coward. He remembered vividly waiting for his first battle engagement. After, when he had dunked his head into a horse trough to wash off some of the dust, dirt, blood, sweat and goodness knows what else, he had held his head under so no one might see his grin of relief. He had always been destined for the army; what else could a third son do? He found battle to his taste. The fear beforehand was tempered with the heavy responsibility of being aware of his orders and of manoeuvring his men, and once battle commenced, there was no fear. Only grit and determination and exhilaration. He wasn't going to take his mind back to the butcher's bills he had submitted, the friends he had lost, the blasted bodies he had witnessed. Now, in fact never, was the time to think about that. But here he was, as screwed to the point as immediately before that first battle. He was sure the Fates were laughing.

But the truth was, he had two half sovereigns to his name. If he wasn't fed and lodged tonight, but chucked out on his arse, he was for sleeping under a hedge in his greatcoat and with air for his dinner. If he hadn't run out of options and ideas, under no circumstances would he be putting himself through this. Joshua's father had once employed him to be, effectively, his son's jailer. He had hated the task and had taken it out on young Joshua.

He didn't even have a card. He stood on the step outside the front door of intricately carved and battered wood, and simply asked if His Grace would see Xavier Hawksworth. Then waited to see if he was ushered into the hall or kicked back out onto the drive. As it was, he stood in a draughty hall staring at dull paintings for a good thirty minutes before being ushered into what was clearly a large study. Joshua sat behind a solid and long table. To Xavier's surprise his wife sat alongside him with her own piles of documents. Hence the table rather than a desk, he supposed. Her Grace on first glance was a small woman of pleasant features with glossy black curls and dark piercing eyes. Joshua himself was clearly far slimmer and fitter looking but had lost a quantity of hair. Xavier stood, feet slightly apart and hands clasped behind his back. He felt rather like a schoolboy in front of his tutor.

'Xavier. I did not expect to see you again. So why do I have this pleasure?' Joshua did not look pleased. In fact, his fists were gripped so tightly they were white and his face was rigid with dislike.

Xavier coughed. 'I have come to see you for two reasons. One I need a job and two, even if I didn't, I needed for my own conscience to come and apologise. I behaved abominably towards you and I have no excuse. My behaviour was neither that of a gentleman nor that of an officer and I utterly disgraced myself.'

To his relief Joshua's fists had relaxed. Xavier had supposed he would have to simply take it if Joshua swung at him, but he was cold, and hungry and tired and didn't look forward to a broken nose or bleeding mouth. Mouth wounds were the very devil.

The interview went better than Xavier expected and to his relief he was escorted to a guest bedroom, a minor one, (at least he hadn't been put with the servants!) and invited to stay for dinner.

The following day more visitors arrived. Xavier was walking in the grounds, making himself scarce until Joshua had time for him, when he saw a bedraggled group of servants trailing up the main drive. He kept out of sight and watched as they were admitted. They looked even more depleted set against the deliberately imposing, if uncared for, front entrance. He was mildly surprised that they hadn't been sent around to the back entrance, but it wasn't his place to reason why. And he wasn't sure his status wasn't equally as lowly as theirs. Right that moment, greeting servants as another servant was rather more than his pride could manage.

Louisa gave her name as Lady Douglas McCloud and hoped beyond hope it would get them through the door. A couple of huge footmen eyed them suspiciously, though she bitterly wondered what harm a woman and a couple of girls could do to the duke and duchess.

The duchess was a small and brisk and the power of her personality arrived first. 'Yes?' she asked abruptly.

Louisa had the sense that the woman had been called from doing something far more important than greeting grubby visitors. Probably looking at fashion plates, she thought viciously. Despite the time between deciding to come and arriving, Louisa was suddenly bereft of an explanation. It was Elena who spoke up. 'I am your niece. Your brother Samuel's daughter. As is my sister, Samantha.'

'Really,' Chantel stated flatly, frowning at Louisa.

'We did meet, but rarely,' murmured Louisa. 'Your mother and father would visit, even dine with us. Then your mother became ill and so it was mostly your father who came over to the Dower House.'

The hall was beginning to spin and oddly, the stone flags in the hall were suddenly spongy. She felt Samantha slide an arm along hers to steady her. Chantel looked up to frown at Elena.

'Humph,' she said. 'Samuel.'

Everything moved fast then. They were ushered up into a suite of rooms. Washing water and food arrived and once clean and fed, all three climbed into one of the canopied beds, holding tightly to each other and fell asleep. It might be early afternoon, but the time of day was hugely unimportant to them at that moment.

The inquisition came the following morning. After eating a breakfast that had been sent to their rooms, Louisa and her girls were ushered into the drawing room by a footman, who was clearly their self-appointed guardian to ensure they did not steal the silver.

Chantel waved an arm at the sofa opposite her seat, 'Please sit. Then perhaps you will explain why you are here.'

Louisa moved to the sofa and sat. Elena moved behind and to one side of her, standing with her hand resting gently on Louisa's shoulder. Samantha sat beside her and took one of her hands. Louisa couldn't have felt more proud of her girls. She lifted her chin and ensured her spine was ram-rod straight.

'So, explain again who you are,' Chantel was asking with a frown.

Louisa swallowed, 'I am Lady Rupert Douglas McCloud she began. I believe I am addressing Her Grace, The Duchess of Daughton, formerly Miss Chantel Causton.' A nod was the response. 'I was your brother, Samuel's mistress until he died. These girls are his daughters.'

'Well. I had not given you a thought,' Chantel said. No, thought Louisa. It is clear that you didn't. 'But I do remember a woman, a companion to Miss B. She was a widow, with a daughter, but I rarely saw the daughter, was rarely in company with either of them.'

'I bore Samuel Elena before I was legally a widow, and Samantha after. Which I am now, by the way. You were just a girl, and a man's mistress is kept away from his legitimate family. Why would you pay any attention to us? The whole of Causton was told I was a widow with children and it was a fiction everyone at the time held to.'

'Despite the fact that you bore Samuel two children while there was no evidence of a husband?'

'People believe what they find comfortable. The truth was plain for all to see, but Sir William and Samuel owned everything for miles around. Who had the nerve to deny it? And Samuel was loved, both as a landlord and a friend.'

Chantel's eyes moved to take in Elena as if measuring her height. 'Sam's girls, are you?' she queried.

Louisa repeated the introductions. 'This is Elena Claire, my eldest girl, named for your mother, and my youngest, here is Samantha, named for her father.'

'I never met him!' Samantha said sharply.

Louisa gave her a sharp look, but it was Chantel who addressed her directly, 'And why was that?'

Louisa could see that Chantel was thinking that Samuel had cast them off before her birth.

'He died. He fell off his horse and was frozen. I was born posthumously.'

Louisa was pleased to see consternation on Chantel's face. If anyone had told her that she would one day be faced with begging for help from Sam's unruly little sister, she would have laughed in their face. Yet here she was.

Chantel was frowning as Louisa continued, 'My husband was Lieutenant Colonel of the 44th Foot. Miss Buckley's brothers in Cambridge had been watching the lists and it was they who informed us that my husband had died. Samuel was on his way to the church to have our banns read. We had received a letter only the day before that meant we were free to marry. He adored Elena,' she added.

'But not me!' Samantha insisted. 'If he had loved me, he would have lived.'

Chantel drew in a breath. 'My brother was a kind and loving man. Had he lived, he would have loved you. He loved me, and I once put a smelly fish in his bed.'

'Did you?' Samantha asked with interest.

'How did you meet?' Chantel demanded.

'I had run away from my husband. Samuel found me and took me to live with Miss Buckley. We fell in love. We couldn't marry, but that seemed unimportant. We lived in half of The Dower House, and Miss B lived in the other half. We had Elena, and were happy. Then he died.'

'I had little sense of your existence. Why are you here now?'

Despite Chantel's reassuring words to Samantha, her voice was still that of an interrogator. Louisa had already conceived a dislike of the younger woman. The door opened and Louisa turned instinctively towards the movement. A man, she presumed Chantel's husband, the duke, entered and went to stand behind Chantel, mirroring Elena. He said nothing, so Louisa continued.

'After Samuel died, your father set us up with a pension, paid from a bank in Bristol. Later, we had to move from Causton as without your father and Samuel to protect us, we were vilified with gossip. You had already been sent to Bath. Life became intolerable. Initially, we settled in a cottage in Bristol, mainly to be near to the bank. Almost two years ago, the pension suddenly stopped, and when I enquired, the bank said they had no information. I had some money, so we have been living on that, but now that has run out, we are, not to put too fine a point on it, starving. You are our only hope. The girls are too young yet to find posts and I am too frail.' Louisa certainly felt frail.

'Joshua, Duke of Daughton,' the man abruptly introduced himself. 'Did you walk here from Bristol'.

'We did sometimes receive lifts,' Elena offered softly. 'On the back of a carts, but people were never going far. But we were very grateful.'

'Why didn't you write?' Chantel asked.

'Why would I? The girls and I were hidden from you as much as possible, and why would you have believed me? I thought once you had seen Elena, there was a chance you would believe I was telling the truth.'

Chantel only frowned, and Louisa's heart sank. She had absolutely nothing to prove her story except Elena's striking resemblance to Sam. She could be any woman off the street. The last time Chantel had even glimpsed her had been years ago, and they were all much changed. Perhaps they were to be shown the door. To her surprise Chantel said,

'Well, for the moment you are welcome to stay. Especially as I was the one to cancel the pension. There was nothing to explain it and so I didn't see why the estate should pay it. I will, of course, immediately reinstate it.'

And that, it seemed, was that. Dinner was to be at seven and they were free to explore; there was a library and of course the grounds. Chantel and Joshua left them then as abruptly, and bad manneredly, as they had arrived. Louisa wanted to remind her girls never to behave in such a fashion, but the huge footman who reminded her of a Viking Berserker remained in the room, so she bit her tongue. Louisa was fairly certain that they would not be out of his sight for the foreseeable future.

Xavier was also interviewed that morning. He was called into the joint study and was asked if he might consider the role of estate manager. As he had been prepared to accept a role far more menial than that as long as he was fed and housed, and it had occurred to him that Joshua might take out some justified spite in offering a post as footman or some such, Xavier accepted without further thought. It seemed there was an estate in Somerset, where the farms flooded every winter but offered excellent grazing in the summer, and he was to research what alterations, if any, might be required to improve management. He was to stay a month and construct a report. As he stood like a school boy once again it occurred to him that a report already existed, and his work would be compared to it. And as he knew square root of fresh air about estate management this was a serious challenge. He walked out of the room feeling relieved and, to his surprise, rather excited. He headed for the library. He had some urgent research to conduct.

Louisa and the girls came down to dinner with trepidation. They owned just the dresses they stood up in. They had left Bristol with more, but as the journey had turned into a trudge of putting one foot ahead of the other, stomachs had passed far beyond rumbling, and light-headedness had set in for hour after hour, clothing had been either sold, exchanged for food, or if neither of those options were possible, discarded, until they between them had some underwear each and one or two possessions that they couldn't bear to part with. For Louisa that had been Sam's gift of a hairbrush. And Lord knew, three women needed a hairbrush. The dust had been beaten out of their clothing, they were clean and decently anticipating a meal rather than dying for it, and so they lifted their chins and attempted to make the best of it.

Dinner, it seemed, was to be in a grand style. The table was laden with porcelain and silver, which surprised Louisa. Chantel and Joshua appeared to be rather plain people, in manners and in dress. However, she supposed a previous generation had probably supplied both the table and the service. When she looked closer, however, the porcelain was mismatched and the silver, though highly polished, battered. There was a number of people that Louisa, Elena and Samantha were introduced to in the drawing room before they entered the dining room. There had been a general agreement that they were to be known as Mrs Causton and her daughters. Louisa was glad to shed the name of Bland and being given the family name seemed to suggest that Joshua and Chantel would not cast them off.

The girls were to remain for the meal and then retire, as they were of an age to behave and there was no governess to join them upstairs for a meal. Most of the faces over dinner blurred to Louisa. She still felt exhausted from the journey, and her feet, knees and hips ached abominably from the miles they had endured. However, there was a dark-haired, dark-browed man of above average height who stood rather like a military man, introduced as Lieutenant Hawksworth. She didn't expect him to pay her any particular attention, but the fact that he clearly hardly noticed her existence when they were introduced flicked at her pride. She had been young once, and reasonably attractive, even, perhaps, lovely with the gleam of youth. His behaviour hurt unreasonably. It forced home on her how bleak and lonely her life had become and she felt that she had entered the realm of the 'overlooked woman of middle years'.

Xavier had indeed hardly noticed her existence. As the woman had nothing to recommend her, he ignored her. He was himself exhausted, brought on by needing to stoop so low he had to beg for employment. His pride was badly wounded.

When the plates were cleared, Louisa took her leave with the girls. She had no conversation and pleaded tiredness. As she climbed the wide stairs, she thought that it was no more than the truth. If she slept for a month, she wasn't sure she would feel any improvement. Xavier watched the three of them leave the room with a frown, and then forgot them.

He left for Somerset the following morning. He had a set amount of time and some living expenses and more importantly, a challenge. He was more than ever certain that he was the second man to be sent to investigate Somerset and he was determined not to be beaten.

Two evenings later, Louisa was at her embroidery sitting close under a candle. Dinner had been cleared away, Joshua was making snuffling noises as he dozed, and Chantel was, as always, frowning over some paper or another. Louisa wanted to scream. The house seemed dull, the rooms pointlessly vacant, the routine even more spirit-sapping, since Hawksworth had blown in and then left. He had been a gust of life, of energy, and given a glimpse of the outside world. The words escaped her mouth before she had properly considered them.

'Did His Grace meet Lieutenant Hawksworth in the army?'

Without looking up Chantel replied, 'Call him Joshua, dear. You are family now.'

Blood roared in Louisa's head. To be called 'dear' by a woman so much younger, and her beloved Samuel's irritating little sister, was beyond enough. And nothing had altered. She wasn't family 'now'; if she was family now, she had always been family. She swallowed hard. 'So, was it the army?' She had never met anyone less 'army' than Joshua, Duke of Daughton.

At this Chantel did look up. 'No. Joshua's father was concerned about Joshua going into society, so he employed Hawksworth as his companion.'

Well! That doesn't explain much, Louisa thought. 'A companion?' she asked, as evenly as possible.

Chantel sighed, and looked at her properly for the first time.

Glancing at Joshua to ensure he was fully asleep, which he confirmed with a shuddering snore, she bit her bottom lip. 'I may as well explain, as you will hear plenty of gossip in town. Joshua's father considered him incapable as he had trouble reading and writing. His father was intolerant and had him beaten for his failure, rather than try to discover why. As you know, Joshua now wears glasses for reading. Because of what his father saw as his imbecility, he was concerned that he might be taken advantage of, so hired Hawksworth to accompany him to social events in the evening.'

'I see,' said Louisa. Though she wasn't sure that she did. But she let it drop. Clearly that was all she was to be told at the moment.

She was not to know Chantel's thoughts as she climbed the stairs much later, which centred around relief that she had brushed through that question. Bitterly resenting his being hired as a spy, still deeply wounded from being pushed out of the army, Xavier had bullied Joshua unmercifully, generally pushing drink on him so that he fell unconscious and he could be free of his charge. Joshua seemed to have forgiven him, but she thought it would be a cold day in hell before she did.

Chapter 12

For Louisa, time slowed down. There was nothing to do. Her fingernails grew to a pretty length for the first time in years, her aches and pains slowly melted away, and Chantel, having grilled her alone for what had felt like days but had actually only been half a day, had given her an allowance to allow her to begin to rebuild a wardrobe for the three of them. With the help of a local seamstress, they now possessed a variety of garments and footwear. Life was immeasurably better, but Louisa was depressed and bitter. She had lost control over her own life, and in reality, that of her girls, and life was dull. She was finding the role of a reluctantly accepted poor relation difficult.

Elena was content. She had clothes that reached the floor and her wrists, her embroidery, and an estate in which to take the air. Samantha was another story. Bored, she took to picking exhausting arguments with either her sister or, more likely, her mother. Where Elena took her bad temper and simply smiled back at her, too wise to either rise to the bait or become impatient, Louisa was the opposite. Samantha's goading had her lashing out, spurred on by years of worry, frustration with her current situation, and anxiety about their futures. Their rows could be heard through half the house, and it was a large house.

Chantel, hearing them one day cocked an ear and calmly remarked to Joshua, not for the first time, that Samantha sounded so like she had done at a similar age. It was Samantha who broke the deadlock by accident. She had been hanging off a ladder looking for something to read in the library that wasn't a religious treatise or book about the geography and farming practises of the counties of England, when Joshua wandered in. He had been hiding from Chantel and looking for a quiet place to curl up and enjoy a nap for an hour or two. Instead, he was accosted by an intense young woman who demanded to know why his library held no volumes of mathematics. 'Why not indeed?' he had murmured and drifted out again, Chantel's throw-away comment about her 'similarity' in his mind.

Chantel wasted no time. She had Samantha settled with a page of mathematics within the hour, the questions of increasing complexity as the page went on. Samantha simply ignored most of the page and settled with the last half dozen questions, striding into the room where Chantel and Joshua worked to point out where Chantel's design of the final question had a mistake. Chantel had taken the wind out of her sales with a brisk, 'I know,' and had then passed the girl a page of workings by an Austrian mathematician she was corresponding with. As the girl whisked out, Joshua had viewed Chantel's smug smile, and thought that losing the chance of a nap was a small price to pay for a harmonious household.

Chantel and Joshua rarely entertained, it seemed. Visitors were greeted cordially but return visits rarely undertaken, until even the most-pushy of the local gentry withdrew. Life was quiet and dull. Louisa had obtained lengths of fabric and was enthusiastically building a wardrobe for her girls, especially Elena. It was clear in order for the three of them to have any kind of life or independence, Elena had to marry well. Louisa didn't spell it out loud and Elena didn't need the explanation. She was ready to do her duty. She wasn't only like Samuel in looks, she also had his calm disposition. Louisa was prepared to sacrifice her eldest daughter, but only if the man was guaranteed kind. Under no circumstances was her precious Elena to be handed to a man like Rupert. How they were going to find a man was uncertain, but willpower would manage, she was sure. She had survived so much she would not be defeated in this. So, Xavier's return sent a ripple of interest through her, not for his marriageability, he was far too hard and cynical-looking for her beloved Elena, but simply for the change in routine.

On his part, Xavier took time only to wash and have the worst of the dust brushed off his clothes before he submitted his report to Joshua and Chantel. He retired to clean up properly but was recalled before he had quite managed the task. His report had already been read, digested and approved. Joshua, he was sure, was not the assessor. He had none of the intense intelligence that rose off Chantel in waves. He was now well aware that the real power of the dukedom was the duchess. Quite what role she allowed Joshua to play was unclear. Xavier felt, not for the first time, rather sorry for the man.

Louisa ensured that both she and her girls were dressed in their best for Xavier's first dinner back. Not because she had given him a thought, but who knew whom he might know? Every new face was an opportunity to be investigated. And one day they needed to escape this dreary life. The moment Elena and Samantha took their leave from the table and were out of the room, Chantel abruptly called down the table to Xavier, 'So why did you leave the army?'

'I resigned my commission,' was Xavier's bland reply.

'Not good enough,' Chantel told him flatly.

Xavier swallowed. Right at that moment he detested the arrogant, mannerless woman. And then he thought how like many of the officers he had known she was. 'You would have fitted perfectly into the Officers' Mess of my regiment,' he told her with a faint smile.

'Oh, I would have wiped the floor with the lot of them,' was Chantel's brisk reply. And then they both laughed. And the atmosphere around the table lightened.

Still smiling, but now ruefully, Xavier sighed and said, 'I suppose it is public knowledge. I seduced a Colonel's lady, which is decidedly bad ton, and I was, not to put too fine a point on it, asked to move regiments or resign my commission. If I had moved regiments, any kind of respect would have been lost before I arrived, so I did what felt like the most honourable thing in the circumstances.'

'It wasn't Grace St John, was it?' Louisa asked suddenly.

Xavier gave her a look of sharp surprise. To Chantel's amusement, he seemed rather embarrassed. Clearly it hadn't occurred to him that anyone might be able to identify the lady from his comment.

'Ah, yes. Did you know her?'

Everyone around the table was hanging onto every word now. 'I did,' Louisa confirmed, 'and knowing the lady, you were more sinned against than sinning.' Her face had lit up with a brilliant laughing smile and altered her completely from a thin-faced nonentity into a lovely woman. Xavier was shocked by a wave of sexual attraction.

'Were you with the same regiment? I don't remember you.' Xavier said.

'No. Our regiment, however, entertained yours on a number of occasions. I heard about her before I married; my father was a major, and after my marriage I was fascinated to meet her. She was stunningly lovely.'

Louisa didn't add, and with a reputation as long as my arm. Xavier might not be aware of it, but Grace had destroyed more than one army career. There couldn't be many colonels' wives like her who preyed on and ate young Lieutenants for breakfast.

Xavier gave a sudden start, 'Good grief. You are Rupert's runaway wife!'

Louisa had frozen. 'He is dead, isn't he?' she asked, rather panicked.

'As a doornail. And no one misses him. When Rupert returned without you the gossipmongers decided he had murdered you. His Colonel, horrified at the gossip, asked quietly around all the other regiments for you.'

'Did he?' Louisa looked appalled at the thought.

'Well yes. People began to talk openly about how you were always bruised and either limping or having an arm tied up. Once his brutality to you became common gossip, the regiment felt it had let you down, and worse, the gossip about a murdering Lieutenant Colonel became rampant. Your Colonel was the one who put you up for marriage, wasn't he?' Louisa nodded, now looking aghast.

Joshua spoke up, 'What do you mean, put her up for marriage?'

'Her father was a serving officer,' explained Xavier. 'Her mother died suddenly and he got so drunk he could hardly stand. Lost everything he owned that night gambling, then fell into a winter stream while on his way home. He died of exposure. Young Louisa here had grown up following the regiment with her parents. The Colonel decided, as she had no other relatives, to marry her off to one of the officers. Rupert wanted her the most and won her.' He turned and said, 'Given the chance I might have offered for you myself. I wouldn't have been much of a catch, but I wouldn't have kicked and beaten you.'

Louisa gave a wry smile at the comment. There had been other Lieutenants at the time who could have sacrificed themselves but had chosen not to. But it had been a gentlemanly thing to say. Joshua was watching Xavier with narrowed eyes. He still didn't trust the man completely, but it had been a pretty comment.

Later that night, Xavier sat with Joshua after the women had retired. The atmosphere between them remained strained, and Xavier wished to mend bridges. He had come to the realisation that he wanted the kind of future Joshua could give him. But, to achieve that, they had to move past his appalling behaviour to Joshua in their previous lives. Mind you, Xavier told himself, Joshua had been no angel either. Also, he was oddly interested in the thin, rather quiet woman called Louisa.

'I take it that the woman introduced to me as Mrs Causton is a relic of one of the duchesses' brothers?' he asked.

'Well, yes, in a way,' Joshua prevaricated. Then shrugged and added, 'It is an honorary title; they were never married.'

'She was with him before her husband died? She was his mistress?'

Xavier's eyebrows were raised. She hadn't looked the mistress type. On the contrary, she appeared somewhat forbidding rather than flirtatious.

'She had left the husband and I am not sure how, but Samuel, the duchess's eldest brother found her. She lived with him for a number of years.'

'So, are the girls Rupert's?'

'No, no, they are Caustons to their fingertips. That brat, the young one, is a severe trial. Too bright by half, my wife says. The elder is the spit, apparently, of the brother. Indigent relatives; father always had a few hanging around.'

Xavier slid a look towards Joshua, but he didn't seem to mean anything particularly disparaging about his wife's relatives in his comment, so Xavier wisely kept his tongue behind his teeth. They sat in companionable silence for a while watching the flames in the fire as Xavier scratched around in his memory for the gossip that had lingered long after Rupert has so carelessly mislaid his wife. The memory, when it did come, was like a sharp blade piercing his mind.

'Grace told me, pillow talk you understand, that Rupert kicked a baby out of her. And she was with child again when she ran away.'

Joshua stared at him. 'Seriously?'

Xavier nodded. 'There is something you need to check.'

'Check?' Joshua asked with a frown.

'Rupert's title was a Scottish one. Rum lot the Scots. Fight like the devil but have some odd customs. His father is an Earl, and I believe he is still alive. Some Scottish titles pass down the distaff side.' He lifted his eyes and gazed at Joshua.

'But Elena and Samantha are not this Rupert's,' Joshua pointed out.

'Not his get, no, but possibly his legally. They were born while Louisa was still married to Rupert, therefore, they are legitimate. I am not saying it is true, but Elena could be on the way to inherit whatever Rupert's father has to leave. Not sure it would be very much but although Rupert wasn't an only child, like you, any brothers predeceased him. I seem to remember that was part of the hoo-ha when the Colonel was looking for your Mrs Causton. There was a widespread belief that she could have been carrying his heir.'

'Grief!' muttered Joshua. What on earth was he going to do about this? He would discuss it with Chantel.

The following morning, Louisa greeted Xavier at the breakfast table with a wide smile before she thought to stop it. This cynical and taciturn man and she had a common thread; the army. Before her face could freeze, he suddenly smiled back. It was so unexpected, Louisa blushed, and had no idea why. From then on, they became polite acquaintances, and began to exchange the common-place comments that people use who regularly run into one another.

For Xavier, Louisa's rare smiles brightened his day, just as her rows with Samantha hurt his ears. Even in the army he had never heard two women who could tear into each other as they could. In public, Louisa was as quiet and reserved as a nun. When the doors were closed and Samantha was shrieking at her, Louisa could give as good as she got. More than once he and Joshua stood at the bottom of the stairs with their eyes upwards waiting to hear if china was to be flung. The footmen who stood with them always struggled to hide their grins. Samantha was a favourite of theirs for some reason. Xavier would ride away afterwards wondering about the woman who was in his thoughts far more than she should be. Her public persona attracted him, though he wasn't sure why. She behaved as mild as milk around him. But the woman who yelled back at Samantha was full of passion, fury and, he suspected, frustration. The more he considered it the more he began to realise how trapped she must feel. This was a woman who had lived her life amidst the noise and turmoil of the army, who had borne Douglas McCloud's beatings without a murmur, escaped, become a man's mistress and then raised two girls on her own. And for all of the voluble rows, Samantha was a credit to her mother in public. Thinking about her kept his mind busy on many a long, lonely journey.

He surprised himself with how much he did think about her. On arrival at a new estate to investigate he found himself often considering it first through Louisa's eyes. Might she like the house? Might she enjoy the countryside here? Was it too flat? Too hilly? Was there society to join in and enjoy? Only then did he ask himself the same questions. He often shook his head at his own foolishness, telling himself that he was indeed looking to settle somewhere, but not necessarily with Louisa. He wasn't sure he convinced himself.

For Louisa, Xavier's constant comings and goings gave interest to her days. When his boot heels could be heard moving rapidly across the hall, she always lifted her head and gave a small smile. Dinner would now be enlivened with tales of his travels. Samantha hectored him mercilessly for stories of the outside world; what places looked like, who he had met, what he had noticed. For his part, Xavier was more than tolerant of Samantha, and gentle and kind to Elena, who while quieter in her enjoyment of his tales had clearly warmed to him; he often ignored Samantha's insistent demands to turn and give his attention back to her.

To Louisa's relief, he appeared to understand Elena's sweet and gentle nature. Louisa was grateful. Elena could be too quiet and shy, but conversing with Xavier was good practice for her for when she made her come out into society and begin her hunt for an eligible husband. How that was to be, Louisa had no idea. But she was determined to make it happen. Her lovely girl deserved a future. She wasn't sure what Samantha deserved. She wondered about her and whether a man had been born yet who could tame her unruly and fierce nature. How it was possible to love someone so much who could drive her insane with frustration, was beyond her. Deep in her memory she remembered Genny, back in the Peninsula, commenting something similar about her offspring. For the moment, she wondered what had become of all of them, then subdued the thought. Like the men who hadn't returned from battle, some things were best not thought about.

Watching her face, Xavier wondered what the mostly reserved Mrs Causton was thinking about. It was rare for her to allow emotion to show. When Louisa raised her eyes to his, perhaps sensing his regard, she blushed, and Xavier felt a shot of emotion himself. She wasn't immune to him. Louisa was becoming sensitive to his presence, and the weight of his gaze when he thought she wouldn't notice. However, she did her best to put his regard in its correct context. She was a woman approaching forty and almost certainly older than him. And he was changing too. He seemed more comfortable in his own skin. He looked well, and he smiled more. And the way he handled her two such different girls had her undying gratitude. His constant comings and goings brought a much-needed breath of life into the whole house.

Xavier was beginning to fathom the workings of The Court and to disapprove of them. More, he began to believe that Louisa disapproved as much as he did. Oh, she did not say a word, but more than once he thought he spotted a look of distaste cross her face. The household was positively rackety. There was no butler, such duties were carried out interchangeably by one of the large senior footmen. The blonde Viking, he now knew was Hugo, while the dark-haired one was Toby. To his horror, they called the duchess, 'Miss'. She, in her turn, called them by their names. They were always utterly polite to him and he suspected no condescension in their manner, on the contrary, they were always cheerful and willing to help. He had come to the conclusion that the fault was that they were seriously untrained in the proper duties of a ducal household. The fact that, from her expression, Louisa thought the same as he did, caused him to warm to her further.

Late in the summer, Louisa was in the main drawing room when Xavier returned to report on his latest spell of estate management. He went as always immediately to the study and she heard the door close from where she had gone to stand by the open door above the stairs. She returned to her seat by the window and gazed out, unable to concentrate on her sewing, or anything else for that matter. She felt over-aware and rather ashamed of how Xavier's return had affected her. Elena was trying to teach Samantha to play the pianoforte by running her fingers up and down the arm of a chair and hadn't appeared to notice her sudden interest in who was crossing the hall below.

'For goodness' sake, girls. Go to the music room and practise there. How on earth is Samantha supposed to understand your fingering on a sofa arm?'

Her voice was unnecessarily sharp. The girls looked at each other, laughed, and skittered out of the room. She didn't then see Xavier until dinner, and then she attempted to ignore him apart from civil niceties.

Once or twice, she felt his gaze on her, but she refused to be discomforted by him, or rather, was too proud to let him see her discomfort. She needed more society. Stranded in this house she was becoming far too interested in the only man who came and went. That was all it was.

The following afternoon, she received her wish. Louisa was surprised to hear the maids muttering about yet another army officer arriving. She slipped up to her room and hiding behind the curtain peered out towards the front drive. Deep inside she still feared that all reports of Rupert's death were a mistake and he might one day suddenly appear. The thought of his rage, if he discovered that his legal wife and chattel had delivered two children from another man, still had the ability to freeze the breath in her chest until she thought she would suffocate. But the man out on the drive, standing by his horse and facing away from the house was definitely not Rupert. Weak with relief she returned downstairs to hide away once more in the little morning room she had made her own.

All that afternoon there were whisperings and the very air of the house seemed to shiver with secrets. At dinner the soldier, a Major Lord James Causton, who it seemed was Chantel's brother, was introduced. Clearly, he had been informed previously that he would be introduced to a 'Mrs Causton', relic of his eldest brother. He said little, smiled mildly, and filled the room with a quiet presence that was diametrically at odds with the brittle irritation that often hung around Chantel. Both Elena and Samantha were clearly charmed by him and appeared unintimidated by the man's size. He was huge. Louisa took her cue from them, and bobbed a small curtsey. Often her girls had a better sense of who was safe than she did, her response coloured as it was by what she knew were often irrational fears.

Major Causton had, it appeared, not just arrived to reintroduce himself to an estranged sister but to inform Chantel of their brother's death. He had visited Causton Manor only to spend a little time with Lucien before he died. Xavier had, incorrectly, assumed that Chantel would be impervious to any such news. The opposite was clearly true. She was not seen for two whole days, and when she reappeared, she seemed thin and fragile. Joshua was quietly solicitous and it occurred to Xavier that perhaps they were closer emotionally than he had assumed. Neither the death, nor the reappearance of a long-lost brother were publicly discussed.

James stayed only a few days. He seemed to spend most of it either in bed asleep or napping in pools of sunlight wherever he found it. Xavier gazed with disfavour at what he considered a great lump of nothing stretching his legs out as he dozed all over the house. The man appeared to have zero personality. When he sent for his horse to travel off on yet another of Chantel's missions, he discovered that, early as it was, James had already left. Xavier was glad. The silent bear of a man had got under his skin somewhat.

To his surprise, Samantha appeared at his side as he checked his horse over before he left. She stood, hands clasped behind her back, swaying slightly from side to side. Xavier straightened and gazed down his nose at her. She grinned up at him.

'Good morning,' she began.

'Good morning.'

'Where are you going?'

'Nottinghamshire, to do some work for the duchess.'

'May I come with you?' From behind her back, she brought out a small satchel.

Xavier leaned forward and pinched her nose lightly. 'No, you may not, brat.' Her grin widened. 'And why might you wish to accompany me?'

Samantha gave it some thought. 'It is exceedingly dull here.'

'Why might Nottinghamshire be any different?'

'I want to see the world. It would be a start,' she tacked on brightly.

He turned and swung into his saddle. Looking down from the height of his horse he told her, 'Be good, and take care of your Mama. She is precious.'

'Is she?' queried the devil child. He grinned and moved his horse forward gently. To his left, her mother stood in the deep early morning shade of the doorway. He lifted his whip and touched his hat as he looked at her. To his surprise, she lifted a hand slowly to shoulder height in farewell. Louisa watched as he increased the speed of the horse and trotted out of view.

'What were you saying to Mr Hawksworth?' she asked Samantha.

'Oh, I thought he might make a suitable Papa.'

Louisa went cold. 'Did you indeed. And what did he say to the idea?'

Samantha was blithe, 'Oh, I haven't asked him yet. I was going to if he had taken me with him, but he didn't.' She stopped her skipping retreat for a moment and turned back to Louisa. 'He did say you were precious though. I am not sure why.' Samantha gave her mother a critical once over, gave her head a small shake, and continued to skip away.

Infanticide, Louisa thought. That is the word for parents who murder their children, wasn't it? Infanticide. She re-entered the house and headed for her breakfast, wondering why, not for the first time, people thought children were a blessing.

Xavier returned a few days later, tired, dusty, but content. As he strode into the hall, soft scampering footsteps raced down the stairs and came to a skidding halt right in front of him. He stopped and gazed down and Samantha grinned back up at him. He recalled asking Joshua how old she was once, and he had answered, at least one hundred and twelve. He was beginning to understand the answer.

'Good afternoon,' she offered brightly, 'did you have a good trip?'

Xavier stood army straight and looked down his nose but the child refused to be cowed. 'The fair was on,' he informed her. And then reached into his capacious outer pocket. In his hand he now had two paper objects, one marked with a S and one with an E.

'No stealing your sister's,' he said firmly as he gave her two packets.

'But what if I like her packet more than my own?'

'One, you shouldn't open something addressed to someone else. Ever. And two, I shall know and will spank you.'

'No, you wouldn't,' said Samantha dismissively, and then, after thanking him prettily and bobbing a neat curtsey, she ran full pelt back up the stairs.

Xavier looked up to see Joshua heading towards him, hand outstretched.

'Exactly what is preventing us sending the devil child against our enemies?' Xavier asked rhetorically.

'We already are, only she doesn't know it. Chantel is working on a code with her. Seems the little beast is a mathematical prodigy.'

'Not what I would call her,' muttered Xavier, and they both laughed.

Nottingham was famous for its lace. As Louisa shook out the two lengths of trim she blinked at the quality. Both lengths were very fine. Samantha's was the plainest with an unusual geometric pattern, and Elena's was more delicate and incorporated flowers and butterflies. Elena was in raptures. Samantha was frowning at hers and trying to work out how it was made. But she seemed pleased. As for the bearer of the gifts, Louisa was frankly surprised. And her mind was whirling as she considered how to use the trim to its best advantage.

Chapter 13

Xavier was marching down the hall towards the main door when in his peripheral vision he saw Louisa sitting sewing in a patch of sunlight in one of the side parlours. He paused mid-step and reversed and entered the room. He had never before been able to catch her completely alone. She lifted her head and gave him a small nod in greeting and said, 'Thank you for the lace trim you bought the girls. It was very kind of you.'

He grunted, then said, 'I am never kind.'

Louisa gave a small smile and continued with her embroidery. It was rare that she didn't have the girls with her. He wasn't going to ask where they were; just as long as they didn't return, he didn't care. He stood for a moment gazing out of the window and knew that Louisa's cheeks had bloomed with a very slight blush. Excellent. He swung around as if to leave, but instead settled in a chair and stretched out his legs and crossed them at the ankles. Then he crossed his arms and closed his eyes, letting the world know he was napping. He had realised that if he wanted to be in a room without having to force a conversation it was an ideal posture. As he lay behind his closed eyes, he wondered about the brother, James, the big lout who dozed all over the house. And wondered about how many conversations he had listened in on while apparently not being present at all. Xavier began to revise his view of the man. It was Louisa who broke the silence.

'How are you enjoying being an estate manager?' she enquired.

Xavier gave an inward grin he hoped he gave no indication of on the outside. 'To my surprise, I am enjoying it. It would have driven me mad at seventeen when I joined the army, but now, I am finding it unexpectedly satisfying.'

She sighed and smiled. 'That was Elena and Samantha's father's occupation. Sam was the most gentle person you could meet. And kind. I adored him.'

Xavier closed his eyes again. He did not want to hear about the paragon of a dead not-quite husband. And besides, he believed himself to be selfish and at times brutal.

'But after a while,' she continued, 'I realised he had a core of iron, he needed one. In the army, if you tell someone what to do and you have the rank, they do it. But farmers appear to be an independent breed. They always called to mind for me the saying about the difficulty of herding cats.' Xavier couldn't help but smile to himself. But she was continuing, 'I then realised that being an estate manager and being an army officer was not so different. It took planning and organisation and the management of men. I began to respect him more, and that was when I truly fell in love with him.'

Xavier snapped his eyes closed and grunted. Bloody man. How could he compete with a bloody dead saint? Especially when his own faults were legion. The room fell quiet again. But he couldn't help himself. Through cracked lids he watched as she stitched away, head down and bathed in sunshine. She had a slight smile on her lips and looked far better than when he had first met her. She had put some weight on, and it suited her, removing that gaunt and grey look she had initially appeared with. He completely believed her story. She and the girls had been starving when they arrived, her most of all.

'Are you watching me?' she asked quietly.

'Yes,' he said, and had to grin. She hadn't lifted her head. 'Were you always an army brat?'

She stopped sewing and gazed into the middle distance. 'Yes. I was born in Ireland strangely enough. My father's regiment was there for a while. Then we went to India. We stayed there when Father was sent to the colonies, but he returned eventually and we were shipped to the Peninsula. That was where I married Rupert, but we were in Plymouth when I left him. He was to report there for a briefing before taking a coastal ship up to the north.'

Plymouth to Wiltshire! he thought, that was a hell of a distance. She had really wanted to put some miles between them. 'Did you enjoy India?'

Her face lit up. 'Oh yes. There was a pack of us, Indian and army children, all mixed up together. We would run around quite naked,' she shot him a wicked grin. 'Our Armahs said it saved on washing! Which made sense, as we were in the river and then in the mud over and over again. It was glorious. And the scents. I still smell India in my dreams sometimes, and see the luscious flowers in their multicoloured glory.'

He couldn't help but shoot her a sharp smile. He too had loved India. Quiet descended once more. Into the silence that had fallen like a heavy blanket between them he asked the question that had been dogging his nights. 'Do you think you will remarry?' He kept his eyes firmly closed and let the density of the silence between them surround his words.

Her voice was soft, "I am not sure. The girls are growing and will leave me one day. I miss Sam. I loved him dearly, and I am wondering if I should like some of that companionship again. It would take a lot of thinking about. I have had a taste of both the good and the bad.'

He opened his eyes in time to recognise that her cheekbones were flying two bright red flags before shutting them again rapidly. He did not wish to embarrass her. Not until they were in bed. He wondered what she would say if he simply came out and said it, 'I want you.' Would she be shocked, repulsed, or might it excite her? Her next question took him totally by surprise.

'Was Gloria very good? As a lover I mean?'

His face cracked into a wide delighted grin. Oh yes, she was the woman for him. His right hand twitched wanting to reach for her wrist and haul her upstairs to a room. Any room. They didn't need a bed, the way he felt a wall would do. As long as it was sturdy.

'Now,' he murmured, 'that would be telling.' She was grinning too, wickedly. He raised his eyebrows. So, Sam had been gentle had he. Well, he wasn't, and he knew in his bones she wouldn't mind one bit. He rose to his feet. He needed to leave. Now. And then he needed an income and a 'yes' to his proposal. He would even take on the girls. Even that bloody awkward Samantha.

A few days later Xavier was standing at the double doors to the dining room. It was a bright autumn day and shafts of gold cut across the room. At the table, Chantel had spread page after page of paper out, and was talking softly to Samantha. The both appeared utterly engrossed. Joshua joined Xavier at the door and enquired softly, 'Mathematics again?'

'Today the monster child and your duchess are exploring advanced mathematics.' Xavier's tone was especially dry. 'Samantha called me a dilettante the other day.'

'I am not sure I can spell dilettante,' Joshua said thoughtfully.

'Nor me,' muttered Xavier.

They both strode away and out into the breezy garden, glad they weren't expected to undertake such arcane activities. Xavier was glad that he and Joshua were beginning to forge a new friendship, leaving the scars of the past behind. It felt, liberating.

Xavier was finding it frustratingly hard to catch Louisa alone. In a house with so few inhabitants he had thought he could manoeuvre some time just with her with no great difficulty, but he was butting against increasing frustration. At least the girls had finally found some friends in the locality that they could hie off and spend time with, but even so, she was proving extraordinarily elusive. And then his chance came.

Louisa was returning from cutting flowers, her face tilted down and admiring the blooms. By the time she lifted her face, he was only a few steps away. She covered her start by saying, 'Good morning. How are you?'

'Well. And you look blooming.' Louisa offered a faint smile and made to go past him. 'Joshua has told me he will take you and the girls for a season eventually,' he told her. Anything to keep her close for a few moments.

'Yes, I hope he keeps his promise. And Elena told me you had been teaching her whist. She said you were extremely patient and kind. I have been meaning to thank you.'

He gave a disgusted grunt, 'I told you I am never kind.' Louisa smiled wryly up at him. 'Joshua came in and thought I was trying to seduce her. He nearly called me out.'

Louisa looked startled then said thoughtfully. 'Well, she is of marriageable age.'

This time the sound he made was utterly disgusted. 'She is a child! Any man who offends her will have half a dozen of us wanting to see him off.'

'You aren't looking for a chit to warm your nights, then?' she queried.

He leant forward and breathed warm air over her ear. 'No. Absolutely not. I want a woman.'

Louisa simply turned her head and gazed into now very close eyes. 'I have borne four children. I no longer have the body of a young woman,' she told him softly.

'Good. I want a body that is as luscious and ripe as a peach.'

She laughed at him. 'Do you indeed.' Her voice dropped low, 'Well I warn you my father was an army major. I grew up surrounded by men like yourself. I would wager I can fire a pistol faster and more accurately than you. And know which end of a knife is which and how and, more importantly, where to use it. My father loved me, and he was absolutely sure if he was not going to be around to defend me, I could care for myself. He was the same with my mother.'

With that she settled her basket of flowers more securely on her arm and walked around him and away. He watched her go and as she disappeared around the side of the house, he considered how his instincts had now been confirmed. She was the one he wanted. Just her. The question wasn't, did she want him? It was, did she want him enough?

Louisa was alone in the drawing room the following morning when the door opened and to her surprise Chantel walked in. The two women nodded to each other. Despite sharing a home for some months, they had not become friends and were each wary of the other. To Louisa, Chantel appeared austere and remote and she could not understand how such an easy-going man such as Joshua had been attracted to such a cold unattractive woman. For her part, Chantel thought Louisa a limp and wan nonentity.

Louisa did what she always did when forced to share a space with Chantel, she dipped her head over her embroidery and ignored her. She heard Chantel order tea and only lifted her head when the maid delivered it.

'Would you like a cup?' Chantel asked.

Louisa was parched. Partly it was nerves. She was on edge listening for Xavier, and wondering if she would see him before he returned to the estate he was working on. 'Yes, please,' she murmured.

Chantel sat sipping and gazing at Louisa over the rim of her cup.

'What on Earth are you working on? You never seem to stop.'

'Pillow case edges for one of the girls. I am trying to make a complete set of bed linen for both of them.' Louisa gazed back at Chantel, a slight challenge in her eyes. What did the woman expect her to do, stuck as she was in someone else's home? If she hadn't set herself an occupation, she might have gone mad. Apart from a brisk walk every afternoon that was all she did, she considered rather resentfully.

'You want them to marry, then?' Chantel's voice was somewhat challenging.

Louisa thought for a moment, 'Elena, yes. She is gentle and loving, just like her father. Samantha, perhaps not for a long while.' She hated being interrogated like this. She had lived much of her adult life alone, making her own decisions and answerable to no one. What she wouldn't give for her own hearth!

Chantel's next approach made her sit more upright in surprise. 'And what about you? You could return to society as Lady Doulas McCloud. You are young still and you could be more than presentable if you smiled once in a while.'

Louisa nearly gasped at the shock. Talk about pots and kettles. When did Chantel ever smile? 'Are you trying to marry me off? Get me out of your home?' Louisa couldn't help asking.

Chantel waved her hand as if batting off a fly. 'Good heavens no. This place will be horribly empty when you and the girls leave, I am certainly not hurrying you all away.'

But perhaps just me, she thought rather resentfully.

But Chantel hadn't finished. 'No, it is not that. I wanted you to consider that there are many men open to a marriage to a woman like you. I was on the town for some years, I do know what I am talking about.'

'Chantel, are you trying to advise me?' Louisa asked. To her amazement Chantel went rather pink.

'Yes,' she admitted, 'and doing a very bad job of it.' To Louisa's further surprise, Chantel laughed softly.

'You know, I am not the only one who looks better with a smile on her face,' Louisa offered gently.

Chantel shot her a rueful glance. 'Perhaps,' she agreed. 'It is just that you are under our roof, and I am concerned.'

'What about?'

'To be blunt, Xavier,' Chantel admitted.

Louisa looked at her curiously. 'What about Xavier?'

'For goodness' sake. His eyes follow you everywhere. Only I am not sure he is a very nice man.'

'You think he is attracted to me?'

'Oh, good heavens. Even the servants know how he feels. He wants you; it is as plain as the nose on your face. What worries me is that he reminds me of a stallion around a mare. Only stallions grip the mare fiercely by the back of the neck, and then once they are done, wander off.'

'Exhausted,' Louisa added to Chantel's description and, with a wicked look on her face, gave a delicious shudder.

Chantel's face registered a moment of shock, before she let out a laugh. Louisa had to join in. 'Perhaps you will cope, after all,' was Chantel's wry comment. 'I didn't tell you the whole truth about him. His job was not just to spy on Joshua, but to be his jailer, to all intents and purposes. He got him drunk regularly. It was his job to escort Joshua in the evenings. It was well known that his father had three sons, and so I suppose he found it prudent to let the third out occasionally.'

Louisa felt her face stiffen but she had to ask, 'Was Xavier cruel to Joshua?'

Chantel shook her head, 'He didn't beat him. He got him drunk. It was his brute of a valet who followed him everywhere in the day hours who was cruel. Joshua said he would cuff him around his head in the presence of his father and brothers.'

'Did Xavier get Joshua drunk? Or did he just not prevent it? If I had been living the life Joshua was living, I would have headed for the bottle too. And they seem to get on together now.'

Chantel looked thoughtful. 'I hadn't really thought about it like that,' she said after a while. 'But seriously, I don't think Xavier is the easiest man around. I am confident you could do better.'

'Because you think he will use me and then leave?' Louisa prodded.

'Yes. Even if he puts a ring on a woman's finger, I can't see him ever being a dutiful husband.'

'He is attractive, however,' Louisa felt she had to add. Personally, she found Xavier gorgeous.

'Well, he is well shaped,' Chantel admitted, 'but I am not sure he is handsome.'

Louisa set her head to one side considering, 'Well, he has a large nose, and heavy eyebrows, but it is a very masculine face.'

'Indeed, but perhaps a cruel one,' Chantel insisted.

'Ah, but you see, I don't see Xavier as a rutting stallion but as a garden bee,' Louisa told her with a wicked grin. She received the response she was expecting.

'A bee! Why on earth do you say that?'

'Have you ever watched the bees bumbling around the garden, wandering seemingly aimlessly from one flower to another. But then, they head off in an absolutely straight line.'

'Can't say I have,' muttered Chantel with a frown, 'but I think you are right.' Already a separate part of her mind was beginning to analyse whether bees really did act like that and if they did, why?

'Well, that is Xavier. At seventeen he was that bee heading in a straight line. The army is all he had ever wanted. Since he was forced to resign his commission completely against his will, he had been bumbling around, lost and directionless. You and Joshua have, it seems, given him a purpose again that he is contented with. He seems to be really enjoying the role you have offered him.'

'Good heavens. I see your reasoning. I must tell Joshua that. He may never recover!'

'Oh please, I shouldn't have said anything. I don't want to embarrass Xavier.' Of all the people to be indiscrete with, why, oh why had she chosen Chantel?

'Well, perhaps this is an analogy we will keep to ourselves,' Chantel agreed with a grin. 'But it is clear you don't feel out of your depth with him at all.'

Louisa took in a deep breath. 'I am not sure. He is bound to be a handful for any woman. But my instinct is that he has some years on him now. He wants a place in the world; somewhere he feels he belongs and a role in life.'

'I am never going to meddle again in my life. It seems I can't read people at all.'

Louisa gave her a wry smile. 'Now, you know full well you aren't going to keep to that.'

They both returned to their cooling tea smiling.

That afternoon, Louisa was heading towards the stairs to fetch a shawl. She walked around the weed-sodden lake every afternoon, or into the village, otherwise she felt she might go insane with inactivity. Elena and Samantha were still off visiting some local girls, so her time was her own. When Xavier appeared from the shadows in the hall, she wasn't in the mood to be particularly pleased. She had been mulling over his approach of the morning and wasn't sure she liked it. She gave him a curt nod and turned around the newel post to head upwards. A large hand reached out and slid a finger along the inside of her bare arm. Louisa glared at him. In times gone past she had often had to put importuning young officers in their place. Ignoring him, she began to climb.

'Where are you going?' he asked.

He might be good-looking to her eyes, but he was a good-looking rogue, and far too pleased with himself. What she wanted to say was, none of your business, but of course that was socially unacceptable. 'For a walk,' she said calmly, and began to trot up the stairs.

'May I come with you?' His eyes were dark and predatory.

She dipped her head to acknowledge the courtesy. 'I prefer to walk alone,' she stated firmly.

Fortunately, social convention also insisted that he respect her wishes and backed away. She watched as he frowned and opened his mouth to protest, then thought better of it. With his own slight bow, he withdrew.

Having seen Louisa head out for her walk from a window, Joshua wandered out of the house to stretch his legs, and his back. He could feel Xavier's bad temper even before he saw him. 'Problems?' he enquired.

Xavier snorted, which made Joshua smile even more. He liked Xavier being out of sorts; seemed justice somehow. In the distance he could see Louisa striding off, her cloak billowing out behind her.

'How far does she go?' Xavier asked.

'She rarely leaves the estate,' Joshua told him, curious as to the question.

'But it's a bloody big estate,' Xavier muttered.

Joshua looked at him, and then away to Louisa. 'And what is your interest in my sister-in-law?' he asked evenly.

'Almost-sister-in-law,' Xavier muttered. Xavier never muttered. He was definitely out of sorts.

'Watch your step, Xav old chap, she isn't alone in the world now.'

It wasn't a threat, not quite. Xavier snorted again. It was a most inelegant sound. 'I want her,' he said bluntly, 'just not sure she wants me.'

Joshua returned to Chantel and his studies with a wide grin on his face. Oh, he did like to see Xavier not getting life all his own way. Xavier too strode off, determined to work off his bad temper. Eventually he slowed his pace and panted to a stop. He was furious. With himself. He had made a tactical mistake. A mistake that could prove fatal. All generals knew that the outcome of any battle could turn on the smallest thing. What child hadn't learnt that for want of a nail a kingdom could be lost? The stroke on the soft inner skin of her arm had been a massive mistake. As an approach to a married woman, bored or disgusted with the oaf she had been married off to, it had proved a tried and tested technique. As an approach to the woman he wanted to marry, it had been a disaster.

Initially, Louisa had been invisible, sitting silently in her chair with her sewing. It had been the girls he had noticed first. Elena, the elder, willowy and shockingly blonde with huge light blue eyes. She was shy and quiet and had no idea of the allure she would offer when she eventually hit the marriage market. Men would be drawn to her like flies to honey. And she had no evident skills to handle such an onslaught. It was that fact that had made him regard the mother. She was pleasant to look at, but no more. But there had been a backbone there well hidden from sight. Perhaps Elena might not be as vulnerable as she appeared with a mother with teeth. He had shrugged and turned away. And then he had become aware of Samantha. Sharp, aggressive even, definitely intelligent. He had found her regarding him through narrowed eyes as if even at her young age she could see right through him; it had been most disconcerting.

Such different personalities had again caused him to regard the mother, and he began to like what he saw. Especially when he found out she had an army background. There was so much about him she would understand instinctively, and that was an attraction in itself. She moved well, with grace and poise, but cautiously, as if the world might bite her at any moment. No surprise there; she hadn't had an easy time of it. He was intrigued. He knew a little about her past. No woman should have survived Rupert Douglas McCloud, let alone find another man and raise two daughters after his early death alone. Backbone indeed. And the girls were a credit to her. The three of them made a tight unit.

The more he watched the more he liked. His eyes began seeking her, his day improving if he managed to entice her into a short conversation. He had recognised he was attracted to her sexually early on, and knew she felt it too. When he had traced his finger tip along her arm it was as if a candle had flared a trail along the whole of his arm. The shock had been intense. But it had been a mistake. She had felt it, no doubt about it, but she didn't trust it, or him.

She was, despite walking out on Rupert and living as another man's mistress, respectable. And independent. Too late, he realised that this was the key to her. She thought and acted for herself, not begging some man's acquiescence. She didn't need a man in her life. She might like one, but she didn't need one. It was a massive difference. Most women needed one to survive. Louisa would spit in their eye. She had been on the point of starving to death before she had come looking for help. Good grief, how he wanted her. He had never met a woman like her, and he was put out with himself that he might have wrecked his chance with her. But battles were not won or lost in one skirmish. He needed to court her properly. Calmly. That went hard against his nature. He knew what he wanted and his instinct was to drag her to bed to prove to her that he was just the man for her. Right now, she would probably kick his teeth in. Turning he began to head back, a plan in place.

Chapter 14

Louisa strode out across the clumpy grass towards the weed-infested lake. As she increased her pace, she realised that, for the first time, she felt alone. And rather lonely. She had instigated the afternoon walks initially in Bristol as a way of wearing out two lively girls so that they would sleep well at night. At that time, they were rarely invited to visit with other girls, her status of 'widow' being rather suspected by a number of gossips who had contacts in Causton. But then she had realised how much better she felt in herself for the fresh air and activity, and it had become a fixed habit. And even when the girls had become old enough to choose not to accompany her on occasion, she had enjoyed the time on her own. But not today. Today she had refused the company of a good-looking man who was single and of a suitable age. She sighed. She felt she had assessed Xavier well. He was a rogue. But if she was correct, if she trusted her judgement, he was a rogue who was ready to settle down. And he was interested in her. The really big question was, was she interested in him? That needed serious consideration. Under no circumstances was she marrying another Rupert Douglas McCloud, wife beater and drunkard.

But as she walked, she began to consider something else. Deep inside she knew was a kernel of bitterness. As a major's daughter, she had been a person of respect. As Lady Douglas McCloud she had been one of the most senior women in the officers' mess. As the mistress of Samuel Causton, she had been the beloved of one of the most important men for miles around. At B's funeral she had been treated with disdain and scorn, and it had insulted her pride, deeply. In Bristol she had been forced to live quietly, with no friends or confidents, and here, she was a poor relation dependent upon her lover's younger sister's patronage. She was angry about it. Furious, in fact.

She stood and gazed out over the rather dismal lake. And then laughed. She was alive. She spun around letting her cloak fly out as she whirled around and around. Dizzy, she stopped and leant forward, her hands on her knees. When her head cleared, she tipped it back and stood gazing up at the scudding clouds as the wind cooled her. She had survived. She had done more than survive, she had lived an amazing life. And it wasn't over. Her girls would settle, somehow, some day, but she would still have a life to lead. Her own life. If people wanted to scorn her, let them. She was more than a match for them. She felt light. She still missed Sam, always would. Love that sweet was rare. But it wasn't the only kind of love.

Her irritation at being stuck in this house living this life, lifted. Chantel had been more than kind, she admitted, and had promised that next year, she would accompany Louisa to London assist Elena in seeking a husband. And she was giving Samantha an education she could probably never find elsewhere. Samantha adored Chantel and hung on her every word. Most of all, she was no longer frustrated and bored, which made Louisa's life so much easier. Joshua had ensured that the girls could ride and had suitable mounts, and that had given them a freedom they revelled in. But more than that, he had given strict instructions that they were never to go anywhere without a groomsman. At first Louisa had fretted when they went off on their own, but when she met the man who went with them, she had relaxed. He was burly, with two grown daughters of his own, and clearly took the care of her girls seriously.

Louisa strode on, feeling oddly happy. Perhaps it was a desirable man making a clumsy overture, or maybe it was the realisation that life really had improved, but whatever it was, it was a wonderful day, and she intended to enjoy it.

Louisa was immediately aware of the alteration in Xavier's intent. That night he escorted her into dinner as if she were a friend's wife he needed to be openly respectful of. In fact, his behaviour was immaculate. And reserved. He was hiding behind good manners and an impenetrable expression. Whereas before he seemed to feel he could bludgeon her into his arms, or more likely his bed, with sheer force of will, now he was courteous. It was like watching a cat smell a chicken roasting, pretending it didn't really care if the wing was thrown its way, while never taking its focus off the dripping meat. She began to enjoy his attentions, and while picturing herself as a roasting joint wasn't particularly flattering, it made her smile to see his clamped down frustration. But she was fair. Clearly, he was trying to make himself attractive to her, and she had to admit, he was succeeding, and if Joshua and Chantel kept their word, he had a future. Besides, she more than liked the idea of bedding with him! But she wasn't sure what she wanted after that. She wasn't alone anymore. If she fell with child, unlikely she felt at her age, Chantel would not throw her out. She was a widow. She could play. Heaven help her, she could enjoy herself! Have fun! The idea made her feel giddy. And a bit faint.

The game grew increasingly intent. Xavier was in and out, learning the skills he needed to be an estate manager, and he always tried to at least see Louisa. And despite his overt good intentions, he knew his gaze fell on her like a burning brand. He hoped she felt it to her core, and the tension between them was, as far as he was concerned, becoming unbearable. And then he ran into her in a downstairs corridor purely by accident. He was in his shirt-sleeves, she was coming in from the pantry where she had hung some herbs to dry. It wasn't planned. But Xavier took one look at her and pounced. He cupped her face in his hands and looked down into her. She didn't move. So, he kissed her, warm, open-mouthed, hungry. And she responded, kissing him back and winding her arms around his neck. He was starved. And so it seemed was she. All of his vaunted self-control vanished. The kiss became frantic, his left hand hauled the neck of her soft dress down so her breast was resting in his palm. Its warm weight nearly caused him to explode then and there, like a randy school boy. He clutched her closer and moved his hand away from her breast to press her firmly against him, so he could feel her warm softness through the fine linen of his shirt, which left his right free to pull at the fabric of her skirts, winding them up and up, until he could find her bare backside.

As he found skin, he groaned into her mouth. The sound seemed to make her as frantic as he. He stroked her, exploring the warmth and softness of her roundness, feeling himself losing control. The fact that they were in a public corridor and it was mid-morning had fled his mind. His hand fumbled, searching for entrance, for wetness, for heat. His hand rubbed her, exploring, entering, mimicking what he was desperate to do, while he pressed his red-hot erection against her thigh. She began to rock against his hand, panting and mewling. And then she exploded. He only just caught her scream in his mouth. It had taken minutes.

As she shuddered to a close, she opened her eyes and stared at him, wide-eyed and shocked. Her mouth was wet and red and open and he moved to kiss her again, desperate to taste her. With a cry she shoved him away and then smacked his face. With a sob she spun out of his arms and ran towards the stairs. Xavier laid his palm on his cheek where she had smacked him, shaken. He took in a breath. Then another. The slap hadn't hurt, she hadn't been able to manage a proper swing.

He stood for a moment confused, as his sense returned. They could have been seen by anyone. No wonder she was upset. He strode off after her, wanting to make it right. Now more than ever he wanted her as his wife. Any wisp of doubt had fled. No one else would do. Everything she was, everything she had been, suited him. His boot heels clattered on the flagstones as he made after her. He heard her bedroom door slam when he was half way up the stairs. He raced to the door, but it was, of course, firmly shut. He reached for the handle but stopped. The sound of sobbing was unmistakable. Heart breaking. Annoyance he could understand, but heartbreak? He put his hands behind his back and stood feet apart facing the door. The sobbing went on. He tipped forward, resting his forehead against the wood, unmoving. He couldn't leave her, and he couldn't go in. So he stood. Behind him a maid scurried past with no doubt curious eyes. He was beyond caring. Why, oh why, was she sobbing?

Louisa appeared at lunch smiling so falsely everyone went along with it, talking a little more brightly to cover up that they had noticed her over bright red-rimmed eyes and brittle manner. Xavier found Joshua glaring at him once and gave a small nod of acknowledgement. Yes, he was the cause, and no it wasn't intentional. Amazing what a glance of an eye and a nod could convey. Lunch was purgatory.

He followed her out of the dining room cautiously. He called her name softly. She turned, and moved into the music room and then she shut the door gently, turning to lean back against it.

'Marry me,' he said.

She gave him a small smile. 'Because of what we did?'

'No. Because I want you for my wife.'

'No one saw. An offer isn't necessary. Or wanted. Anyway, I am not sure you are marriageable material, Xavier.'

He just stood and looked at her. He couldn't argue with that. He wasn't. He knew himself to be selfish and cared little for the opinion of others. He wasn't a kind man. Or a gentle one. Not like her not-quite-husband, the sainted Samuel. And then air shot into his lungs. Ah. She hadn't known. She hadn't thought there was more to what a man and woman could do with each other. She had been contented with their lovemaking because she hadn't known that a woman, too, could fall from the precipice. A surge of triumph swept through him but he tamped it down. Hard. Now was not the time to enjoy his conceit.

'May we please go back to being how we were? To being friends?' she asked softly, her tone clearly showing how upset she still was.

Not in this lifetime, he thought, but he nodded. 'I apologise,' he said.

She gave a small laugh, but there were tears in her eyes, 'It took two, Xavier, it took two. No apology is necessary.'

With that she spun out of the room, leaving him thinking. Back to slow courtship then, he thought, but he walked out of the room with determination in his step.

They didn't quite go back to how they were. Louisa was like a cat prowling a hot oven, decidedly flighty around him. He wasn't sure what it meant. Did it mean she was frightened of him? Of herself? Or had what had happened given her a distaste of him? He had no idea and he was working constantly to learn all he could from Chantel, so hardly ever saw her. Gradually over the autumn they worked their way back into being comfortable friends. Well, she might be comfortable, he certainly wasn't. He had never felt so wrong-footed by a woman.

Then at last he had the certainty of a future. It was time to make his bid. She was softening towards him. He had felt it. Sensed the warmth in her greeting, the way her eyes followed him around the room sometimes, the blush that crept up her neck when she found him gazing intently at her. Nothing had been said, but he was confident their silent courtship had progressed.

Chapter 15

Louisa was sewing in the side parlour frowning in the poor light. She hadn't heard Xavier come in. He had been away for ten days and she had missed him.

'Walk with me?'

At the sound of his voice, she jerked with a small shock. She gazed up and her insides tensed.

'I am rather busy,' she murmured, and returned to her needle.

He strode across to her and gently lifted the fabric from her hands.

'If you puncture yourself with a needle, it will be your own fault,' she told him.

'Come. Don't you want to hear my news?'

Louisa thinned her lips in exasperation, then rose and brushed threads from her skirts. Glancing out of the window she said coolly, 'Well, I suppose it might rain soon, so some fresh air now might be a good idea.'

He lifted her hand onto his arm and led the way out of the room. It felt somewhat less of a walk and more like a route march. They strode around the house and along to one of the side walls to a servants' entrance. There was no one around but Louisa felt more than a little suspicious. She deliberately stepped away from him and narrowed her eyes. It was the first time she had been totally alone with him since their time in the corridor. Xavier was not deterred, he simply stepped closer.

'I have been offered a permanent role. I have, it seems, proved myself and have been offered an estate to manage.' His eyes were laughing and she couldn't help but feel infected by his optimism.

'I am pleased for you,' she offered politely, pretending not to be delighted for him. He was too confident by far and she was not going to give him any fuel.

Xavier stepped closer. 'I have missed you,' he breathed into her ear.

'Nonsense,' she said, but she couldn't help the effect it had on her. Every inch of her skin was aware of him.

'Did you miss me?' he asked softly.

'Of course not.'

'Liar,' he whispered, his breath moist on her ear. He lifted her chin with a finger and raised her mouth to his. His kiss was warm and intense but Louisa remained standing still and unbending. He lifted his mouth and breathed, 'Tease.'

At that she couldn't help it, she giggled. She, Louisa, giggled! His delighted face was lit from inside. She had been hungry for so long. She stepped forward slightly, pressed against him and wrapped her arms around his neck. This time the kiss was as intense and as heated as she remembered. More so, in fact.

He released her and spun around grasping her wrist. It happened so fast Louisa's head was whirling. What was he up to now? He tugged her through the door and checked no one was around. Louisa opened her mouth to protest, then shut it. She felt alive. And naughty! He crossed to the stairs, still tugging her along. The light was dim and full of dust motes, with sunshine rods cutting the gloom. Together they raced up the stairs, Louisa still allowing the pretence that she was being pulled along. Suddenly he stopped and she knocked into him. 'Where are the girls,' he whispered, his tone intense.

'Out,' she whispered back. They had gone riding with Joshua to a farm to visit some other youngsters of their own ages.

'Good job I never made General,' he commented, and carried on tugging her up the stairs.

She grinned, 'Insufficient planning and aforethought?'

'Exactly,' was his dry response.

A small part of her mind wondered why she was going so willingly up these stairs with him. Truth was, she wanted to. She felt alive, and she had been dead for so long! His room was at the top of the stairs. And there was, she was relieved to see, a key in the lock. She knew exactly why she was crossing this threshold. If it was going to be a repeat of the corridor episode, she was ready for a replay. And she wanted to. Very much. As if that wasn't an understatement. He didn't hesitate. He spun her into the room, shoved her against the wall and hauled up her skirts. 'No drawers again,' he whispered into her neck. 'I knew you were the woman for me.'

He fumbled with his flap, and then he was inside. And she was ready for him, as hot and wet as he was. Her spine hurt as he banged her against the plasterwork and she didn't care. She wrapped her legs around his waist and tipped her head back as far as she could so he could ravish her neck. There was inconvenient fabric and buttons that dug in but it was glorious. He spent quickly. And she rested back against the wall panting, wanting more. Much more. But even if that was all he was offering, it had been worth it.

'I have fantasised about doing this ever since I first met you,' he told her neck.

'When you first met me, I was half-starved and terrified.'

'Ah, but your eyes weren't starved,' he disagreed, and gazed into them.

She began to slide down the wall, and was decidedly uncomfortable and wet down her thighs. She needed to go back to her room and clean herself up. She began to wriggle out of his grip.

'Oh, no,' he whispered, and hauled her into his arms. With two strides he was across the room and then he threw her high in the air until she landed with a flurry of skirts and petticoats on the bed. And then he launched himself on top of her. 'I haven't finished with you yet,' he told her.

'Thank goodness for that,' she replied, 'I was beginning to think you were the sort of pistol that went off on its own.' And he laughed. And she hadn't known he could laugh. By the time they had divested themselves of their clothes he was ready again.

'Hungry, I see,' she breathed in his ear.

'Starved,' he breathed back into her mouth.

He rode her hard, and she raised herself up and took it and gave back more. Then they slept for a while. He woke because she was heaving against him to roll him over onto his back. He watched her through slitted eyes, her cheeks flushed, her dark blonde hair tousled, and her eyes intent. He shifted so she could position him and then she slid down his body and took him in her mouth. He gave an involuntary groan, arched his back and spiked his fingers through her hair until he could cup her head. The woman might kill him with pleasure yet.

When she was satisfied she had his attention, she straddled him and sat on her knees. Then she rose up and slid down on top of him. His eyes were closed but behind his lids scarlet and black flares were racing in every direction. She leaned forward with her palms on his chest. 'Am I too heavy?'

'No.' His voice was husky. 'But let me position you.' He pushed her upright gently, so she was straddling him, then moved her arms even further back. He let his palms fall to rest on her thighs. 'Lift yourself up and down.' His voice was now a growl.

She began to move as directed, clumsy as first and then found a rhythm and lost her frown of concentration. 'Oh,' she muttered, then 'Oh!'

Her body leaned back even further and her movements began to speed up. Her eyes were closed and she was frowning again, but he knew now it was for a different reason. Her mouth was slightly open and her concentration was absolute. Xavier kept his eyes open and watched. He had heard that this position was particularly pleasurable for women, but to hell with what she was feeling, he had just died and gone to heaven. If she was finding pleasure, then he was doubly delighted. The joy of lust roared through him and he matched her thrusts with his own gripping her thighs as his own pleasure roared. Her eyes were closed tight now and her skin glowed rosy in the soft light of the early afternoon. He could see the outline of her ribs as she leaned back, and her hair covered her shoulders and fell in a wave down her back. Taut in places and soft in others her body was no longer young, and he adored every inch of it. He had some years on him himself. Then she jerked forward, her face contorted in what might have been agony, but wasn't, and screamed. He supported her as her completion rocketed through her. He couldn't help his climax. Seeing her in the throes of extreme pleasure had shot him through the roof. She collapsed onto him and then rolled sideways. He held her close and smothered her in small kisses, murmuring words without thought to soothe and comfort her. She continued to shudder for a while. As she quietened, he cupped her face in his hands and kissed her softly.

'Thank you,' she whispered.

'And thank you,' he whispered back. If this woman thought she was not going to become his wife, she would have to think again. They fell asleep curled into each other, hot, sticky with sweat, but unable to allow even the smallest parting.

When they woke the shadows were lengthening. Louisa reached up to stroke his face, then shifted to once again sit astride him.

'You like that?'

She didn't deign to reply but settled herself to straddle his stomach. Hers was now soft and cushiony but his was a slab of warm oak. Riding, she supposed; her middle had been as hard when she had spent days in the saddle. He lay under her, relaxed and still sleepy. She stroked the gap between his eyebrows with one finger then let the tip slide down the beak of his nose. A glitter of eyes suggested he was watching her through almost closed lids. Now she slid two finger tips across his mouth. It was beautifully-shaped, she hadn't realised just how beautifully so she traced the bow of the top lip and the warm plumbness of the lower. His mouth opened and he sucked both fingers in. She let him for a moment, relishing the warm shudder that shot through her. She had believed herself satisfied, possibly for the next year or so, but that warm sucking was changing her mind. Withdrawing her fingers, she let her dry thumb stroke down his chin to rub across his afternoon beard. Back and forth she rubbed, exploring the sensation of bristle on thumbpad. Something bumped into her back. She looked up and into his eyes. He was hard again and his eyes were laughing and intent.

'More?' she whispered.

With a quick twist he had thrown her up into the air like so much washing and was on top of her. She landed gasping and grinning at the speed and power with which he had manhandled her. It took all her scattered wits to breathe a soft, 'Oh!'

Their lovemaking was sleepy and slow. An endless dance of stroke and counter-stroke. She explored the hair on his chest, rubbing it into kiss-curls before stroking it out again, then testing the different texture of the dense hair on his thighs. She shoved him onto his front and let her fingers find the bumps of his spine and the slabs of muscle in his back, but he grew impatient and tossed her onto her back again so she explored his arms and his wide shoulders with her palms. Then he began to explore her in earnest. His hands roamed and delved and showed her places that gave her pleasure that she had never known existed. By the time he entered her she was arching up off the mattress, grinding into his hand, ready to beg for release. He surprised her, entering slowly with a tantalising glimpse of what he might give, if he were so inclined.

'Bastard,' she hissed.

'Perhaps.'

His face was taut and she was relieved to know that he was struggling to maintain control; she didn't want this to be too easy for him, she wanted him to long as she longed. Her memory of wondering if he was a rapid shot when she was now almost screaming with impatience returned to mock her. By the time he increased his pace and began to hammer into her she was empty of thought and simply wanted him to hammer forever. And then she exploded, and her body convulsed around his over and over again as it tried to jack-knife upwards. She had no energy for speech after, she just plunged into a black abyss of unconsciousness.

They didn't reawaken for a long time.

'We missed lunch,' she muttered into his shoulder. He kept toying with her hair, too exhausted to move. Dinner might be essential however, he thought, or he might expire.

'The estate is in Lincolnshire,' he said.

'What estate?' she murmured sleepily.

'The one Joshua and Chantel have invited me to permanently manage.'

'Will you like living there?' she asked, raising her head. 'It isn't somewhere I know anything about.'

'Nor I. But it has a manor house, not too large, not too small. And income. Some, but not much society. In the winter we can travel to London, or anywhere else you would like now the war is over. Italy? From spring through to autumn, I shall not wish to go away. I will be a farmer, you know, tied to the land and the seasons. I have come to the conclusion it is not so different from being in the army. One is tied to a place the army chooses and have restricted movement there too.'

She had shifted to lie with her head on her arms on his chest, gazing up at him. She was frowning. 'What do you mean, 'we'?'

'When we are married.' He suddenly felt a bucket of cold water swish round his guts. She had to say yes, hadn't she?

'One, you haven't asked. And two, maybe I don't wish to be tied to a man again. My first husband was violent, and my second died on me. Both of which in my book are unforgivable.'

'You loved him?' Where had that come from? Xavier couldn't believe he had been so gauche.

'Sam? Oh yes. Deeply. I adored him; I still do. And, always will, to my last breath.' She looked at him gravely. 'And I love my girls. And I loved Miss Buckley who took me in. And I loved my mother and father. And if today results in another child, I will love that child too. Love doesn't fit into boxes or containers, it is eternally expansive.'

'A child? From today? But that is why you have to marry me.' His tone was firm. A man telling a subordinate what to do. Besides, he couldn't believe after such an explosive climax he hadn't made her pregnant.

Louisa sucked in her cheeks and gazed back at him. 'No, I don't. I know Joshua and Chantel will look after me. I have raised two girls alone. I can manage a third.'

'Did you think I wanted you as just my mistress?'

She gave him a wicked look. 'You wouldn't be able to afford me.'

He threw his head back onto the pillows and gave a huff of breath. He had thought she was playing. He had assumed her refusal was a game. But as she used his wash bowl to clean herself down, he realised she still hadn't agreed to his proposal.

'I am serious, you know,' he said from the bed. She raised her eyebrows and tied a bow to her shift. 'I am asking you to marry me.'

She smiled. He didn't like that smile. It was the sort one gave to a foolish child. 'I know. And I am appreciative of the honour. But no. We wouldn't suit.'

Xavier sat up sharply. He threw out an arm wide in exasperation. 'Not suit! You can say that after this afternoon?'

'There is more to marriage than bed.' With that she walked calmly across the room and left.

He crept down to find food in the kitchens when it was dark. He hadn't known what to do after she left. They hadn't used a touch of caution; the whole household would know they had spent since late morning to late afternoon in bed. He had assumed they could join everyone at dinner and be congratulated on their engagement. Not for the first time he had badly misjudged her. 'Definitely lost your touch, old man,' he muttered to himself in castigation.

He rose before dawn. He found out his best clothes and his most polished boots. He shaved himself and made himself as smart as he could be in civilian clothes. Then he marched down to the hall and stood in its centre, legs slightly apart and hands behind his back, unmoving, unseeing.

If he had ever wondered what a footman did, he was now enlightened. The two big ones, Hugo and Toby were the first to appear as the light began to arrive. They both saw him, but acted as if he were invisible, and he was horribly aware he was grateful. Large baskets of logs arrived at doors and they were the ones who carried them to the hearths for other staff to unload and use. They were the ones who returned the baskets to the door. They shifted furniture, fetched and carried. They were never still, and clearly had the running of the house down to a fine art. Whether it was a jammed door that required muscle to force it ajar or a huge cupboard that needed moving so a silver knife could be recovered, they were the ones who solved the problem, speaking little and appearing to know each other's minds with nothing said. He admitted he had seen them as louts who needed putting in their place, but as he stood, unmoving, appearing unaware of the activity as cans of water were hauled upstairs and maids bustled cleaning grates and furniture, he was forced to admit he would have been proud to have them in his regiment. They were good lads. Clearly hard-working and intelligent. If he hadn't been so determined not to move a muscle he would have sighed. He had got them wrong too.

Joshua clattered down the stairs two hours later. He skidded to a halt when he spotted Xavier standing stationary in the hall. He met Xavier's eyes with a glare. Xavier didn't move. Then he gave a curt nod towards the study. Xavier fell into step and followed him into the room. As the door banged shut Joshua swung towards him, his face tight with anger.

'She refused me,' Xavier said. And that, it seemed, finished the argument.

It was not far past daybreak but they both sank into chairs side-by-side with brandies in hand. Joshua wasn't drinking his, but Xavier didn't notice as he was downing his like water. 'I miscalculated,' he admitted, 'I thought once I got her into bed, she would have to accept me. She told me to think again.'

Joshua watched Xavier's face and felt an unholy glee. It was ungentlemanly, but he really did enjoy seeing Xavier so out of all countenance.

'Do you still want to marry her?'

The look Xavier shot him was filthy. 'More than ever.'

'Do you think she will have you in the end?'

'No idea,' he muttered, and sank more brandy.

Even Chantel was impressed with how Louisa brazened her behaviour out. She acted as if nothing had happened, which did, in fact, make it easier to pretend that they were all unaware of her vanishing with Xavier for most of a day and then him riding away looking like thunder. Joshua, however, couldn't leave it like that. For a mess of reasons, he knew he had to have a talk with her. He dreaded it, however. 'What do you wish me to do?' he asked her at last.

'Do?'

'Louisa, you are under my protection and Xavier is now employed by me. Should I ensure he never stays under the same roof as you?'

Louisa looked both shocked and surprised. 'I was willing,' she informed him. He had never heard her voice so hard. But at least her cheeks had gone pink. That made him feel a little better though he wasn't sure why.

'So, you wouldn't mind him staying here again, if you and the girls were still here.' He watched as her brave face slipped and he saw again the woman he thought he knew.

'No,' she said softly, 'it wasn't his fault. He offered marriage and I turned him down. He honestly thought we would be engaged and married so there would be neither blame nor shame.' And then she asked with a note of pleading in her voice, 'Has he gone far?'

'I have sent him to Gloucestershire. He is looking into a badly run estate there.' He couldn't help it. 'Do you not care for him?'

She offered a wan smile, 'Too much so. He is too much like Rupert. Arrogant, dictatorial and blind to other people's needs or wishes.'

Joshua wasn't sure what to say. It wasn't his place to plead Xavier's cause, and everything she said was correct. 'You think he would treat you cruelly?'

'I don't know. When he asked, he was so sure of himself. He didn't actually ask, he told. He looked so confident. I was suddenly filled with doubt. Marriage is more than bed, and so I walked away. I had a lovely afternoon, but it wasn't enough to gamble my and my daughter's futures. I don't trust him enough, and without that, I cannot marry him. I am sorry if I have given you a disgust of me.' Once again, her face hardened.

'Far from it. You are both past youth. I think, for what it is worth, you are wise.' They parted, he thought, as friends, but it wasn't an interview he wished to repeat in a hurry.

Chapter 16

Louisa was crossing the hall when Xavier strode in. She hadn't known he was due to arrive and stopped dead in her tracks, not sure how to react. The main doors were wide open while Hugo and Toby, Chantel's huge footmen, hauled his bags, the grey light and blustering cold of a damp and miserable day swirling around. He saw her and did not break stride. Stopping just in front of her he set his feet apart and clasped his hands behind his back. She was not short, but she tipped her head back to look up at him.

'Louisa.'

'Xavier,' she replied coolly.

He didn't shift. Leaning forward from the waist he lowered his mouth to her ear and said softly. 'I have missed you.' He paused, letting his breath warm her skin before adding, 'horribly.'

At that point a clattering on the stairs brought Samantha into view. 'Xavier!' she shrieked. 'How lovely to see you. Welcome back!'

'Brat,' he drawled, with a grin.

'I am learning Newton's calculus. Shall I teach it to you?'

Xavier gave a theatrical shudder. 'Perhaps not.' Drawing himself upright he said to Louisa, 'I have to report to Joshua,' before bowing very correctly and heading around her to the study.

Louisa knew she had flushed a vivid red and was breathing more rapidly than she needed to. Hugo and Toby pointedly ignored her. So much so she knew that they had seen and heard everything. What had he meant by, horribly? That it was horrible to miss her? That missing her was an unwanted emotion and therefore horrible? That she was horrible? Oh, she hated him! Of course, she did. Suddenly totally flustered, she forgot what she had been doing and where she had been going and fled upstairs to her room. She felt both sets of eyes from the footmen burn into her back. Oh, she hated them too!

Xavier at dinner was perfectly correct. He had met many of the people on the estate in Gloucestershire and brought back a good report. Yields looked like being up, and there was a general air of contentment and quiet effectiveness all around the estate. The young manager Chantel had put in place wished to marry a local clergyman's daughter and appeared well settled. He was articulate about the golden cottages made of local stone that many of the estate workers lived in and described the rolling countryside eloquently. Louisa listened to it all, and used his account as an excuse to gaze at his face, but his private thoughts were well hidden. She went to bed in a thoroughly bad temper.

Louisa slept badly and rose early. She came down the stairs for breakfast and was the first to walk into the dining room. The table was set as it always was but as it was so early nothing was laid upon the sideboard as yet. The Court was the only home Louisa had ever known that served water with meals. Most households of any size considered water for horses and fish, but there was always spring water available here, usually subtly flavoured with sprigs of rosemary or lemon balm. She walked into the room to find a pitcher and help herself to a drink. As she poured a glassful she glanced at the place where she usually sat. Something was laid out across her knife and fork. Moving slowly, she stepped closer, then looked around. Hard against the wall opposite her was a footman. The dark one; Toby. Louisa disapproved of the way Chantel managed her household. To Louisa's mind, Chantel's familiarity with the staff, the two senior footmen in particular, was wholly inappropriate. Although she would never admit it aloud, to her it clearly indicated Chantel's inadequate upbringing and total unsuitability to be a duchess.

She crossed to her place setting. A sheet of paper covered her cutlery and where her plate would go. On it, right in the centre, was a small mess of straw or grass, a construction that would fit easily in the palm of her hand. She looked across to Toby. He was absolutely still and totally impassive, as was correct. She looked back at the plate. 'Did you put this here?' she demanded.

Toby's eyes moved from straight ahead to hers. 'No, ma'am,' he said softly before returning his eyes to the front.

Exasperated she asked, 'Well, do you know what it is?'

The response was made in exactly the same way. 'Yes, ma'am.'

Louisa had a strong urge to smack him. 'Well, what is it?'

This time his whole head moved to face her. 'A dormouse nest, ma'am.'

At that Louisa's mouth fell open in a way that was quite unladylike. 'But why is it here?' But even as the words left her mouth, she suspected the answer. Again she was afforded the whole-head turn.

'I believe ma'am,' he said in his soft tone, 'you are being courted.' Then he returned to his rigid posture and she had the distinct impression that she had been dismissed.

Louisa said little over breakfast. Who on earth courted with dormouse nests? Of course, the question was rhetorical. The tiny home was now nestled in one of her cabinets. The one nearest her bed. What did he mean by it? And how did he expect her to respond? And how should she respond? Xavier too was quiet over the meal, and did not appear to be attempting to seek any response from her.

Xavier, contrary to Louisa's observations, was watching her closely. He had wrong-footed her on his arrival and he had a shrewd idea he had managed to wrong-foot her again. But he wasn't sanguine. The little nest had vanished and Toby had assured him that it had been Louisa who had removed it. For all he knew she had thrown it on the fire.

His contact with Louisa during the day was minimal and always in company and as such was wholly social and public. She said all that was proper and behaved as if they were merely social acquaintances, which, he admitted to himself, he admired. To behave so coolly when they had for one unforgettable day explored every inch of each other's bodies was almost beyond him. For his part he wanted to howl at the moon in pain at his loss! He had no idea if his strategy might work, but it was all he had been able to come up with. In the evening Louisa saw that neither he nor Joshua appeared, eating their meal over discussions about estate business. She had no idea of how long he might stay. Perhaps he would leave again in the morning? It gave her another restless night and this time she was last to arrive to the breakfast table.

She found her seat and there was another sheet of paper but this time lying on top was a tiny bouquet of grasses and seed heads tied together with a further length of dry grass. As it was late November and even seed heads and grasses had been destroyed by winds and rain by now, the tiny, pristine, bunch was a minor miracle. Louisa lifted the fragile gift, laid it alongside her wine glass, folded the paper and held it up by her right shoulder where Hugo expertly made it vanish. Neither Samantha nor Elena said a word, let alone everyone else. She felt her cheeks flush slightly and the room took on an over-warm feeling, as she realised that either every soul in the house was either aware of her strange courtship or had gone dumb, deaf and blind.

That night Xavier sought her out after dinner and conversed with her in a wholly unexceptional manner about Gloucestershire, his journey, and a host of other matters that drifted into their minds. Louisa found herself relaxing and enjoying his company and even laughed at his witticisms. It wasn't that she didn't like him, she kept telling herself, she just didn't trust that he was safe. Not for her, nor for her daughters. Neither Elena nor Samantha appeared to have any reservations whatsoever. She frowned severely at them, but they continued to flirt and chatter with him as if he were a favourite uncle! There was no small gift on her bed cover, and she smothered a sense of disappointment.

Nest day at breakfast it was a beautiful shell no smaller than the little dormouse home. It was swirled with colours of soft brown and pink and cream and when she examined it, she could find no flaw. At dinner it was a stone. It looked like it had come from a river bed, being perfectly round and smooth, and coloured in blues and greys. On her bed that night was an embroidered handkerchief, too large to be for a woman, and with a large flowing H crossing and entwined with an X. She climbed into bed and once again found sleep hard.

The next morning James, Chantel's brother arrived. He had bought his fiancé, Lady Mary Swann. It was her estate in Lincolnshire that Xavier might be managing. They pulled up with two coaches and a cart. The wind had died down, though even in its less blustery form it was evilly bitter. James emerged first, reaching in to take in his arms a little poppet with white blonde hair that flew around her head like thistledown. The little one sat secure in his grasp, her arms around his neck and her head on his shoulder. Louisa thought if James wasn't taken, she could fall for him herself. She glanced up to see that Xavier was watching her, and if she wasn't mistaken, reading her thoughts.

Lady Mary stepped down next, followed by a young boy. She was tall and had dark upswept hair that was perfectly in place. She stood and gazed at the assembled throng on the steps and Louisa felt her gaze move up and down her before she assessed Chantel. Louisa wondered if Chantel had come off any better in the woman's opinion? Then her eyes met Joshua's and she returned his wide grin with a gracious smile, but her longest gaze was for Xavier. Louisa felt a hot flash of fury and experienced the sudden desire to rip the woman's head from her body. Xavier stood looking back with narrowed eyes and a sardonic twist to his lips.

Louisa went to sew in the drawing room, hiding in plain sight while the new arrivals were shown around and settled in. Chantel entered and rang for tea with an irritated yank on the bell pull. Louisa dared to comment, 'Your brother is to marry Lady Mary, I understand.'

'Indeed,' was Chantel's crisp comment. And then they shared an unusually conspiratorial smile. It was clear Chantel was as unimpressed with the woman as Louisa was. To Louisa's surprise Chantel had been seeking out her company as she had some questions she wished to ask.

James was not the man on this visit that he had been on his last. Far from napping all day and sleeping all night he was up at cock crow and never stopped to draw breath. He had, it seemed, taken on the determination to learn all he could about estate management as rapidly as possible. Mary was refusing to marry him until they had resolved on the pattern of their future lives. James privately detested the fens and had all his hopes pinned on Xavier being employed by Mary to run her estates. He wanted his own lands and the challenge of seeing if he could bring his family estates back into profit. It was clear to them all that as Mary refused to sleep alone presumably the matter wasn't too urgent at present.

Late that afternoon, Louisa entered one of the long dark corridors upstairs and realised James and Mary were further along. It looked as if Mary had just left their room and he was heading towards it. James took a fast step forward, grasped Mary around the waist and swung her around. Louisa stepped back into the shadows embarrassed to be forced into spying on them. James walked Mary back and up against the wall. He bent and kissed her with heat. Louisa felt herself blushing and wondered how quiet her footsteps would be if she backed away. Worse, Mary hung round his neck and swung her legs up off the floor and gripped him around the middle. Louisa swallowed, wishing she were anywhere else. She heard James growl and walk her, still hanging on back to their room. Where did they get the energy, she wondered? They had been out riding for hours!

With the arrival of Mary and James, Louisa's strange small gifts had stopped appearing. After two days had gone by Louisa was feeling decidedly unsettled and more than a little resentful about the couple's arrival. What had the gifts meant? And did their cessation mean she hadn't responded how he had hoped? How should she have responded? Xavier's behaviour was immaculate towards her, as it was with everyone, and not once did his eyes or his demeanour suggest that he regarded her any differently to anyone else, or any other lady. Louisa felt definitely out of sorts.

That night she paced her room, the curtains open so the draft from the window chilled her bones, in the light of the large moon that hung over the gardens. The cold felt appropriate somehow, though she had no idea why. Her bare feet were turning to ice blocks and her thoughts rather than whirling, were stuck in a kind of frozen immobility. Winter was not just outside the window but felt as if it had invaded her internally. Eventually she took up a candle and let herself out of her room and down the corridor. She entered his room as quietly as possible.

He wasn't asleep. He had a whole candelabra burning beside him and had papers strewn about the bed as he sat perusing them. As she entered, turning to click the door shut as gently as she could, she could hear the rustle as he gathered them up and put them to one side. As she turned, he was removing a pair of steel-wire eyeglasses from his face and laying them on the side. Joshua's were gold-rimmed she thought with a flash of resentment. As she walked to the bed, he pinched out two of the candles beside him, so she spat on her fingers and pinched hers out too.

He was sitting up cushioned behind with pillows against the carved oak headboard. Louisa reached for another pillow and set it against her back and settled to lean against the post diagonally across from him. Settled she said, 'I didn't know you needed eyeglasses.'

'Just for reading.'

'Joshua wears his all of the time now,' she commented. He gave a small nod. He knew she hadn't come for pleasantries. 'It is a dormouse nest, isn't it?' It wasn't really a question.

He had linked his fingers in his lap and was looking down at them, not at her. The soft gold of the candlelight limned his bare chest and shoulders. His chest hair was fine but dense and in a defined vee. 'It is,' he agreed after a while.

'Why?' It summed up everything. Just the one word, why?

His gaze never left his linked fingers. 'I found it the first day after I arrived in Lincolnshire. It is a particularly small one, I was told. It was so beautifully wrought and tiny. I had thought it was a bird's nest. There had been many of those in the hedgerows I climbed in and out of as a boy every summer.'

'Why give it to me?'

He tipped his head back and gave a sigh to the canopy over his head. 'It struck me that it was a home. Something neither of us have. And I knew that if I had a home, I wanted you in it. Otherwise, it would just be a house.' For the first time he looked at her, unsmiling, his face giving nothing away.

'And the grass bouquet?'

At that he smiled, 'Ah well, if it had been a different season, it would have held wild flowers, but that morning all I could find was dried evidence of the earlier year.'

He had gone out that morning! To find a tiny bouquet. For her! 'And the shell?' she was beginning to enjoy this.

'Only that it was beautiful, and the colours reminded me of you. Some of the browns in the shell are like strands of your hair.'

Louisa blinked. 'And the stone?'

'Even more tenuous, it was pretty, and I have no money for jewels.'

'Have you ever bought a woman jewels?' The question was out before she could stop it and she instantly regretted it.

'Once. It took everything I had. It was a brooch with a lozenge ruby, a wonderful colour, framed in pearls.' His fingers traced a shape. Louisa gazed at him and he met her eyes properly for the first time.

'You bought it for Grace St John.'

'Yes.'

'You were in love with her.' He simply looked at her. 'Of course, you were,' she went on. 'You wouldn't have let them throw you out of the army if you hadn't been.' His face made no reaction and so they sat, looking at each other. A sick feeling surged in Louisa's insides. 'Do you still love her?'

At that he laughed. 'Heavens no. I was experienced in war, but remarkably inexperienced in love and women. I fell so hard. I was obsessed with her, couldn't concentrate on anything else. I ached for her. Not only her body, her scent, her glance, just to catch a glimpse of her made my day. That I was her lover made me insane with delight.' He paused then added, 'Looking back, I was very young.'

'We aren't young now,' she said.

'Young enough.'

At that she rose and crawled up the bed towards him. As she slid in beside him, he gave a grunt. 'Might it be possible for you to remove those feet?' he asked. 'They have to be the coldest limbs I have ever encountered.'

'All of me is cold,' she told him. 'Might you be able to warm me?'

There was a deep tenderness to their lovemaking that hadn't been there before. In the morning they awoke and smiled at each other.

'What do you want out of life?' she asked him.

He raised his brows. 'Philosophy? This early in the morning?'

'I am not at all sure it is early. I heard a valet creep in hours ago with warm water, but I am sure it is cold by now. I didn't lock the door.'

Xavier rolled onto his back and sighed. 'I used to want glory. To race into battle and earn medals and approbation. Now, now I want contentment.' He rolled back towards her.

'Are you going to ask me to marry you now?' she enquired.

Xavier looked away and out of the window across the room. 'If I don't, Joshua will definitely call me out this time. I am not at all in the mood for terminating the existence of the man who is going to allow me the means to keep my wife and daughters. However, I am not sure I dare ask, you might refuse again.'

'I never took you for a man lacking in courage,' she told him, and punched his stomach lightly. She was grinning at him.

He gave a deep sigh, 'You are going to give me a devil of a time, aren't you?'

'I hope so,' she told him.

'Well?' he said. 'When we eventually do go downstairs, am I going to be able to announce that you are to be my wife? Because I refuse to face everyone if you are not. I shall have to creep down to the stables and make away into the night like a thief. And then I will be in utter disgrace and will soon fade away and die under a hedge.'

Louisa laughed. It was going to be good, she thought. He wasn't handsome to many women. He was too stern, too dark, too intimidating. But he had loved her with an intense passion that had caring at its core. A man who wasn't selfish in bed was unlikely to be selfish out of it, she mused.

'Yes, I will marry you,' she said, 'it is time I became respectable again.'

'After last night,' he muttered, 'that is asking for a lot.' But he was smiling slyly at her. So, she kissed him to shut him up.

Chapter 17

Louisa believed her life was settled. She would marry Xavier, live in Lincolnshire, find a decent husband for Elena, send Samantha to rule a colony somewhere, and live a turbulent life with her husband. Then the coach arrived.

It had crests on the doors, two postilions covered in gold braid hanging on the back, and twelve outriders. Clearly someone who considered himself important, Xavier thought, as he watched the coach draw to a halt by the steps. He was due to leave this morning for another investigation on behalf of Chantel, but he had lingered, enjoying his status as a newly engaged man, which meant he could tumble Louisa as often as they thought prudent. That was what he had been telling himself. If he was brutally honest with himself, he was reluctant to leave. He would miss all three of them. His new family. He was slightly ashamed to admit he was happy.

He wasn't so sure about Joshua who had been summoned from his study by one of Chantel's bodyguard footmen and had looked rather white as he crossed the hall to greet the coach, so Xavier had placed himself outside the doorway behind him. He turned his head at a slight sound to discover Chantel's pair, Toby and Hugo, also aligned in the opening. Joshua turned to see his personal regiment at his back. Xavier gave him a reassuring nod and Joshua looked vastly relieved.

A lackey announced the Earl of Fyte. The man who eventually emerged from the coach was old, very old, and leaned on a cane not for the reason James had used one, because he was recovering from injury, but simply because of age.

After he had allowed the lackey to properly announce him, the old man declared, 'I believe you have my son's wife here.' His voice was surprisingly strong from such a frail body, and clearly used to giving orders.

Joshua frowned, giving it some thought. 'Louisa?' he asked.

'I believe that is her name, yes.'

Xavier suddenly felt sick.

'She may not wish to see you,' he heard Joshua say, 'and no one here will force her.'

'No, I quite understand. But you will inform her I am standing on the steps.'

'Tea?' he heard Joshua offering, and he looked again, and saw how very old and frail the man was.

'Bloody coach was bloody uncomfortable, something stronger, I hope. Might un-numb my arse.'

Joshua was grinning as he escorted the man into the house. Xavier felt frozen in place. Joshua and Xavier stood outside the open door as the Earl, clearly tired, sat in the drawing room. When Louisa arrived, with Elena and Samantha, they ushered them in with smiles but did not move. Louisa was entitled to privacy, but they were not going to shut her in a room with the father of the man who had beaten her black and blue and worse, however old he appeared. Words too could wound. Louisa had not wanted to receive him and had been terrified the Earl could take her daughters from her. Joshua had reassured her as best he could, but Xavier had remained quiet. He was suddenly uncertain of his status. Did he have a claim on Louisa or not? Did he have a right to step in?

They watched as the Earl tried to rise, but it was so clearly an effort Louisa waved him down again and sat herself opposite him. Just as before, Joshua noticed, willowy Elena stood behind her mother with one hand on her shoulder while Samantha sat beside her, frowning deeply.

The Earl, it seemed, had intended to come some months previously, but had been brought to bed with the influenza, and only now had felt well enough to travel. It was just earlier that year that he had discovered about the existence of Lady Douglas McCloud, and was anxious to meet both her and now that he knew of their existence, her daughters. Xavier heard Louisa say, with her back ram-rod straight and her chin lifted, that Elena had been born when Rupert was alive and Samantha after his death. The old man waved such niceties away with his hand.

'Don't matter a damn. Wise man that knows his own father, as they say. The eldest chit is my heir. Been mightily anxious to meet you and see if there was one. We inherit down the distaff side, y'know, when necessary. Lawyers all informed.'

The Earl declined to stay, he had, he said, arranged to visit an old friend a few miles away and would reside there. If Louisa and her daughters would care to visit him, he would send a coach. He left, leaning heavily on his stick.

'Think he will last the journey?' Xavier muttered.

'Oh yes,' Joshua muttered back, 'men like him go on forever.'

After they had seen the Earl off, they all returned to the saloon.

'I am, it seems, a rich woman,' Louisa began. Xavier felt himself go white. 'The title belongs to Elena, as Rupert's legitimate daughter, her legitimacy being determined as she was born while we were still married. According to the Earl, the fact that we were living apart does not affect the legalities. Samantha, meanwhile is illegitimate as she was born after Rupert died and before I could marry her father.'

Samantha folded her arms and threw herself back on the seat with a loud, 'humph', causing them all to smile. 'As the relic, I have a Dower house and small estate in Scotland. Elena, meanwhile, will inherit all the Earl has on his death, all of his sons predeceasing him. She is, he insisted, an heiress of considerable fortune and I should be wary of fortune hunters.'

Louisa looked up at the two men who had stood guardian just out of ear-shot as she had listened to the Earl.

'I am free!' she declared. And then she looked at her girls, 'We all are!'

Xavier had never seen such delight on her face. Ever. He spun on his heel and strode from the room. Distantly, he heard Joshua run after him.

'Where are you going?' Joshua demanded.

'You have entrusted me with a job. Time I got on with it. If I don't swallow a pistol first.'

'Oh, don't do that,' Joshua told him, 'they taste disgusting.'

Xavier threw him a glowering look and strode on. Joshua was spun around as Louisa hurtled past.

Xavier had reached his horse which had already been standing for far too long. As he tightened the girth, Louisa reached him. He didn't turn around to face her, instead he dipped his forehead to rest on the saddle.

'Xavier?' Her voice broke.

He didn't turn. 'I have work to do.' Better end it now and end it quickly. He tightened his muscles in order to vault up but felt her hand grasping his jacket, her head hitting hard against his back.

'Coward.' Her voice was muffled by the tweed.

He took a deep breath and turned around. He couldn't help himself, his arms slid around her. Her face was anguished. 'You are free. Financially independent, which is the only way a woman can be truly free. Free in a way almost no woman ever is. Enjoy it, Louisa. Go out into the world and enjoy your freedom. Revel in your new life. I wish you every joy. Truly I do.'

'Oh, you idiot!'

He had to smile. 'A coward and an idiot. How highly you rate me.'

'You deserve it. Why are you running away?'

'Oh, worse and worse. Isn't it obvious? You are now free to find a decent man. One who can care for you and the girls.'

'Better than you?'

'God damn it, yes.' The words were wrenched from him. 'I will only ever have a moderate income. I can offer you an employed husband in Lincolnshire and a yearly short spell in London. A few new gowns. A life watching the pennies as I am more afraid of debt than a foreign bullet.'

'Are you too proud, then, to marry a wealthy wife?'

He shook his head, his face rigid.

'Do you love me?'

Xavier closed his eyes. 'Ah, Louisa. Your father taught you knife work well. That goes deep.'

'Well, do you?'

'Yes,' he whispered. 'Dear god, yes.'

'Good,' she said. 'I lost Sam and could do nothing about it. Oddly enough, willpower does not defeat death. I won't lose you. I never dreamt I would care for anyone like this again. I love you Xavier Hawksworth, and I want to live my life with you. So kiss me, get on that horse, go and do your job and then come back and marry me.'

And Xavier laughed. Because if he hadn't, the strain in his throat might defeat him. 'Perhaps the girls first,' he murmured.

They turned. Elena was standing hugging herself with her arms tight around her torso, her face bone white against her hair, while Samantha was standing scowling with her fists so tightly against her sides, he could count her white knuckles even from here. He tipped his head and smiled, and they both ran towards him.

'Are you still going to be my Papa?' Samantha demanded.

Xavier's grin widened. Straight to the point, this one. 'Yes,' he said, 'so give me a hug before I go.' To his surprise she threw herself at him and wrapped him tight. He stroked her hair and hugged her back. Elena stood a little apart, tears sliding quietly down her cheeks. 'Ah little one,' he murmured, and kissed her forehead. 'Do you want me too?' She only nodded, but a smile broke out. Louisa tipped her head and he kissed her mouth, and tasted a future he wanted and was glad to walk into.

'Don't you dare not come back!' Louisa admonished him. 'I'll chase you into hell if you don't!'

'I hope you would,' he whispered, and kissed her again.

For the first time he rode out with a party of loved ones at his back watching him go. He was already thinking that three weeks for the banns was going to take too long. He was past thirty. He needed to get on with his life.

Louisa watched him until he was out of sight. She had so far refused Joshua's offer of a mount. She had hardly ridden at all for years, not since she had left Rupert years ago. It was time she got back into the saddle. The next time Xavier left she was going with him. She wrapped her arms around her precious girls and they walked back to the house. They all, it seemed, had a future.

Acknowledgements

Thanks are due to, Janet, who read everything first. Caroline Mylon, copyeditor extraordinaire who checks that all of my full stops and commas are in the right place, and Keith Abbott of Michael Terence Publishing who is the rock who takes my imaginings and turns them into a saleable product. And finally to John, who supports me throughout.

Thank you all.

Book Group Questions

1. Should Louisa have left Rupert earlier?

2. Do abused women now have life any easier than she did?

3. What do you think about the fact that alongside her grief she is angry at Sam for dying?

   Does that surprise you?

4. Independence for women only comes in the book because of financial independence. How much has life changed for women?

5. Did it surprise you that although the war with the French eventually ended, prices rose alarmingly?

6. Did you know that the French continued to fight the British by proxy in the American War of Independence and that the new colony would not have won without their financial and other support? Support that almost bankrupted France.

7. Do you think Xavier Hawksworth will make a good husband for Louisa?

Available worldwide online and from all good bookstores

---

www.mtp.agency

www.facebook.com/mtp.agency

@mtp_agency

Michael Terence Publishing

Printed in Great Britain
by Amazon

16426990R00140